One of These Nights

by

Roni Denholtz

One of These Nights

Cover Art by *Kristian Norris*

The Wild Rose Press, Inc.
PO Box 708
Adams Basin, NY 14410-0708
Visit us at www.thewildrosepress.com

Publishing History
First Fantasy Rose Edition, 2018
Print ISBN 978-1-5092-2030-4
Digital ISBN 978-1-5092-2031-1

Published in the United States of America

Dedication

For my critique/brainstorming partners/friends:

~*~

Karen Bryan,
who helped me deepen the conflict of this story after we
attended Alice Orr's workshop;

~*~

Christina Lynn Whited & Kat Mancos,
I was with the two of you in Christina's backyard when
I first got the idea for this story;

~*~

Carmel DeJohn O'Brien,
who as an avid reader always has insights;

~*~

and Mo Boylan,
who always has invaluable revision suggestions.

~*~

Thank you all!

Prologue

When was he going to finally contact his brother?

Drew stared at the now empty, round table where they had just tried another séance. Another unsuccessful séance, as far as he was concerned.

Yes, they had contacted an entity…an older cousin, Frederick, who had died a few years ago, and liked to come through every once in a while. But not Charles, his brother. He was desperate to contact him, to hear from him…to see his brother's familiar face.

Drew sighed heavily. Here he was a scientist in this modern age of 1898, one of the few people in the area to have successful séances on a regular basis…but he could not contact the one person he wanted to. *Needed to.*

He knew they were getting close; he could taste it, like a fine French brandy on his tongue. Even last week a guide had told them Charles was near, straining to reach them. But try as he might, Charles had not come through. They had asked repeatedly for his presence at many of the séances he'd either conducted or attended. But Charles had not appeared.

They had to get through. *He* had to. How else was he going to find out who had murdered Charles? The detectives on the case had been unsuccessful. It was only logical that he go to the source, his dead brother. Charles would know who had killed him.

1

Drew moved to extinguish the two candles in the room. They wavered as wind gusted against the window, creeping through the spot where it didn't quite meet the sill. It sounded unusually loud to his ears.

He wondered about his Aunt Patricia's suggestion, that perhaps with a secretary to help he could make better notes and figure out what was working and what was not.

Perhaps she was correct. Maybe an assistant—a fresh set of eyes and ears to give him an additional perspective, would help him to achieve better success and finally contact Charles.

He resolved to go to his study and put pen to paper to compose an advertisement for just such a person…a research assistant.

With the candles out, he strode rapidly toward the main house and his study there, already composing the advertisement in his head.

Wanted: research assistant and secretary, to take notes, research and assist at séances.

He *would* be successful in his quest, he determined. *One of these nights,* he would contact Charles…

Chapter One

Violet alighted from the train, clutching her bag tightly. A soft wind gusted, the September air unexpectedly cool as clouds scooted across the sky. The train depot ahead was neat and appeared fairly new, with *Twin Bridges* lettered in gold against black.

The older couple ahead of her greeted a man of similar age. She glanced around, wondering who from the Covington household would appear to meet her. Mr. Covington had assured her someone would be awaiting the train.

She swallowed. The train ride from Morristown had been pleasant and was not her first ride alone. But now she was here, completely on her own for the very first time, away from what was left of her family. Here to do a job.

A rather unusual job.

Of course, she reassured herself, the job was not forever. And Morristown and her sister were only a two-hour train ride away. She could even visit her sister. And once her job here was done, she would be back home before she knew it—and probably wishing to be on her own again.

And, of course, she had to worry about the secrets she was keeping. Secrets she had not revealed to Mr. Covington when she applied for the position.

The air was clean, and she breathed deeply, the

fumes from the train not overwhelming here. There were no other trains in sight, but the pleasant sounds of people talking and horses clip-clopping nearby were familiar, if more subdued than at home.

She glanced back to see the conductor and another train employee bringing her trunk off the train. She smiled and thanked them.

"Someone meeting you, miss?" the conductor enquired as they set her trunk on the wooden platform.

"Yes, thank you," she answered.

"Miss Moore?" The cultured, soft tone came from her right.

Violet turned to find herself face to face with a woman who was probably in her fifties. The woman was of small stature, shorter than Violet herself, with brown hair streaked with gray, swept up under an elegant brown hat.

"Yes," Violet replied.

The woman smiled. "I am Patricia Covington, Drew Covington's aunt. I'm here to escort you to Covington Manor. Welcome."

Her smile was warm, but Violet noticed Patricia Covington eyed her carefully. She got the impression that Drew's aunt was a shrewd woman. She wondered, fleetingly, what this woman thought about Drew's experiments.

Or what she would think of Violet's carefully guarded secrets.

Behind her stood two young men. "Is this your trunk?" Mrs. Covington asked, gesturing to Violet's belongings.

When Violet nodded, she turned slightly. "Gerard, Simon, please bring the trunk." Not waiting to see if they did her bidding, she said to Violet, "Follow me."

Violet carried her carpet bag, full of several books and other sundries, as she followed Patricia Covington. The woman walked briskly through the door of the station.

The Twin Bridges station was modern, and gleaming. She inhaled the smell of beeswax polish. The town obviously took pride in the railroad station and kept it scrupulously clean. Inside were two men, conversing, and a man behind the ticket window. She followed Drew's aunt and stepped through the small station and out onto another platform which faced the main street of Twin Bridges.

Here, a large but simple carriage awaited, a man standing near the four horses, talking to them. As soon as he saw Mrs. Covington, he snapped to attention.

"Good afternoon," he said, opening the door. Behind the coach stood a wagon, also with four horses.

Mrs. Covington allowed herself to be helped into the large but simple carriage.

The main street of Twin Bridges was level but wound upward several blocks from the train station. Along this main road were a bank, a dry goods store, a milliner, a candle-maker and farther down, a blacksmith. Several large and stylish homes were situated on the street, past the businesses. The street was narrower and less busy than the streets of Morristown, and the town appeared quite a bit smaller—something she had already known.

Violet glanced the other way and saw a coaching inn and hotel, which was bustling with people going in and out.

"Miss?" The coachman offered her his hand. "Your

trunk will follow on the wagon behind us."

Violet gave him her hand so she could be helped up. She swallowed. *I have nothing to fear*, she told herself firmly. Just because she was on her own for the first time in her life—that was no cause for alarm. She *wanted* this independence. She *wanted* this job.

Violet slid into the seat. She should not have been surprised to note that the dark blue interior of the coach was comfortable. It obviously belonged to a family which had money and taste. "Thank you," she murmured.

"I hope you had a pleasant journey," Mrs. Covington said once Violet was seated opposite her.

"Yes, I did, Mrs. Covington," Violet answered.

She waved her hand. "Please, call me Patricia." She pointed out the window. "If you look out, you'll see most of the center of our town. And you can see Covington Manor up there."

Violet peered out the window. Up the main street, the road became steeper, then disappeared behind some trees. Patricia was pointing toward the top of the hill.

Although the house was situated less than a mile away, from its height, it probably overlooked the small town. It was a large, white structure, with several turrets and a large porch. The house was lovely, though imposing as it looked down on its neighbors.

"It's beautiful," Violet murmured.

"Our family is quite proud of it. Drew's father and mother had it built according to their plans soon after they migrated from England. They came first to New York, then to New Jersey, and traveled for several months before they decided on the place they wanted to live and build their home—and the factory. They felt

Twin Bridges was picturesque yet convenient." Patricia smiled. "My husband was Drew's father's younger brother, and he came over several years later."

"Are you from England too?" Violet asked. Patricia had no discernable British accent.

She shook her head. "No. I grew up in New York City."

Drew's last letter had described the members of the Covington household, and Violet knew that his aunt had been widowed when her husband took ill more than ten years ago. Childless, Patricia had moved into the home of her brother-in-law and his family.

The carriage started smoothly and they turned, then proceeded up the street. Violet heard the clip clop of the horses, echoed by the same sound from the wagon traveling behind them. The wagon with her trunk, holding almost all her belongings in the world. For although her sister Rose had reiterated that she was always welcome at her childhood home—now owned by Rose and her husband—and that she wanted Violet to reconsider her decision to live on her own, whether it was this job or another—Violet was quite certain she was not going back—at least not permanently. Whether it was logic or instinct, she was sure that she was going to be on her own from this moment on. It was an exhilarating, but frightening, thought.

They passed the stores and several homes and then wound up through trees. Here the homes were larger, farther apart, and the hum of activity from the center of town faded away. They passed under trees which were just beginning to shed leaves. The road wound gradually upward and approached a bend.

"Look out the window on the other side, and you'll

get a good look at Covington Manor," Patricia declared.

Violet did as she suggested. They came out from a canopy of trees and there ahead, on the left, was the house.

Closer up it was even more beautiful and majestic. The three-storied white home had turrets, a wide porch, and a slanted roof. White trim with dark blue shutters decorated the home. It was quite the largest in the area, possibly larger than most of the mansions in Morristown that Violet had passed by many times.

The lawn was well manicured. It appeared there were several small outbuildings in the back—perhaps a stable and something else. Violet spotted a group of deer farther up the hill.

"The house was built in the shape of an E lying on its side," Patricia described. "It is a popular style back in England."

The carriage turned up the drive and rolled toward the front of the house.

"Here we are," Patricia said cheerfully as the carriage halted.

One of the coachmen helped Mrs. Covington, then Violet, down from the carriage. Patricia Covington led the way up four steps to the porch. The porch was all gleaming wood, chairs, and tables and gave a welcoming feel to the large home.

"Madam," a voice said formally. A white-haired butler bowed slightly as they entered the wide hallway.

Violet looked about in awe. It was the largest house she'd been in, she was certain. The hall was wide, with a grand staircase halfway toward the back, and many doors opening along the hall. It appeared that two smaller hallways branched off on each side part of the way down the hall which ran front to back. Several Oriental rugs lay on the polished wood flooring, and landscape and portrait paintings lined the walls, carefully spaced. One table held a bowl of flowers.

"The house is beautiful," Violet murmured.

"I will be glad to show you around, and we can have tea. Would you like to see your room first and refresh yourself?" Patricia asked, pulling off her gloves.

"Yes, thank you," Violet said.

Patricia introduced Mrs. Durham, the housekeeper, a stout woman with faded red hair.

"This way, please, miss," Mrs. Durham said and started up the stairs. "They'll bring your trunk straight away."

Violet wondered as they ascended the stairs where her room would be. She stepped onto the landing, where a window let in lots of light. Then they went up the continuing flight of stairs. As her sister Rose had pointed out, she was not family nor a guest; so she might end up on the third floor, with other servants, or even close to any nursery quarters.

At the top of the stairs was a wide hallway that went left and right. A staircase, smaller than the one they'd climbed, also went up to the left, presumably to quarters on the third floor. Violet took a step toward it.

"This way," Mrs. Durham said, indicating the corridor to the left. Violet followed the housekeeper down the hall. Once again, there was polished wood, some small carpets at intervals, and a table or two. They passed a number of doors on both sides. "The family's bedrooms are on both sides of the house," Mrs. Durham said. "We are now in the east wing." The corridor ended, but another branched off to the left. "There are some guestrooms here."

This corridor was slightly narrower. Mrs. Durham walked briskly ahead and opened the second door to the right.

Violet entered the room. It had been painted a cream color. Blue draperies, blue and gold pillows, and a blue and cream rug gave the room touches of warmth and color.

"It's lovely," Violet remarked, surprised at the size. Well, perhaps not for a guest room—but for her? She was here to work, not as a guest. "Quite lovely," she repeated.

Mrs. Durham looked pleased. "I hope you find it comfortable."

The room had a small fireplace, a generous bed, a wardrobe, night stand, and chest of drawers all of a medium-toned oak wood. A ceramic bowl and pitcher, decorated with painted blue flowers, stood on a side table.

But what she liked the best was the small writing desk in a corner. "A desk!" she exclaimed, delighted. She would have a place to sit and make notes in her room! Something she had dearly wanted while growing up. But sharing a room with Rose did not allow for an excess of furniture. Their home hadn't been tiny, but it hadn't been large either, and the desk her father used—and she used when she could—had been situated in the sitting room, where she could not always work quietly. She had had to resort to writing on tables or strange places many times.

She moved closer, running her hand over the smooth wood. The desk did not appear very old. There was a blotter and several pens, and a few cubbyholes with paper.

"Mr. Covington thought you might like having one in your room," Mrs. Durham said. "He said he will be providing you with tableaus, or notebooks, or loose paper if you prefer."

"How kind." Violet stepped back and glanced at the housekeeper. "The desk will be useful."

"Is there anything you'd like me to send up?" the housekeeper asked.

Violet shook her head. "I'll freshen up, and join Mrs. Covington. She said she'll show me about the house and then we'll have tea."

"Very good, miss. Oh, the water closet is across the hall and one door down," she added hastily. "There are four bedrooms in this section of the east wing, and they all share that water closet. But you are the only one occupying any of the rooms right now, so you'll have it to yourself."

That was a nice feature, Violet reflected, and thanked the woman again as she left.

Inside the water closet was a large tub, a sink, and toilet. Fresh towels and a lavender soap had been laid out, as if for an honored guest.

Violet took a few minutes to refresh herself and comb her hair. Her dark curls were escaping the knot she'd drawn her hair into so she redid her knot. She attempted to smooth the wrinkles that traveling had put in her dress. Satisfied, she left the room and proceeded down the short hall, turning to the right and the main upstairs hall.

Where she almost ran straight into a solid mass of wool suit, and masculine shoulders.

Chapter Two

Violet let out a small gasp. The man's hands shot out to steady her, dropping a rolled paper.

Handsome. That was her first thought. She recognized him at once. And—younger than she'd expected. Quite a bit younger.

She'd seen one photograph of Drew Covington in a newspaper last year. He'd won some award—not his first apparently—for a scientific invention, a machine or something. At this moment she didn't recall the details. His hair had appeared light in the newspaper, and she'd thought perhaps it was gray.

But this was no middle-aged man. This was a tall, good looking man with dark blond hair which was wavy and rather long. His bluish-gray eyes were keen as they looked her over. He looked to be in his late twenties, or perhaps early thirties, she thought.

And his shoulders! Broad and masculine-looking, his shoulders—his stature—were those of a man who was more than pleasing to the eye. The newspaper photograph had not done him justice.

"Are you all right?" he asked, gripping her elbows. Holding her up.

"Yes." Her voice sounded breathless to her own ears. "Yes, thank you. I apologize—"

"Nonsense, I was rushing about as usual."

She was acutely conscious of his hands, their

warmth penetrating through her simple traveling dress.

He stepped back suddenly and bent to retrieve his rolled up paper. Straightening, he eyed her carefully, a smile on his face. "You must be Miss Violet Moore. I'm Drew Covington."

Violet gave a little curtsy. "Mr. Covington. Your home is lovely. And my room—"

"It's suitable?" he asked.

"Yes—very! It's charming."

"Good, very good. My aunt told me she's ordered tea and then she's giving you a tour. I will try to join you presently."

"Yes, she is," Violet began, when he took another step away.

"I must check something. I will see you in a short while." And he all but dashed to a door across the hall, opening it and shutting it behind him.

The room faced the front of the house but appeared to be a corner room. His bedroom, she guessed. She wondered what was on the rolled up paper. Notes, perhaps, on his experiments? But the paper had been a large one. Plans, perhaps? For his family's factory? A new machine?

Plans for a séance?

He certainly was a handsome man. She had expected him to be older, more staid. More like the scientist she'd pictured in her mind.

A scientist who was now exploring some very peculiar things.

Well, she had hoped that this job would prove to be interesting. Extraordinarily interesting.

Or it could be a big disappointment. If his experiments were anything like her own experiences with the occult.

At least, most of them. She swallowed. There had been that one time—

Sighing, she went toward the stairs and descended them, thinking about the handsome, younger-than-expected man who was her employer.

The hall downstairs was quiet. She was just wondering which room Patricia might be in, when she heard her voice from behind her.

"Come, let's have some tea," Patricia said.

Violet turned to find Patricia sitting in a small chair down the hall, apparently waiting for her. She led the way down the hall to the left of the entrance. "I prefer to take tea in the afternoon in this small sitting room. It is a favorite of mine and was my sister-in-law's favorite too," she said. "If I am alone, or we have only one or two visitors who are close friends, this is my room of choice. We call it the green room."

The room faced the back yard of the house and was cozy. A green sofa and two green chairs dominated the room, surrounding a marble table set with a silver tea set. A thick carpet and several paintings added a touch of elegance. There were a few side tables, one of them piled with several books. A small fireplace was unlit, but Violet guessed it would keep the room nice and toasty during cold weather.

"Cook made some lemon biscuits—I mean cookies," Patricia said. "You must excuse me; I sometimes do refer to things by their English names, since so many of our family members do so."

"That's quite all right," Violet said, seating herself on the sofa, which turned out to be quite comfortable.

Patricia sat in the chair nearest the table holding the

books and poured tea for them both. "I shall give you a tour of the house after tea."

"I would like that very much," Violet said. "It's quite large, and I don't want to get lost."

"You won't," Patricia said, smiling. "The house is shaped like a large letter "E", lying on its side. There are many homes in England shaped thusly. The front of the house is the largest part of the "E". On either side, toward the back, are two small wings." She pointed out the windows of the green room. "We are in the west wing, at the back of the house. Your bedroom is in the east wing, but in the back section—the arm of the E."

Violet stirred sugar into the hot tea and then lifted the flowered china cup to her lips. Steam from the cup touched her face, and she sipped carefully. The brew was hot and strong.

Setting her cup back down to cool some more, she said, "I am excited to be working on Mr. Covington's research."

Patricia waved a hand slightly, then reached for her own cup. "Yes. This research—I've never seen him so absorbed in a project. *Ever*. Not even when he was working on a machine to help hammer boot heels into the boots. That was an important invention and helped the Covington Shoe and Boot Factory enormously, but—I digress." She sipped her tea. "This— experiment—could also have enormous implications, but it is consuming him. More than anything else." She frowned, lines of concern edging her face.

"The experiment—" Violet began. Of course, Drew Covington had described the experiments briefly in his letters, but he had not said precisely what he was working on—except that it had to do with the séances being conducted.

"But please tell me about your background," Patricia said, as if wanting to change the subject. "Drew told us only a little about you. Your father was in the printing business, he said, and you are well-read. And that you had done some academic work, so being a research assistant for Drew will be a perfect fit."

"Not exactly academic work," Violet said slowly. "Yes, my father owned a printing press. I grew up with many books and materials available for my reading." And she had read—everything, although novels of romance and mystery and fantasy remained her favorites. "He and my mother passed on two years ago—they succumbed to the fever that was so prevalent that year and died only two days apart. My brother had gone to Arizona to seek his fortune and didn't want to return. My younger sister Rose and my father's assistant were sweet on each other, so they took over the business, and they married in the spring."

"No other family?" Patricia asked, picking up her cup again and sipping.

"We had another sister, Lilly, who died when I was only a tot," Violet said. "I can barely remember her. She was about two years older than I. Rose was an infant and doesn't remember her at all. Lilly, too, had a fever. In fact, we were all ill that winter; but Lilly was the only one of us who didn't survive that sickness."

"So many children don't," Patricia said, with a sigh. "I'm sorry. I lost two of my four sisters at young ages, and one of my two brothers."

"I'm sorry." Violet inclined her head. "As for other family—my mother has no remaining family. My father has some cousins, but they all live in Connecticut, and we see them infrequently."

"Tell me about your academic work," Patricia said.

She seemed genuinely interested, so Violet elaborated. "I enjoy working with books and papers. One of our neighbors was a professor at a nearby college. His eyesight was going bad, so he let me help him. I would read the students' papers to him and help him grade them. Eventually he let me do some of the grading and comments myself. He even let me come in and speak about some topics—books I'd read, to his literature classes, for instance." It was hard to keep the pride from her voice. If she'd had the money to study at college, she could have envisioned herself lecturing and teaching too after receiving a degree.

"How interesting!" Patricia exclaimed.

"A few of his colleagues asked my help, too, and they paid me well. I helped a history teacher who had injured his arm for a semester, and I read an astronomy text and helped explain it to some students at the request of a professor who had to be away for part of the year, studying himself. That was fascinating. I enjoy reading astronomy books."

"Oh, you will love it here," Patricia said enthusiastically. "Drew has a telescope and is quite knowledgeable on the subject. And the sky is so beautiful and clear in this part of western New Jersey. You can see so many stars at night. It is breathtaking!"

Violet's heartbeat quickened at the idea of studying the heavens through a telescope. "I would love to see stars through the telescope."

Especially if it involved observing them with the handsome Mr. Covington.

Patricia offered her the platter of cookies, and

Violet accepted one. Biting into it, she found it to be delicious, not overly sweet, and after finishing it, helped herself to a second. Patricia munched along with her, gazing out at the garden, where a squirrel ran up a nearby tree. She asked her a little bit about Morristown, and Violet described the small, bustling city.

After a few minutes, Patricia Covington put aside her teacup and saucer. "Perhaps you would like to see the house now?" she queried.

"Yes, I would," Violet answered, hastily putting down her china. She wiped crumbs from her fingers with a linen napkin.

"We'll begin here, in the west wing," Patricia said. "The green room is one of our small salons, used mostly by family, not very much for entertaining, except for an occasional small group of friends. The room before it"—she moved closer to the main part of the hall—"is what we refer to as the men's parlor." She made a slight smirk. "It started as a place where the men would go for cigars and brandy after dinner. After Drew's parents died, Drew and Charles began using it as a place where they could sit and talk. It became their room, and no one else used it much. On the rare occasions we entertained, maybe the gentlemen would have port there, but mostly it was Drew and Charles' retreat." She opened the door and Violet peeked in.

The room was not large—slightly larger than the size of the green parlor—and it was masculine in furnishings and atmosphere. Violet caught the slight tang of expensive cigars. The sofa and chairs were deep, a dark brown, and the furniture heavy. A hunting scene hung over the fireplace. On a sideboard were decanters and glasses.

"It does look exactly like a masculine retreat," Violet observed.

"Indeed." They left the room, and Patricia closed the door after them. She moved across the hall to the front of the house. "This is the main parlor for entertaining, the gold room."

The room was plush but not overdone, its colors a mix of gold, cream, and some rose tones. From there they went on the blue parlor, which Patricia informed her was used more by the family and for casual entertaining. Then they crossed the hall to a small study.

"It doesn't seem very used," Violet said, somewhat disappointed. The huge desk held only a few books and one neat stack of papers. There were two armchairs by the fireplace but it seemed rather empty.

"That is because Drew uses his study in the laboratory most often," Patricia proclaimed.

Violet raised her eyebrows. "The laboratory?"

Patricia pointed out the window, which looked out to the backyard of the house, to a wooden structure that Violet had thought was a barn. "Drew had it built many years ago so he could have plenty of space to work on his inventions, and work quietly into the night. This way he did not wake people in the family—and we did not have to smell the fumes from experiments that went wrong." She wrinkled her nose, smiling.

Violet returned her smile. "I guess he has been working on inventions for a long time?"

"Oh, yes, since he was a child. He certainly has helped things to run smoother at the factory with some of his findings."

Violet knew exactly what she was speaking of.

Everyone, far and wide, knew of Covington shoes and boots. The factory had been built by Drew's father, John, and later his brother had joined the company.

"The factory is half a mile from this house, west of the railroad station," Patricia continued. "With the leaves on the trees you can't see it right now, but if you go to the third floor, or when the leaves come down in the fall, you will be able to see the building."

There was a door in the corner of the study. "That leads to the library, or we can enter from the hall," Patricia said. She led the way back to the hall, then opened the next door.

Violet gasped. The library was splendid! Bookcases, some quite full of volumes, lined the walls. A large table stood in the center, and here were scattered some books and papers. A globe presided over one corner, along with a sideboard again sporting decanters and glasses. Several comfortable looking armchairs and a small red and gold sofa were grouped together, and plush rugs covered the floor. The room looked comfortable and well-used.

"This is delightful," Violet breathed. She could imagine herself sitting at the large table, carefully making notes on Drew Covington's experiments, or better yet, sitting in one of the comfortable chairs with an exciting novel on a cold night, the fireplace logs snapping.

Patricia was studying her. "I gather you enjoy reading?"

"I love it above all things," Violet said, then paused, realizing she was gushing. "I was fortunate that at the building which housed my father's printing press; there were many things I could get my hands on to read."

Violet moved forward. At random she stood before one bookshelf and skimmed the titles. Plays of Shakespeare, poets she recognized from England. She moved to the next bookcase. Here were texts on scientific subjects—astronomy, meteorology, physics, chemistry.

Patricia was smiling when Violet turned around. "I can see this is a room you will enjoy."

"Yes," Violet said. "If Mr. Covington doesn't mind my using it in my spare time—"

"Of course he won't." She waved away any objections. "I'm sure he'll be delighted if you want to use it."

Violet stayed as long as she could, studying the shelves, but sensing that Patricia wanted to continue, she slowly left the room.

Patricia showed her the rest of the downstairs rooms. The house was even bigger than Violet had realized. In the center area was a music room, complete with a grand piano, and a billiard room. The east wing contained a large dining room, a smaller breakfast room and the morning room—the room that got the most sun in the morning, perfect for cold winter mornings, Patricia told her.

"Of course, on a hot summer day we prefer the green room," she added.

The back part of the east wing was devoted to the huge kitchen and butler's pantry. Patricia propped open the door so that Violet had a quick peek at the large space.

"You've already met our butler, Mr. Durham, and housekeeper, Mrs. Durham," Patricia said as she led the way upstairs. "We have Cook—Mrs. White, and her assistants the Misses Ames and Lewes. We also have two servant girls, our head of the stables, Stanley Hodes; and two lads who help him; and the two groomsmen who double as servants in the house. Not a very big staff, really."

The staff seemed a huge number of people to Violet, who was used to the one servant who had helped her parents. But she said nothing.

Once they reached the second floor, Patricia began rapidly pointing out rooms but didn't open most.

"The other stairs lead up to the nursery, schoolrooms, and several servants' rooms, plus the attics," she told Violet. "There's no need for us to go upstairs right now. You may explore by yourself later, if you wish. Right now, all the servants have quarters over the stables and in the small house beyond. John and Claire, Drew's parents, preferred that the servants not be underfoot all night." She shrugged. "Now here"—she indicated doors across from the main stairs—"at the front of the house are their rooms. No one uses them since their passing."

"Did they die recently?" Violet asked.

"A carriage accident while they were visiting Italy four years ago." She sighed heavily. "They hadn't taken a vacation for ages, and they carefully planned this one. Such a tragedy."

"How sad," Violet said quietly.

"Well, they died together. They were a devoted couple," Patricia said matter-of-factly. "Now here," she continued, turning toward the west wing," is the room of Drew's older sister, Mary, who is married now. But when she and her husband visit they stay here. And this"—she pointed to a room at the back—"is mine. It overlooks the gardens."

Violet observed the location of the room. It must be directly over the green parlor. Perhaps Patricia liked the view of the backyard from this angle.

She pointed out the red and green guestrooms, as they were called, and several water closets. In the section that was a mirror to the one Violet's room occupied in the east wing, Patricia pointed out a gallery, holding many portraits and other paintings. Turning back, she led the way to the center of the hall and then to the east wing.

"This is Cousin Betsey's favorite room, when she visits," she said, opening the door to disclose a buttercup yellow room overlooking the back of the house.

"How cheerful," Violet said, peeking in. The room was large, larger than hers.

"Yes, she always asks to stay there. She lives in New York, is a little older than Drew but younger than Mary, and a favorite with all of us. Her mother is Claire's sister. Betsey's mother hasn't been well and hasn't been here for a few years, but Betsey comes several times a year. We expect her in a few weeks." She shut the door. "Now over here"—she pointed to a door next to John and Claire's suite—"that was Charles' room." Sadness touched her voice.

Charles. The brother who had died so suddenly last year. The brother—

"And in the corner, that is Drew's room. His suite, actually. He took the small room next to his and made it into a sitting room for him and Charles many years ago. But they still preferred the men's parlor. I think he is using this one more now, since Charles passed away." She continued past the doors, turning to the area where Violet's room was. "And we have several guest bedrooms here, and"—she strode to the end of the section and opened the door—"the conservatory."

Surprised, Violet followed Patricia in. The room was a garden room of sorts, with some indoor plants and chairs. Large windows faced the backyard. The view would be especially beautiful and romantic in the moonlight, Violet thought, then wondered why that thought had occurred to her.

"Sometimes Drew looks at the stars from here," Patricia said, and pointed to the telescope in the corner. "When he was alive, Charles would often join him."

Violet moved over to the telescope and touched it gingerly. She'd seen one of these instruments in the office of the science professor but had never gazed through it. How exciting to see one in real life—and think that she might have the opportunity to use it some night!

"I would love to see how it works," she said softly.

"Tell Drew. I'm sure he'll be glad to show you," Patricia said. "Well, that is the end of the tour."

"The house is wonderful," Violet said enthusiastically. "Beautiful and spacious and decorated tastefully."

Patricia smiled sadly. "Yes, John and Claire are to thank for that. My husband and I," she continued as they turned to go back, "lived close to the factory, but after my husband died John and Claire convinced me to move in here so I wouldn't be lonely. I do love this house." She sighed.

They were just approaching the staircase when a

door opened behind them. Violet and Patricia both turned to see Drew Covington striding toward them.

"I'm sorry I forgot about tea," he said quickly. "But I will see you at dinner."

"We dine rather early here in the country," Patricia said to Violet. "Six o'clock."

"I'm used to eating about that time," Violet told her.

"I'm looking forward to your taking over the note-taking for me," Drew began, gazing at Violet. "You're not tired from your journey, I hope?" He regarded her carefully.

She found herself smiling at him. "No, I'm fine," she said. He probably wanted her to begin straight away in the morning.

"I hope you don't mind," he continued, "if we begin right away. Tonight."

Tonight?

Chapter Three

Violet stared at Drew Covington. "Tonight?" Her voice squeaked as her pulse increased.

Eagerness highlighted his face as he regarded her.

"Really, Drew, perhaps Miss Moore is tired from her travels," Patricia said in an almost-scolding voice.

His face fell. "Are you?"

While Violet would have preferred to retire early—perhaps with a book from the wonderful library—she was not fatigued. And she wanted to please her new employer.

"That would be fine," she said.

"Good. I'll send word to Harriet O'Grady—our medium," he explained. "I told her yesterday I hoped we could begin right away. She lives close by, not even a half mile from here."

He started to turn to the stairs, then turned back. "Thank you. I'll see you at supper." Then he moved swiftly and left them.

"Well," Patricia said. "Perhaps you'll want to rest in your room until supper?"

"I believe I will," Violet said. It would give her some time to unpack and relax before the evening began.

She took advantage of the time to put her clothing away, then relaxed with her brand new journal, purchased for this adventure. This job. She made notes

26

on what had occurred so far.

A knock on her door sounded shortly after she put it aside, and a servant girl announced that Patricia had asked that she be told that supper would be served in ten minutes.

It was a quiet dinner. Drew, Patricia, and Violet were the only ones present in the dining room. The food was simple but delicious—roast chicken, potatoes, and zucchini, with a blueberry tart for dessert. They spoke a little about the community of Twin Bridges, and Drew remarked that they would visit his sister Mary soon. "She is eager to meet you," he said.

Violet wondered why. She had been hired by Drew to be his assistant, specifically to make notes on some experiments he was conducting on a new invention—and on the séances he was holding. His letters had said that his work was fascinating, but he was finding the note-taking to be time-consuming and a chore, especially since he still ran the shoe and boot factory.

Mr. Covington had sounded most enthusiastic when she wrote that she had attended a number of séances after her parents had died. She had told him little, because she wanted this job badly. It would be so much more interesting than being a governess or a tutor! So she skirted around the issue that most of the séances she had attended had brought forth few results.

Except for that one instance...

And, of course, she didn't reveal anything about her other purpose in being here, that tied in with the one successful séance she had attended.

As they finished coffee and dessert, Drew said suddenly, "We'll meet shortly before eight o'clock in my laboratory. I have set up a room there that we've been using specifically for séances. Mrs. O'Grady will be there at eight. You know where the building is?"

"Yes," Violet answered.

"Good." He drained his cup. "I have some work to do before then. Aunt Patricia, Miss Moore. I will see you later." He stood, gave a small bow, and almost dashed from the room, already looking like his mind was miles away.

Patricia sighed when he departed. "He is so consumed lately. He only had a mild interest in séances until—until Charles died." She met Violet's eye, a frown on her face.

"He said Charles was murdered?" Violet asked. Drew's admission in his letter had started her looking through the newspapers for information regarding the death of his younger brother.

"Yes, and he's been driven to find some answers since. He has even begun corresponding with Sir Arthur Conan Doyle about his séances." Patricia sighed again, then gave a brief smile. "I hope you liked dinner?"

"Delicious. Your cook is very talented," Violet said. Mr. Covington had said he was corresponding with several scientists and well-known people regarding their séance experiences but had not mentioned who they were. Arthur Conan Doyle? She was impressed.

Patricia smiled. "Thank you." She pushed her chair away. "Breakfast is on the sideboard from seven o'clock until nine. We generally eat when we want."

"Thank you," Violet said.

Patricia rose. "After dinner I usually take a walk, then I like to read in the green room."

"I think I will gather some papers and go over to the laboratory a little early," Violet said.

Back in her room, she freshened up, then selected some paper and pens. She put on the jacket that went with her traveling dress again and found her way to the back door from the large hall.

The moon was a sliver, shining over the stone porch and the steps down to a walkway. She smelled some flowers vaguely, ones she couldn't identify as she walked along. There were trees farther back from the house, and she heard the faint hoot of an owl. There was little wind, and the air was clean and comfortably cool.

Lights shone in one part of the laboratory building. Violet approached, feeling a little twinge in her stomach. Excitement? Nervousness? Perhaps a little of both.

The front door was partially open. She rapped on the wood and called out "Hello? Mr. Covington?" as she entered.

The door led into a large room. Her first impression was that there were a dozen different projects being worked on simultaneously. Several large tables held everything from instruments, tools, microscopes, bowls, stones—it was as if each table was a combination of kitchen, woodworker's shop, and scientific laboratory. The tables held papers and books too—many of the books lying open.

On one side of the room were cabinets, a sink, and countertops also littered with equipment. On another side of the room were tall bookcases, some books standing straight, and others lying down. There were three doors at the back of the room, two of them opened to rooms with lights on.

"Mr. Covington?" Violet called.

"Oh, yes!" The voice came from the room on the left. "Please come in."

Violet moved around two of the large tables and entered the room, which was a study with a large desk, two more bookcases—also chock full of books—and two wooden filing cabinets. Drew Covington was seated at the desk, wearing glasses and peering down at some notes.

"I just received a letter from Arthur Conan Doyle yesterday," he declared enthusiastically, looking up at her and smiling. "I am going to incorporate some of his suggestions starting tonight!"

"It's wonderful that he is so helpful," Violet said. She noticed that on his desk, lying face up, was a framed photograph of a gentlemen. His brother Charles?

He must have seen her stare at it. He picked up the framed photograph, gazing at it, his expression instantly sad, his mouth turned downward. Then he met her eyes.

"My brother," he told her quietly. "Charles." He passed her the photograph.

Violet studied it. The young man was tall and had light hair like Drew's. His face was rounder, where Drew's was more oval; but still, the eyes, nose and mouth were similar. He was leaning against a fireplace, his posture casual, smiling at the camera as if he had no cares.

"That was taken at a restaurant and bar he frequented in New York City," said Drew.

"He resembles you. And he appears to have been a happy person," Violet said, raising her eyes to regard Drew.

Drew sighed. "He was. Very happy, not a worrier

at all. Why someone should murder a man so liked by so many—I cannot understand it."

"What happened?" she probed, although she knew a little bit of the story. He had been in New York City, and was set upon by thieves, the newspapers reported.

"Sit down," Drew said, indicating the chair in front of his desk. As she took the seat, he reached out, and she handed him back the picture.

"The police believe he came out of this very restaurant and bar in that photograph, late at night. Usually he was with friends, but that night his friends left before he did. He had been drinking more than usual, I am told." He sighed, his face drawn.

"And..." Violet said.

"And...he left, and someone approached him from behind and hit him on the head with a heavy object. That object was never found. Charles died instantly, and his watch and cufflinks and all his cash were taken from him. The police believe he was simply robbed, that the robber probably meant to stun him and take his belongings, but the way he was hit, the blow was fatal."

"I am so sorry," she murmured. "That is indeed terrible."

"I might as well tell you, because I am hoping we will have some luck contacting him. There is more to the story than the newspapers have reported." His voice took on a decidedly grim note.

"Oh?"

He folded his hands in front of him and stared at her, peering through his glasses. "My brother had left Twin Bridges to do business two days before his death. He was the head of the business aspect of Covington Shoes and Boots. He was brilliant when it came to business and bookkeeping. He was meeting some buyers from stores, showing them some of our new merchandise. The day he departed—a Tuesday—he left me a short letter on my desk in our study in the main house. I did not find it until the following morning, since I was working at the factory and then in my study here, in the laboratory."

"What did it say?"

Mr. Covington opened a drawer in his desk, and reached inside, moving some papers. He took out a leather case, and opening it, removed a letter. "You may see for yourself."

Violet grasped the one page note, written with a scrawl on thick paper.

"Drew, I am most concerned," she read aloud. "I have learned something that leads me to believe we are in danger. As soon as I return, we must discuss this and take measures to protect ourselves. I shall be returning on the Friday train and hope to arrive home early in the afternoon. Yours, Charles"

"He never returned home," Drew said, his voice suddenly thick.

Violet met his eyes. "I am so sorry," she whispered.

"Now you see why I wish to contact him. It is not simply because I miss my brother, and want to hear his voice, see him. Although I *do*. But—it's also because I believe he was murdered."

A shiver coursed up her spine. "And you want to find his killer," she added.

"Yes." Desperation edged his tone. "I believe my brother was cold-bloodedly killed, and I want to find the killer and bring him to justice. I need answers!"

"And do you think your family may be in danger?" she asked, leaning closer.

"I don't believe so," he said, "But I am unwilling to take chances. I need to speak to Charles, to learn what he was afraid of."

"Have you had any success so far?" Violet asked.

"Only of a minor sort. Once, I could have sworn I heard his voice calling me, saying 'Drew' two times. But we—we lost the connection." His voice dropped, and the disappointment on his face was evident. "I have tried with several mediums. Mrs. O'Grady lives nearby and knew Charles slightly. She has been the only medium to reach him both times." He sighed. "The second time—about six weeks ago—we were having a thunderstorm. For one moment, I saw Charles, during a lightning flash. But then he was gone, and we heard nothing." His shoulders drooped.

"Perhaps we will be more successful tonight," Violet said encouragingly.

He smiled suddenly, his face taking on a boyish, charming expression. She could see the resemblance to his brother's face in the photograph. "Perhaps we will. I knew when I saw your letter that you were the exact person I needed as my assistant."

Violet responded with her own smile. "Thank you. I have brought paper and a pen, to make notes during the séance."

"Very good." He pulled out a gold pocket watch, consulting it. "Mrs. O'Grady should be here in a few minutes. Let's set up the room."

He stood, and she followed as he led the way back to the main room, past another smaller room, that he showed her was used for storage, and to the third door.

Inside that room stood a round table, covered with a dark blue cloth. A side table held an oil lamp, a large white candle, a trumpet, and a drum with a wooden stick.

Violet was not surprised to see the trumpet. Many mediums used them, with varying success, in contacting those who had passed on.

She had only read once of anyone using a drum to help the dead communicate but had never seen it at any of the séances she'd attended.

Drew Covington lit the candle but left the oil lamp alone. Then he moved to the small window and opened it slightly. Wind stirred the curtains, gusting in the small room, bringing clean, cool air.

"Some people prefer to keep the windows closed during a séance so there are no distractions," he said, glancing outside. "But I prefer to open them. I feel it lets any spirits outside know they are welcome—although the walls wouldn't stop them. And I believe when the moon is out, it is more conducive to spirits coming through. According to my research, more of them do reach us during the full moon."

"How interesting!" Violet said. "Was there a full moon when your brother communicated?"

"No, but we shall have one in ten days," he said.

Footsteps sounded in the large room, and a woman's voice called out "Good evening, Mr. Covington."

"Ah, Mrs. O'Grady," Drew responded.

Harriet O'Grady appeared in the doorway, a shawl over her dark red dress. She was dressed simply and appeared to be in her mid-forties. A small, thin woman, with brown hair touched by gray, she nevertheless had a pleasant smile and demeanor.

Drew introduced her to Violet.

"It is a pleasure to meet you," Violet told her.

"Likewise," Mrs. O'Grady murmured with a shy smile.

Drew's face took on a solemn expression.

"Shall we get started?"

****

Drew placed the candle and its holder on the sideboard, right in the middle, then indicated that the two women should take seats. He went into the large, main room and dimmed the oil lamps there, leaving only one on near the end of the room, where it barely penetrated the darkness near them. Harriet O'Grady sat in her usual seat. Facing the sideboard, the door at her back, the window to her right.

He glanced at Violet Moore, who was calmly seating herself. She placed her pencil and papers on the table in front of her. So far, he'd been impressed by her, despite the fact that she was not what he had expected.

When he'd first advertised in several newspapers for a research assistant, he'd gotten about a dozen letters applying for the job. Some of the people— mostly men—were clearly not right for the job. Their English was poor, which made him wonder about their note-taking skills. Or they had a slightly scoffing attitude about séances and research that came through in their letters.

He'd asked Violet and two others to write to him again; of the three, Violet had impressed him the most and he'd offered her the job on a trial basis for several months, to see if she could do the work he wanted.

He had expected an older woman, a bookish,

spinster type. After all, she had expressed that she loved to write, and learn, and do research and work with college professors.

Instead, she had appeared in his home, a young woman of about twenty, small-boned and very pretty. She had dark blue, almost violet colored eyes (perhaps that was why her parents gave her that name?) and a pert nose. Her dark, almost-black hair was thick and lustrous, even pulled back as it was now. He had a sudden, absurd desire to run his fingers through her beautiful locks and had to quell the desire. And though she dressed in plain, serviceable clothes, they hinted at a feminine figure.

"Shall I take notes during the séance or immediately afterward?" she asked him now.

"Right afterward. We do not want to interrupt the proceedings," he answered in a low voice.

They sat quietly. From the window, which was open only slightly, they could hear the low chirping of the crickets that were still around. Once an owl hooted, and he saw Violet move slightly, as if she'd been startled. Her breathing was more rapid than his, but gradually it slowed, as if she were relaxing.

Slowly, Mrs. O'Grady's breathing deepened, and he knew she was going into a trance. Now if only someone would come through.

He glanced from the corner of his eyes at the sideboard, where the trumpet and drum sat near the window, far from the candle. Perhaps a spirit would use them tonight. The last four séances had resulted in nothing, no contacts at all. But he continued to hope.

The breeze touched his face, and then he realized suddenly it was coming from the door, not the window.

There was a sound, and the empty chair on the right of Violet moved a few inches.

Violet sucked in a breath.

Harriet O'Grady opened her mouth.

"Top of the evenin' to you, friends!" a masculine voice declared jovially.

Chapter Four

Violet gasped.

Drew found his body tensing as his pulse speeded up.

Someone had come through!

It wasn't Charles—this voice was unknown to him. An Irishman, judging from the words and accent.

Excitement leaped through Drew's veins.

"Good evening," he addressed the entity. He peered through the dim light, but he saw nothing.

And yet, the chair had moved.

Violet was staring at the chair, too, her face a mix of surprise and awe.

"Whom do we have the honor of addressing?" Drew asked cautiously, striving to make his voice welcoming.

"Edward. Edward Rourke," was the answer, in a strong voice.

"Thank you for joining us, Mr. Rourke," Drew said, his tone belying his rapid pulse. The stranger sounded quite cheerful.

He glanced at Mrs. O'Grady. Could this man be related to her in some way?

"Welcome, Mr. Rourke. Do you have a message for us?" Drew asked, after a moment of silence.

There were a few seconds in which he thought that both he and Violet were holding their breaths. He knew he was. No one moved, no one spoke. Even Mrs. O'Grady seemed still.

"Be careful." The voice was now more serious.

"Be careful?" Drew repeated.

"Yes. *Be careful.*"

The voice seemed to be coming, not from Mrs. O'Grady, but from the air around the chair. Drew waited for something further.

The voice was not forthcoming.

"Be careful—of what?" Drew asked slowly, not wanting to disturb the entity in any way.

"Danger," was the un-helpful reply.

For a moment, Drew gritted his teeth. Of course, he should be careful of danger. But then, he thought, this spirit was trying to tell him something.

"What kind of danger?"

There was another moment of silence. Suddenly he smelled a hint of tobacco.

"Danger from close by," the Irishman replied.

That wasn't too helpful either, but he refrained from pointing that out. Sometimes those who crossed over found it hard to tell you what they wanted. He had seen that once or twice at different séances.

Sometimes a specific question would help. "Is the danger imminent?"

A pause, then, "No. But—not far away."

He waited, but the man did not elaborate.

Drew tried again with a specific question. "Do you perhaps have a message from my brother? Charles Covington?"

He heard Violet take a long breath.

For a minute, there was no answer. They waited, and he could see her hand tense on the table, as she leaned forward just the slightest bit.

At last, there was a response. "No." The voice sounded regretful. "Sorry, lad. Not tonight."

But that in itself was interesting. "But—in the future?" Drew asked, trying to tamp down on his eagerness.

Again, there was a brief moment of silence. Then, "Yes. I can't reach him now, though."

Excitement shot through Drew. This spirit had some contact with his brother! He might reach him soon!

"Thank you, Mr. Rourke," Drew said. "Thank you very much."

"Sorry I can't help tonight, m'boy." Then they heard a chuckle, and the chair scraped against the floor. "I wanted ta say good evening to the young lady here." The tobacco scent grew stronger, then began to fade.

"Good evening, Eddie," Violet said suddenly. "I am so glad to—hear you."

Drew stared at her.

The wind blew. "Goodnight, friends." The voice was fading now.

Mrs. O'Grady made a snorting sound.

And Drew felt a peculiar feeling, one he'd felt only a few times before. It was as if a weight, a *something*, in the room had melted away, disappearing, leaving an empty spot in the room, in the very air around them.

As if someone had been there, and gone.

Violet's eyes were wide.

Harriett O'Grady shuddered suddenly, and her breathing changed, became less slow and deep. A minute later, she opened her eyes and straightened.

She looked from Drew to Violet and back.

"I feel—I feel tired," she murmured. "Did—did someone come through?"

Violet nodded her head as Drew answered "Yes!"

He turned to Violet. "Did you know Mr. Rourke?"

"Yes." Her voice was uneven, and her breath came out in a rush. "He was—he was our neighbor from two houses down the street. He passed on about six months ago." She took a deep breath. "My family always liked him."

"Fascinating, how he came through—perhaps to see you! But he did say—," he turned to include Harriett in his remarks—, "that we might get a message from my brother in the future." He did not include anything about danger. Why worry Mrs. O'Grady? She did not remember more than fleeting impressions from her trances.

He was pleased. True, they hadn't reached Charles. But they had reached someone. Someone with a message!

He could definitely hope that, in the future, Charles would join them.

He faced Violet. "I will walk Mrs. O'Grady home, since it is late and she usually is tired after a séance," he told her. "Can you make notes right away? So nothing is forgotten? We can review them in the morning."

As she nodded in response, he was thinking he might still make some of his own notes. This had been a successful evening, with the promise of more. "I will lock up when I return. You may make your notes inside the house, if you wish."

"Yes," Violet said and blew out the candle. The three walked together outside, up to the back door, where Violet let herself in, clutching her papers. Drew continued on the path around the house with Mrs. O'Grady.

****

What an exciting evening!

Violet hurried into the library, eager to make her notes. She had chosen to write them here, rather than in her own room, hoping to see the fascinating Mr. Covington when he returned from escorting Mrs. O'Grady home.

There was a small oil lamp lit in the room, as if someone had anticipated that perhaps Mr. Covington would return here. She had passed no servants, and she thought that since it was nearly ten o'clock, most must be abed now. She placed her materials on the table and set to work.

But her mind was rolling rapidly, going over the evening's events.

Eddie Rourke had been present!

She had no doubt that Eddie's spirit had indeed, if not shown itself, at least made itself known this night. His voice, the odor of the cigars he sometimes smoked, the exact lilt to his speech—that had been Eddie, and she had felt shivers from the moment he greeted them.

Eddie had always been warm to their family and gently teased her and her sister when he did see them. He had lost his wife a number of years ago, when Violet was young. Eddie's two sons were grown now, one living only a few miles away, another living farther north in New Jersey. She and Rose had been saddened when Eddie died of sudden heart failure.

It was amazing, now, to think that Eddie had gotten through to them. They'd wanted to speak to and see Charles Covington—but Eddie Rourke had shown up, in a manner of speaking.

To see her?

And...with a warning for Drew.

She shivered as she remembered that.

Quickly, Violet wrote down the exact occurrences as they happened, the breeze, Mrs. O'Grady's breathing, the sound of the chair, Eddie's voice and what he said. At the end, she added her impressions, that she had felt someone sitting in the chair beside her, as if the air was displaced, that she had been aware of this other presence in the room, and that she had smelled the cigars he used to favor smoking each evening.

When she finished, she glanced up. The clock over the mantel said ten thirty.

She stood, her awe-struck mood suddenly replaced with fatigue. It had been a long day of traveling, the excitement of her new job, and then the séance. It was time to turn in.

She went to the window and looked out at Drew Covington's laboratory. As she watched, she saw him walking up the path. He entered the building.

But instead of locking up, he must have moved into the room and turned on the oil lamp, because the window grew brighter there. He did not come out, and she guessed he had decided to do some further work there. Perhaps he wanted to mull over the events of the evening.

Weary, Violet hesitated, then left the light on, should he decide to come and work here. Either he or a servant would douse the light, she surmised.

She took her notes and went upstairs. Preparing for bed, she wondered if the events of the night would keep her up.

The bed was wonderfully comfortable, and she quickly fell asleep.

She awoke as usual at seven a.m. For a moment, Violet lay on the comfortable mattress, the wisps of a dream surrounding her. She had seen her sister Lilly, with her long, light brown hair and dark blue eyes, coming down the stairs of their home in her nightgown.

It had been a long time since she dreamt of Lilly. It must have been because she'd spoken of her yesterday.

Stretching, she got out of bed and went to wash and dress. As she approached the water closet, two young maids were bringing up pails of steaming water.

"We thought you might want a bath, ma'am," one said.

"Thank you," Violet murmured. "That would be lovely." She usually bathed in the evening before bed; but with the work Mr. Covington did, it might be easier to bathe in the morning. Besides, she did not want to disrupt the household routine.

Once she had bathed, she went downstairs to the small breakfast room. A breakfast of eggs, sausage, toast, and jellies was laid out along with both coffee and tea.

For the moment, she was alone. Violet helped herself to some toast and eggs and coffee. As she sat down, Patricia entered the room.

"Good morning," Violet greeted her.

"Good morning! I thought perhaps you would sleep late after your busy day yesterday," Patricia remarked, pouring herself some tea.

"I usually wake the same time every morning," Valerie said. She sipped her coffee, which was rather strong and invigorating. "I am eager to get to work. I made notes last night right after the séance, but I want to review them and see if there's anything else I should add." She sipped some more.

"Were you successful?" Patricia sounded genuinely interested. She paused in buttering her toast to look at Violet.

"In contacting an entity, yes," Violet told her, "although it wasn't Mr. Covington's late brother."

Patricia raised her eyebrows. "Oh?"

"It was—a neighbor of mine, who passed on several months ago," Violet said. She set down her coffee cup and picked up her fork.

"How interesting," Patricia murmured.

Violet got the impression that Patricia was truly interested. She described the séance.

"Perhaps I will join you for the next one," Patricia said. "I used to go to many of them; but since the last several have been without any occurrences at all, I stopped participating."

"This séance was certainly eventful, although it was not the person we expected," Violet admitted.

They finished breakfast, and Patricia excused herself to visit a neighbor who was recovering from an illness. Violet returned to her room and took out her papers, seating herself by the lovely desk.

She read over her work, then began to copy it more neatly in pen. She was proud to note she had not forgotten any details of the evening. She wanted to show them to Drew Covington when he returned home. Perhaps he would have some impressions of his own to add.

Patricia had said her nephew worked at the factory

in the morning and early afternoons; he usually returned then and worked on his own inventions and research later in the day. Lunch was usually also laid out for people to eat as they wished; Drew took lunch at the factory most days.

By ten thirty, Violet was finished with copying her notes. Leaving both copies on her desk, she went down to the library, hoping to find a book or two. She would love to read some of the research books Drew Covington was studying and a fictional book as well. She would ask him which books he recommended and could spare for her to read.

In the meantime, his library awaited. With great anticipation, she went downstairs and entered the room.

The room was bright and inviting. She soon found a shelf with mystery novels and selected one to begin with. She ensconced herself on a comfortable, overstuffed crimson and gold chair and was soon absorbed.

It wasn't until a grandfather clock in the room chimed noon that she realized the time. She stood, stretched, and glanced around. The story of a young woman who found a body of the town's most prominent citizen by the clock tower had kept her riveted. It was by an author who was unfamiliar to Violet; the copyright date on the book was only the year before. The well-written story had kept her in suspense, and she was eager to read more.

She decided to eat lunch now. Taking the book with her, she went back to the breakfast room.

Lunch was laid out. It was simple, consisting of breads, cheeses, some cold luncheon meats, and fruit. Violet usually had a small sandwich and fruit for lunch at home so was used to a smaller meal. She made herself a sandwich now with turkey, cut some cheese to have on the side, and poured herself water form a china pitcher. She added an apple and sat at the table and began.

Patricia entered the room. With a glance at the book on the table, she said, "Ah. I read that when it first came out. A very good mystery, I thought. What do you think of it?"

"I like it very much," Violet answered. "I cannot imagine who murdered Mr. Jackson."

"I won't tell," Patricia said with a smile.

After lunch, Patricia said she was going to read in the green room and invited Violet to join her. Patricia was reading a Charles Dickens novel that Violet had read already, and Violet continued to read the book she had started. It was cozy and companionable, and that was where Drew Covington found them both several hours later.

"Hello," he said, his voice rising with a jovial note.

"Hello," Patricia said, as Violet stood hastily and curtsied.

"Hello, Mr. Covington," Violet said, not sure how formal to be with her employer.

He waved his hand. "No need for formalities. And again, please call me Drew.'

"Only if you call me Violet." The words seemed to come from her mouth of their own accord. Violet smiled, slightly nervous at her own boldness.

"But of course." He inclined his head, and grinned. "I am exceedingly pleased by our results from last night's séance."

"You are? But we couldn't contact your brother,"

Violet blurted.

"Ah, but we did get someone else, and it was a strong visitation, despite no visuals," Drew declared. Despite the fact his brother had not appeared, he was pleased by last night's séance. "Edward's presence was accompanied by the tobacco scent. A satisfying visitation, for certain."

"When would you like to see my notes?" Violet asked. "Perhaps you will have further impressions I can add."

"In ten minutes? I can meet you in my lab," he said.

"That would be fine." Violet hurried to her room to get her notes.

Drew watched her leave the room, and then, aware that his aunt was watching them both, turned to her.

"She is a nice young woman," Patricia murmured. "Well read, too." She tapped her novel by Dickens. "She has already read this book and is now reading the mystery I enjoyed so much last year, *The Clock Strikes Twelve*."

Drew looked at the doorway. "Yes, she seems intelligent. I hope she is as industrious as her references stated."

"And pretty, too."

He knew that. He certainly didn't need his aunt pointing out that his new assistant was beautiful and feminine. He gave his aunt a sardonic look. "I hired her because I need an assistant with the right skills to participate in the séances and take notes. Not for any other reason."

Patricia tsked. "Of course I know you'd never do anything that wasn't above board. But a thought occurred to me. She knows no one here except for us. Perhaps she would enjoy going to the apple festival this weekend?"

He hesitated. He had forgotten about the festival in the orchard two miles outside of town. He had planned only to put in a brief appearance as befitted a community member; but now he thought it might be a nice diversion for Miss Moore. "I can escort her, if she'd like," he said to his aunt. "And you too, of course."

"I should very much like that," Patricia said, beaming.

He wondered if she liked the idea so much because Violet would be joining them. Did his aunt perhaps miss feminine company since his sister had married and moved away?

Or did she think she could do some matchmaking now?

****

When Violet appeared in Drew's laboratory, he was already sitting at his desk in his study there. He invited her to have a seat and look over his notes while he read hers. "Then you can add my impressions to yours," he said.

He read in silence for several minutes. Finally he looked up. "These are good," he said enthusiastically. "Very detailed. You remembered everything that occurred."

Violet felt warmth flow through her. He was pleased with her work!

"Thank you," she murmured. "Your notes were much the same, except you forgot to mention the smell of the cigars."

"Yes. That is why I need a research assistant, someone who can immediately capture all the details while I walk Mrs. O'Grady home. I don't want to miss a single thing. I shall write to Arthur Conan Doyle immediately and tell him of these results."

"I will add your impressions to my report now," Violet said. "Will Mrs. O'Grady return tonight for another séance?"

"She gets tired afterward and does not like to do them two nights in a row," Drew said. "And tomorrow night she is busy getting ready for our local annual Apple Harvest Festival. But she has agreed to return on Friday evening."

"Perhaps," Violet began, hoping he would not mind her making a suggestion, "we could try a séance without her, just you and I and your aunt Patricia. She said she used to attend them until recently when you didn't get results."

"A splendid idea!" he said heartily. "Can you ask her when you return to the house?"

"Certainly. And may I borrow one of your volumes on séances, or ghosts, to read? I have read several books on the topic, of course, but would like to read additional ones."

"Of course." He got up, went into the main room, and returned with a slim volume moments later. "Here is a treatise by Heyword. It is informative and well-written, good basic information. I recommend this book to many people."

Violet reached for the well-read volume. "I am unfamiliar with his work."

For one moment, his fingertips brushed hers as they both held the book. Warmth sparked her at his touch.

"I think you will find it informative," he said, his voice quiet.

"Yes." The word came out breathlessly. "I am sure I will."

Taking a deep breath, she turned to go.

"Oh, Violet?"

She turned back.

"Our town participates with several others in the annual Apple Harvest Festival on Saturday. Would you like to go with me? And my aunt," he added.

A thrill out of proportion to the simple invitation—with his aunt—sped through Violet. An Apple Festival with the handsome and charming Mr. Covington? Of course! Even if it was with his aunt. In a way, that was even better. It was as if Patricia was chaperoning.

"I would be delighted," she said, and smiled.

"Good. Then I will see you at dinner."

Absurdly pleased by his praise and the invitation, Violet hurried back to the main room to add his impressions to her notes.

****

It was quiet as Violet, Patricia and Drew waited in the darkened room. Waited for something.

Patricia had agreed to sit with them, and now, at eight o'clock, they sat in the room where the séance had been held last night. Drew had expressed doubts as to how successful they would be without Mrs. O'Grady. But he, Violet, and Patricia had all been willing to try to contact Charles—or whoever chose to come through.

A cool breeze from the window touched Violet's face. It was damp, holding the promise of rain to come. Like last night, they did not hold hands. The room was hushed. As they waited, Violet became conscious of Drew's slow breathing and Patricia's slightly more rapid breaths. And her own, which were somewhere in between.

They sat quietly. About ten or fifteen minutes passed. Violet tried hard not to fidget. Once or twice, she found her fingers gripping her blue gown or smoothing the fabric, and had to stop herself.

A sudden wind gusted, chilling the air. Violet became aware of a certain heaviness nearby.

The empty chair scraped back slightly.

She held her breath. Was it Charles? Her old neighbor Eddie? Someone else?

There was further silence. After another minute, Drew said quietly, "Hello."

There was more silence. Then a voice came out of the darkness, sounding low and slurred.

"Hel-lo…" The voice was hard to understand.

She sat up straighter. It didn't sound like Eddie— no Irish lilt. She sniffed. No scent of tobacco smoke either.

"Who do I have the pleasure of addressing?" Drew asked. His tone was cautious.

There was a garbled response. Could it be Charles? Someone else?

There was another garbled word, and then, stronger this time, "M-m-urray."

"Murray? Samuel Murray?" Drew sounded excited. He paused, and she heard him draw a deep breath. "Is that you, Samuel Murray?"

Someone Drew knew fairly well, Violet surmised. They listened.

Another minute passed. Then the chair moved

again.

"Samuel, thank you for joining us," Drew said.

There was no reply.

They waited. Perhaps three or four minutes went by, and then Violet heard a strange, popping noise.

And the heaviness in the room suddenly disappeared.

She saw Drew sag, as if disappointed.

They sat quietly. But after ten minutes or so, Drew spoke.

"I believe he has left us; and that is the only visitation we are going to get tonight." He moved his chair back and brought the candle on the sideboard to the table.

"That was Samuel Murray, wasn't it?" Patricia asked.

"I believe so. He always had a deep voice," Drew concurred.

"Who was he?" Violet asked.

"A foreman at the factory for many years. He died about four years ago," Drew said. "He was elderly and his health began to deteriorate."

"Our family was very fond of him," Patricia added.

"Has he come through before?" Violet asked.

"No, never," Drew said. He sounded excited at the thought. "It seems that although we haven't contacted Charles, some other spirits have been able to get through. This is most interesting!"

"I suggest we all quickly write down our impressions, and then I will copy them tomorrow," Violet suggested.

"Yes, we should," Drew agreed.

They went into the main room, and Drew turned on

the oil lamps so there was bright light. They sat at one of the tables and each scribbled down notes on what had transpired.

Finally Violet looked up to see both Drew and Patricia were regarding her silently.

"Would you prefer that I take notes while the séance is going on?" she questioned.

Drew shook his head. "I have tried that. It seems to distract the spirits. Although," he added, "I suppose we could try it again."

Patricia yawned and covered her mouth. "I am tired. I think I will go to sleep now."

"Would you like me to escort you to the house?" Drew asked.

She smiled. "Nonsense. But if you'd like," she said, seeing his concerned expression, "you can watch me from the window."

Violet said goodnight to her, and Drew gave his aunt a hug. "Thank you." Then he stood at the main window of the laboratory and watched his aunt return to the house.

After two minutes, he turned back to Violet. "She's inside." Drew looked tired but happy. "Well, although tonight was not as successful as our previous séance, I would say it was quite satisfactory."

"Yes," Violet agreed. Then she voiced the question that had been on her mind since yesterday. "You do not hold hands at your séances. Have you tried to?"

He shrugged. "I did try séances with and without the holding of hands. In my experience it did not make any discernible difference."

"The séances I attended where there was the holding of hands, in general, were more successful than the ones without," Violet stated.

"Well, we can certainly try it again," Drew said. "In fact, we can try it with Mrs. O'Grady on Friday evening."

"I think it would be a good idea to try," Violet said. "And—one more question, if you don't mind."

"Questions are always good," Drew told her. "It helps us search for answers."

"Does Mrs. O'Grady ever have a control?" she asked, referring to the experience of a spirit taking over the medium's body to guide them to further spirit communications.

"Sometimes," Drew answered. "Quite a few times we have been guided by Red Feather, an Indian spirit."

"How interesting," Violet said. "In my reading, it appears many mediums are guided by Indian persons."

"Yes," he agreed.

She found herself stifling a yawn.

"You are tired," he said. "Why don't you copy all our notes tomorrow morning, and we can meet when I return from the factory."

"That will be good," she agreed.

"I'll walk you to the house," he volunteered.

She couldn't help the slight thrill that went up her spine. Of course, he had offered the same to his aunt.

"I can walk back myself," she said.

"It's all right. I want to get a book which I believe is on my desk in the house," he told her.

They walked through the dark, damp air in silence. Violet was acutely conscious of Drew's close proximity. She wished she dared step closer to him, but she kept a respectful employee-employer distance. Once inside the house, he bowed slightly as she said goodnight.

She brought the papers upstairs and placed them on her small desk. Then, impulsively, she went to the conservatory and looked out the window toward the laboratory building.

Drew was striding toward it, a book in his hand. She watched as he opened the door and went inside.

With a sigh, she returned to her bedroom. Pausing to make notes on her questions about trying the holding of hands and taking of notes during the actual séance, she then prepared for bed.

Her last conscious thought was of Drew Covington, and how appealing a man he was…

****

"Are we ready?" Drew asked.

"Yes," Violet and Patricia both replied.

It was Thursday evening, and they sat once again in the dim candlelight of what Violet thought of as the séance room. This time she had a sheaf of papers and a pencil by her right hand so she could take notes while the séance was in session.

The day had been much like the day before. In the morning, she'd copied all their notes neatly into the notebook she'd started on Wednesday. Then she'd gone over the notes after lunch with Drew, who had nothing more to add. It was a pleasant, partly sunny and partly cloudy day, so Patricia had suggested they walk into town. She wanted to get some candy.

They'd taken Louisa, one of the serving girls, with them, and Violet enjoyed the exercise and the brisk, almost-fall air. After shopping for the peppermint candy that Patricia admitted was a favorite, they strolled into other parts of the mercantile. Patricia purchased some yarn to knit a blanket for a neighbor who was expecting a baby. Violet had had little extra spending money in the last year, but her salary for the next month or so was excellent; so she decided to splurge on a new shawl. With Patricia's help, she selected one in tones of dark blue, medium blue, green, and gold.

Pleased with their purchases, they'd returned to the house, and Violet had spent some time continuing to read the book Drew recommended, which she had started that morning.

Now, sitting in the séance room, she was reminded of the book and how the author had stated it was important to take notes because later something which seemed minor at the time might be significant. He'd cited the example of an Indian guide who had predicted the gold rush in California some twenty years before it occurred.

The author had suggested making notes immediately after the séance, but Drew had agreed to try note taking during the séance tonight to see what results they obtained.

They sat quietly now. After about ten minutes, the wind gusted into the room. Violet found herself holding her breath.

A minute or two passed, and she let out her breath. Nothing.

Then, slowly, the chair to her right wobbled. She felt the now familiar heaviness in the room. Then the chair scraped back.

It was dark, but she made notes about the wind, the movement of the chair and its scraping, plus the heavy feeling.

There was a garbled voice nearby. Violet couldn't

be sure, but she thought it said "—Tree—-sha" or something like that.

Tricia? For Patricia? She scribbled.

"Samuel? Is that you?" Drew's voice was pleasant.

Nothing. Violet began to write again when suddenly she felt a tug on her pencil. It flew from her hand.

"Oh!" she gasped as it rolled across the table.

The wind gusted again.

Then nothing. They waited for at least ten minutes, perhaps fifteen.

Drew sighed. "I believe that is the end of our brief visitation."

Patricia moved to light another candle. "I think that was Samuel's voice again."

"Yes." Drew rubbed his eyes, looking suddenly weary. "What happened to the pencil?" he asked Violet.

She hoped he wasn't accusing her of something untoward. He sounded merely curious—but she didn't know him well enough to be sure.

"I felt something tug on the pencil and pull it from my fingers," she said.

Patricia gave a small exclamation. "Indeed! Perhaps he didn't like your note taking while we were sitting."

"I'm afraid you're right, Aunt," Drew agreed. He sighed heavily.

"I'm sorry," Violet said quickly. "I just thought we should try—"

Drew waved his hand. "It's all right, Violet. It is good to try different methods of conducting a séance. That is the scientific approach. I suggest that next time, we go back to taking notes after the actual event."

Violet nodded, and so did his aunt.

"And," he continued, "even though the contact ended rather abruptly, this was still a somewhat successful séance."

"It was?" Violet asked cautiously.

"Yes." He looked directly at her. "We did make some contact. Do you realize," his voice was earnest, "that in the last three days we have made some sort of contact each time?"

For a moment Violet regarded him. It was true, she thought. They had had some success, however meager.

"I would say we have been *wildly* successful," Patricia put in. "There have been times when we went weeks without any contact at all—despite having two or three séances each week."

"Oh," Violet said. "Yes, I have been to séances without any contact whatsoever too…but this contact tonight was so brief…"

"But," Drew said, and this time he smiled, an excited gleam in his eye, "we have had three nights out of three with some kind of contact. Not the person we had hoped for, but *something*. This is amazing!" he added.

Violet observed how pleased Drew looked. Unexpectedly a wave of warmth washed over her. Perhaps she had contributed to this success, even in a small way.

"Let us make our notes and then retire," Drew suggested. "Tomorrow, with Mrs. O'Grady joining us, I am hopeful that we will be successful again. Perhaps even more so!"

They sat in the larger room. There were few notes to make, so they finished quickly. Then Drew escorted both Violet and Patricia back to the house.

"Goodnight Aunt, Violet," he said.

"You must be tired," his aunt pointed out. "You have been working every night this week."

"I shall only be in the laboratory a short time—I want to look up something," he told them, and disappeared out the rear door.

"Well, I am tired," Patricia said. "Goodnight, Violet."

"Goodnight," Violet said, and followed Patricia up the stairs.

****

Friday passed swiftly. After copying their notes, Violet read more of the book Drew had loaned her, then went to help Patricia with some preparations for the Apple Festival. Patricia was taking some blankets and scarves she'd knitted to donate to a booth for the church, and Violet made a list for her of the donations. Patricia went over with the cook the food items they were taking in a basket. "There will be plenty of pies and cakes for sale so we need only sandwiches, fruit and, cheese," she told Violet. Turning to Cook, she added, "Make sure you pack plenty for the rest of the household." She'd indicated to Violet that all the servants joined in the fun.

"Yes, ma'am," Cook said, smiling happily.

Once Drew went over the notes and had nothing further to add, Violet continued her reading and research until suppertime. She spent an hour reading the mystery novel she had borrowed as well. By seven thirty, she was at Drew's laboratory, preparing the séance room with him—a new task for her. She observed how he checked the candle, the drum, and trumpet, and how he checked the table and chairs to make sure nothing had been tampered with, as he put it. She knew he'd never want to be accused of any falsifications in his work.

Patricia and Harriet O'Grady both arrived shortly before eight o'clock, and they sat down at the table.

"We shall try holding hands this evening," Drew announced as they took their seats.

They sat quietly. The air in the room was still and warm for the late September evening. Violet waited, hoping that once again they would have a visitor. Mrs. O'Grady's breathing became slower and more sleep-like.

They did not have to wait more than ten minutes when wind gusted through the window, and Violet felt that heaviness in the air she'd become accustomed to associating with a spirit presence.

The chair in between herself and Mrs. O'Grady moved. Violet felt Patricia's hand gripping hers tightly.

"Good evening, friends," said a masculine voice. The voice seemed to come from Mrs. O'Grady.

"Good evening," Drew and Patricia said, and Violet hastily added her own "good evening." She had never had a spirit greet all the sitters quite this way and had been unsure how to react until she heard her fellow sitters greeting the presence.

"Do we have the honor of addressing Red Feather?" Drew asked after a moment's silence.

"Yes," the deep voice answered from Harriet O'Grady's lips.

"We are honored. Will I be able to speak to my brother Charles?" Drew asked. His voice was so eager, so hopeful, that Violet's heart went out to him.

There was a minute of silence. Then the answer, "Not tonight, friends."

She saw Drew's shoulders sag in disappointment in the semi-darkness.

"But," Red Feather added, "there *is* one who wants to come through. He has tried before but is having some trouble."

"Yes?" Drew asked, his voice still holding a note of hope.

There was another pause, of two or three minutes, and then the low voice from the day before reappeared.

"Tricia, Drew…young lady." There was another pause, and Violet wondered if the spirit was gathering his strength. And then, "It is I, Sam—uel…Murr—ayyy…" the voice faded.

"I'm glad to hear you, Samuel," Drew said. "I was sorry we experienced—difficulties—hearing you the last two nights."

There was another pause, shorter this time.

"Trying to…warn you." Samuel's voice was more clear than it had been the last two nights, but still not distinct. The words were slurred, slow, as if coming from a distance.

"Warn us?" Drew asked.

Another pause and then, "Dan…ger."

Chapter Five

The entire Covington household headed to the Apple Festival, seated in the carriage plus two wagons at approximately eleven on Saturday morning.

Drew had helped Violet and Patricia into the carriage along with Cook, and then the housekeeper Mrs. Durham and her husband boarded. The rest of the staff followed in the two wagons.

Had Violet imagined it, or had his hand lingered on hers a shade longer than necessary? Tingles had run up her arm as he touched her hand.

She sat in between him and Patricia with Cook and the Durhams sitting across from them. In the spacious carriage, they were not squeezed in tightly, but there was no extra room on the seat. They'd placed the baskets on the floor and in the wagons.

"You will enjoy the day," Patricia told her, smiling as she smoothed out her skirts.

Violet was wearing a serviceable blue gown whose color she liked and she'd brought her new shawl. Patricia had warned her that the temperature could rise or dip suddenly as the day wore on.

As the carriage moved forward, she tried not to study Drew too openly.

He'd been excited about the séance when it ended last night. Right after the "danger" warning, Samuel Murray had disappeared, and Red Feather had

63

announced he'd "gone back." Then, Red Feather had said goodnight and disappeared just as quickly.

Afterward Drew walked Mrs. O'Grady home while Violet and Patricia returned to the house and made their notes. Drew had joined them and written his own notes. Violet had sat in the library copying most of the notes, leaving only the final sentences for today, and she'd finished them up this morning. Drew had declared he wanted to review them before the Apple Festival.

"I see you put in your notes that the chair moved," he'd said with approval. "I had forgotten that." He'd looked at her and smiled. "This is why I need someone who can take meticulous notes."

Warmth suffused Violet. "It seems that we are more successful when I don't take notes at the actual séance," she said, pleased by his approval.

He nodded. "Yes, although we should experiment at least one more time with the note taking during the séance just to be sure."

"I agree," she concurred.

It took less than fifteen minutes to get to the large fields where the three adjoining towns held their Apple Festival. Alighting from the carriage, Violet was struck by the sounds of people chattering, music from a band, and someone calling out "Peanuts! Get yer peanuts!" She could smell freshly baked goods and feel the warmth of the sun, which was surprisingly strong today.

As Patricia led the way into the area, Violet saw several tables lined with pies and cakes, pastie sandwiches, and homemade bread. Another table nearby held all kinds of hard candies. There were tables farther down piled with knitted goods and others with ribbons and hats. She wasn't sure where to look first.

"Let us go put a blanket down in the picnic area and have lunch," Patricia suggested, waving her hand grandly. "Then we can walk around."

"I will show you the many booths and exhibits," Drew offered. "And there is much to buy." He fell into step beside Violet.

"I see. Perhaps I will purchase some ribbons," she said, spotting some red and white ones that would look lovely on her old, worn, gray hat. She slanted a look at him. "Are you planning to buy anything?"

"I always look," he said. "I have nothing special in mind, but last year I bought an unusual rock that was purported to come from a meteor shower in Canada."

The servants followed them after hitching up the horses and watering them. They soon had several blankets spread out and ate alongside the help. Neighbors from down the road—the Donnelly family— parents, two teenaged boys, and two younger girls, sat near them, and they traded some sandwiches.

Somehow the cheese, the meat pies, and apples that Cook had packed were tastier outdoors, Violet thought as she bit into her apple. She sipped some lemonade and remarked that Cook had outdone herself.

The woman looked pleased. "Thank you, Miss Violet."

"We shall buy some pies and such to have later," Patricia told Violet.

Some of the servants wandered off, either to look at the booths or to hear the band. Drew had finished eating and appeared to be waiting for Violet and Patricia.

When Violet finished, Patricia said to her and Drew, "Why don't you look at the exhibits? I will stay here for a while with the Donnellys and catch up on the latest gossip." She smiled at Mrs. Donnelly.

Violet felt herself flush. It seemed rather obvious that Patricia wanted her to spend some time alone with Drew. As she hesitated, Patricia made a shooing motion "Go on, now."

Drew stood and held out his hand to help Violet up. He did not seem to mind being alone with her in the least, Violet thought, brushing at her skirts.

And she certainly was glad about it, she admitted to herself.

He took her elbow and guided her to the busier section of the fields. "Have you ever been to anything like this?'

"I have been to a county fair," Violet said, "but not for several years." She had always enjoyed them. "The Apple Festival appears similar to the fairs I attended with my parents and siblings."

They walked among the booths and tables, stopping to look. Violet found the red and white ribbons that had attracted her and purchased them. They strolled past a candy display, and Drew purchased her some rock candy. When she protested that it was unnecessary, he said "Nonsense. It is my pleasure," and she grew warm at his words.

A wind had sprung up, making the warm sun quite comfortable as they strolled along. Drew stopped to look at some magnifying glasses. They moved past a booth where a man juggled several balls, and then another with a "bearded lady" that Violet thought looked fake. They passed some boisterous lads of about twenty or so, and then a young blonde woman strolling with an older woman who must be her mother.

"Drew!" the young woman exclaimed, smiling.

The older woman shot her a quelling look and then looked Violet up and down before saying "Mr. Covington," in a subdued voice.

Drew bowed. "Millicent, Mrs. Brown. So nice to see you." His voice was friendly but not, Violet thought, overly so.

Mrs. Brown raised her eyebrows and stared at Violet.

"Oh, this is Violet Moore, my new research assistant," Drew introduced her.

"A pleasure," Violet said.

Mrs. Brown was frowning. "Research? Not your occult research again?"

"Yes, I'm afraid so," Drew said, smiling, and Violet caught a gleam in his eyes.

"Hmph." Mrs. Brown tugged her daughter. "Let us go see the candy they are selling, Millicent. Good day, Mr. Covington."

Millicent, who had looked so eager before, now followed her mother, her face crestfallen. Violet heard something from the older woman's mouth that sounded like "the devil's work" as she moved away.

She glanced back at Drew. His lips were folded together.

He turned them both away, and he chuckled. "You will find," he told her, "that some of the people hereabouts are a superstitious lot, small-minded, and think anything to do with the occult or paranormal is like playing with the devil."

"Yes, there are those who believe the same in Morristown," Violet admitted.

"Ah, at least you are more educated and open-minded," he said, and now he laughed. "Come, let us continue."

Violet wondered if he was aware that Miss Brown appeared to be sweet on him. She continued on the topic of superstition instead of discussing the Browns. "What about Mrs. O'Grady? Do people hereabouts seem upset because she takes part in séances?"

"No," he said. "But I believe that is mostly because she has lived here all her life, and people know her outstanding character. Her father was a physician, and her mother a nurse. She helped her parents with healing even as a young girl. So many people in this area respect her."

They approached a tent with a painted picture of a woman gazing at a crystal ball. "Madame Versailles Sees All!" the sign next to the picture said.

Impulsively, Violet stopped. "I'd like to hear what she says," she told Drew.

He raised his eyebrows. "You do know, Violet, that unlike the serious research we do, the people at these fairs often are frauds?" He kept his voice to a whisper.

"I know, but it is fun to get your fortune told," she said in a hushed voice. "I have experienced this only twice before."

He shrugged. "If you would like to."

A man appeared from around the tent. He had a long mustache, dark hair, and a decidedly gypsy-like appearance.

"Good afternoon!" he declared jovially. "Do you want to see what the future holds for you? Madame Versailles knows all!"

"Yes," Violet answered simply.

"She is almost finished with a customer, if you can

wait but a few minutes," the man began.

Two minutes later, after paying the man the reasonable sum he quoted, the flaps of the tent parted, and an older woman in her forties left, smiling. A satisfied customer, apparently, Violet thought.

There was the jingling sound of bracelets clanging together, and the flap of the tent parted again. An attractive woman of perhaps thirty poked her head out. She wore a scarf around her curly dark locks and gold hoop earrings. Bracelets slid up and down her arms and the gown she wore was a colorful swirl of red, yellowish-gold, dark blue and turquoise.

"Madame, another customer for you," the man said, indicating Violet.

Violet glanced at Drew. His expression was neutral, neither approving nor disapproving.

"I'll wait out here," he said, tilting his head toward several benches near the side of the tent.

"All right," Violet said, and followed the woman into the tent.

The tent was dark, and Violet paused for a moment while her eyes adjusted.

The scent of incense wafted up to reach her, and she spotted an incense stick in a large bowl on a table to the side of the entrance.

In the center was a round table covered with a dark blue cloth. In the middle of the table stood a large crystal ball.

She had seen them before, of course. She had had her fortune told twice in the past; once using her hand and once with a crystal ball. This was larger than the ball she remembered from when she was fourteen or so. She had sneaked away during a county fair with a friend so they could have their fortunes told, but she'd been disappointed by the vague fortune of meeting a tall handsome man.

"Please sit," Madame Versailles said, indicating a chair. She took the one opposite. "Let us see what the future holds for you."

Violet sat, and Madame sat opposite her.

"What is your given name?" the gypsy asked.

"Violet."

"A lovely flower." She nodded sagely.

The woman put her hands together and closed her eyes. "I will now pray for clear sight and guidance." She chanted something in an unknown tongue.

Then she fell silent.

The slightly spicy, unique scent form the incense stick tickled Violet's nose. The sounds of the festival seemed very muted here, and she could hear the woman's breathing, slow and steady, just as Mrs. O'Grady's had been at the séance.

The crystal ball looked clouded and hazy.

Two minutes passed, and then the woman opened her eyes. "Let us begin." She leaned forward and peered into the glass.

Violet watched as white foggy wisps swirled in the crystal ball.

Then, they began to collect together.

She caught her breath. An image was forming.

Although it was white and grayish, the form of a man in an overcoat appeared. He tilted his face up, and it seemed to grow larger.

Charles!

Violet gasped. The man seemed to open his mouth, and then, quite suddenly, the image began to fade.

"Do you know him?" the gypsy asked.

"He is the relative of someone I know." Violet's voice was shaky.

"He is coming from the Great Beyond!" The gypsy sound excited. "He is trying to reach you and his family."

"I shall tell his brother."

"The man outside?"

"Yes," Violet whispered.

The woman peered into the globe, where white wisps once again swirled. "He is trying to send you a message. I heard the word 'danger' in my ear."

Violet started. Danger. The same thing Eddie and Samuel Murray had told them during the séances.

"Danger?" she asked.

"Yes." The woman continued to peer into the globe. "There is danger in the future for his brother; he must be very careful." She looked up. "And for you, too."

"Will we succeed in our quest?" Violet asked eagerly.

The gypsy woman studied the crystal ball. "You have the ability to succeed, but you will face trials and danger." She leaned closer. "You must beware. This man we saw"—she waved at the globe—"came to a tragic end. Murdered." She looked at Violet.

Violet sucked in her breath. The gypsy *did* have some kind of powers. "Yes."

"And…" she hesitated. "I believe the same person or persons threaten the man you are with—the brother—and you as well."

"Who are they?" Violet heard the fright in her voice.

The woman stared. "I would say someone who is closely associated with the man we saw in the crystal ball. I feel a connection of some kind, perhaps work, or family...the danger is not from a stranger."

Once again Violet drew in a sharp breath. "Do you have a name for this person?"

The woman studied the globe. "I am sorry, no," she said after a minute, shaking her head. She looked at Violet. "But...I do see the possibility of great happiness if you can triumph over this threat."

"You do?" Violet knew not to give much away; that she should draw the woman out, see what she came up with on her own. But her heart beat rapidly as she waited.

Madame Versailles nodded, her earrings swinging through her curly hair. "Yes. There is a connection—an emotional bond—between you and the man who waits outside."

Violet had to force her mouth not to drop open, but her heartbeat quickened further.

The woman smiled. "You must be careful," she emphasized. "But if you can meet and triumph over this danger, you have a rosy future." She rested a finger on the globe.

The clouds had taken on a pink hue.

"Just—be very careful," Madame Versailles finished. Her eyes met Violet's. "There is great danger. Someone means you both harm."

Chapter Six

Emerging from the tent, Violet found Drew sitting in a chair, chatting with the mustached man.

Drew stood up as she approached. He was smiling. "How was your fortune?" he asked. Clearly he expected that Violet had a gotten a fortune filled with predictions of true love or monetary gains—the kind one often got at a carnival.

"Very interesting," Violet said.

He gave her his elbow, and she slipped her hand inside it, giving one glance back toward the gypsy woman.

Madame Versailles was watching her, a worried look on her face. Beside her the man sidled up, said something in a low tone, and she looked at him.

Violet didn't understand the language they spoke—it was nothing she was familiar with. Certainly not French, as her name would indicate—or was that perhaps an alias used for fairs and carnivals?—nor did it sound like Spanish or Italian, both languages she had heard spoken when she had visited New York City.

Perhaps it was the language of the Romany.

"So tell me, what did she see in your future?" asked Drew.

Violet took a deep breath and began to describe the events that occurred during her visit with the fortune teller.

When she came to the part about the man in the crystal ball and recognizing his face, Drew stood stock still.

"You did not describe him?"

"No." Violet shook her head. "I said little. I wanted to see what she foretold on her own."

"And you recognized him from the photograph. Could it be you expected to see him?"

"I don't think so. I was expecting the usual fortune, about money or perhaps romance."

Perhaps, she thought, she had even been hoping for a fortune involving romance and a certain blond haired, blue-eyed stranger who liked to hold séances and explore the occult.

He let out a low whistle. "This is fascinating."

"I am glad you do not discount the possibility of being able to predict the future. I believe some people have the gift, although there *are* many charlatans about."

"I agree with you," he said simply. "There are too many who do a stage act involving trickery and vague predictions. But I was speaking to Madame's brother— the man out there—and he told me she has predicted many things which came true, including the exact details of several battles."

"My goodness," Violet breathed.

"She comes from Romania, but she and her brother came to the United States when their parents died," he continued. "He believes he has somewhat of a gift himself, but that hers is much stronger. He told me—" Drew paused, then continued. "He told me I was seeking a truth. Although anyone might presume that, he went on to say it was a truth about the death of someone near and dear to me."

Violet gave a little gasp.

They continued to walk together. "Please tell me the rest about your visit.'

She finished describing the session as he listened intently. People jostled past them, some holding baskets plied with items they'd bought, children licking candy. They paused to watch a booth featuring a fire-eating man, which Violet found quite amazing.

"It is stage trickery," Drew whispered, but they stayed and watched with the growing crowd.

When the man finished, there was loud applause, and then Drew led the way forward again. They moved to a corner of the field on the outskirts of the fair.

"Perhaps you did see Charles," he mused. "And the fortune teller—or Charles—is warning us of danger. As did your former neighbor." There was a note of excitement in his voice. "I may meet with danger on my quest."

"You must be careful." Violet's voice was low. She stopped, and he stopped too and looked down at her upturned face.

For a moment, they just stared at each other. Violet's heartbeat quickened.

"Please be careful," she urged. "If those who caused Charles' death were to find out you are searching for them..." her voice dwindled.

Something passed over his face—concern, she thought. He dipped his head lower.

"Violet..." he began. He hesitated, then took her hand in his. His large hand was warm and reassuring. "You must be careful too," he said. "You are helping me search for answers."

"I am in no danger," she protested. The words seemed to carry on the wind. Here in this corner, with fewer people about and the jovial sounds of the festival more muted, even their low tones were clear. "It was not my relative who was killed."

"But you are helping me," he insisted. "Therefore—" He bent closer.

For one moment, Violet held her breath. Was Drew Covington going to kiss her in this secluded place?

His breath touched her face. His eyes held hers.

"Ahh, Covington," said a masculine voice nearby, and they both jumped.

A man strode toward them.

Drew stepped back, letting go of her hand. Violet felt herself flushing.

"Violet, may I introduce my friend Billy Simmons," he said.

The man lifted his hat off his medium brown hair. He appeared to be about Drew's age.

"Billy, this is Violet Moore, my new research assistant," Drew continued.

"A pleasure," Billy said as Violet murmured hello.

"I was hoping to see you here," Billy said. "Now that I am back from my trip to Boston, I was hoping I might attend another séance?"

Drew turned to Violet. "Billy works as one of our salesmen, representing our company and supplying a good many stores in Boston, Providence, and Connecticut with our shoes and boots."

"I have tried several times to contact my father, who passed on three years ago," Billy said. "However, we have had no success—yet."

"We have been having some successes," Drew

said. "Although not, unfortunately, in contacting Charles. Do you remember old Samuel Murray?" At Billy's nod, he went on. "Twice he has tried to get through to us, the second time—last night in fact, with more success."

"You don't say!" Billy looked impressed.

"We plan another séance on Tuesday night," Drew continued. "If you would care to join us."

"I wouldn't miss it. May I bring my sister? Although she does scare easily," he added.

Drew frowned. "She fainted that last time ,and we had no success—"

"Oh, righto, that was a disaster," he said. "She always asks to come, you know, but you are quite right, Drew, she will only get scared. I will tell her you have enough people so as not to hurt her feelings. I believe Hope just wants to see *you*," he added, a mischievous look on his face.

Violet looked from one to another. First Millicent, now Billy's sister Hope—it seemed that many women wanted to spend time with the handsome Drew Covington.

Drew glanced over at Violet. "Why don't you have Hope come to visit Miss Moore one afternoon?" he asked his friend. "Perhaps she would enjoy the company of someone other than my aunt. And Cousin Betsey will be arriving soon."

"Certainly, I will tell her," Billy said. "He turned to Violet. "My sister is a somewhat shy young woman, and she doesn't go out much."

"I'd be pleased to meet her," Violet said cautiously, "so long as it does not interfere with my work for Mr. Covington."

"Of course," Billy agreed.

"Is she here?" Violet asked.

He shook his head as wind gusted, almost taking his and Drew's hats with it. They clutched their hats simultaneously. The air was soft but the wind held a decided dampness to it. Violet guessed they might have rain by late tonight.

"No, she doesn't care for crowds," Billy said. "Now my brothers Todd and Freddie, on the other hand, are gadding about, and my mum's with your aunt at the moment." He looked toward the nearest booth, where a group of people were strolling by. "They were close behind me a few minutes ago."

"Let us go find them," Drew suggested. "Perhaps it's time for some pie?" He quirked his eyebrows at Violet.

"I should like that," she said, and accepted his arm. They moved toward the crowd with Billy falling into step beside them.

They walked past several people, and then heard "Drew! There you are!"

Patricia stood beside a stout woman of about her age. The woman's coloring was exactly like Billy's, and when they drew near, Patricia introduced Mrs. Simmons to Violet.

"I am glad to meet you," Violet said simply.

Mrs. Simmons turned out to be as cheerful as Billy himself. With Billy and his mother, they returned to their blanket. Patricia had purchased an apple and a blueberry pie. They dug into them, the men with gusto. As they ate they were joined by Freddie and Todd, who proceeded to dig into their slices of pie even faster than Drew and Billy.

The pie was delicious, with sweet apples liberally seasoned with brown sugar and cinnamon in a flaky crust. Within minutes the men were all having second helpings of either the apple or blueberry pies, and Patricia declared they would need to purchase more pies to bring home.

On the blanket nearby, the Covington servants had gathered. They had their own cakes and pies they were passing around, and from the conversation she gathered that Drew had given them money to purchase the desserts.

Once they had snacked on the delicious desserts, the younger Simmons boys ran off to enjoy the festival again. The rest of them returned in a more leisurely manner.

Violet found herself once more walking around and enjoying the sights with Drew as Patricia wandered off with Mrs. Simmons. They paused to examine a booth with various cures for all that could ail you—including something to give you more "insight and powers" called "Dr. Jones' Brain Syrup." They chuckled about that one.

"If I believed it would help with our séances, I would purchase it," Drew whispered as they continued along.

They did stop at a booth that displayed unusual rocks, gems, and crystals. Drew looked these over carefully. "They were here last year, and I purchased a few items," he told Violet.

She was attracted to a beautiful pale pink crystal.

"That's quartz," Drew said. "So is that." He pointed to a clear and white crystal. "They are supposed to bring positive energy and clear thinking." He reached over to a group of clear crystals. His hand hovered for a moment, then he selected one.

"You must pick the one which speaks to you—which seems to call to you." A man who looked like he was another gypsy said.

"It's for her," Drew said, tilting his head toward Violet. "And—the pink one too." He pointed at the one she'd admired.

"A good choice," the man said.

Violet was flattered. "Thank you, Drew."

He smiled, then continued to look at the other rocks and crystals. He finally selected several crystals and another highly unusual-looking rock.

They haggled a bit over the prices, and then Drew paid the man, who placed most of the rocks in a rough cloth bag but put Violet's in a prettier blue bag.

"Thank you,' she repeated as they moved down the line of booths.

He grinned. "I hope they bring you good fortune. These—," he held up his bag, "—may be useful in some of our séances. We will experiment with them and see."

The wind had picked up, and more clouds were covering the blue sky. They strolled along, meeting a few neighbors whom Drew introduced. They saw Mrs. O'Grady with her son and daughter-in-law, who was obviously expecting a baby. They passed by Billy, who was now walking with a young woman about Violet's age who he introduced as Catherine.

Violet enjoyed the clean, cool air, the sun on her face interspersed with the clouds, the breeze, the sights and smells of the festival. The camaraderie among the people—gentry, farmers, tradespeople—was warm and friendly, and she wasn't aware of the time until Drew glanced at his pocket watch.

"Almost five o'clock," he said. "I promised my aunt we would meet at half-past five at the blanket in the field. The festival closes at six."

"Time passed so quickly!" Violet observed.

And it had—in Drew's company.

They went back to the booths featuring baked goods. There were only a few cakes and pies left, so Drew bought another apple pie and placed it in the basket Violet carried.

They started back to where they had left the family's blankets, and Violet thought what a fun afternoon it had been!

Especially since she'd spent it with Drew Covington.

She glanced at his profile as they strolled along. He was handsome, but it was more than that. Intelligent, personable…if only the shadow of his brother's death didn't seem to pass over his face so often. This was the first afternoon when she hadn't seen him stop, frown, and seem to be a million miles away. The festival had been good for him, she decided. It had taken his mind off his loss.

They met up at their blankets and folded them, the servants nearby doing the same. It was nearly six o'clock when they joined the long line of carriages and wagons exiting the fields where the festival was being packed up by the various vendors.

Patricia glanced out the window of the carriage. "I believe it shall rain later tonight." The sky had grown overcast.

"Yes," Drew agreed.

The ride back was quiet, and they discussed some of the highlights of the fair. Cook told them one of the maids, Loretta, had had her fortune told, and the gypsy "saw true love coming within the next year."

Once back at Covington House, the few remaining pieces of food were put away by Cook, the horses stabled, and everyone scattered.

"We always give the servants the rest of the evening off after the festival," Patricia said. "There are more meat pies, sandwiches, and pastries in the kitchen if anyone does get hungry."

"I am full," Violet declared.

"We will have breakfast as usual tomorrow, and then we attend church," Patricia continued.

"May I attend with you?" Violet asked.

Patricia nodded approvingly.

"I'm going to the lab," Drew said. As Patricia nodded and moved to give the extra pies they'd bought to Cook to put away, he said in a low voice, "I enjoyed this afternoon, Violet."

"I did too," she responded.

He smiled briefly and disappeared to the back of the house.

Violet went upstairs to put her new purchases away. She left the ribbons and her bonnet out to work on another day, then carefully laid the crystals in the drawer of the chest she was using.

After freshening up, she took the book Drew had recommended and went downstairs to read in the library.

She passed the green room, where Patricia was already absorbed in a book. Entering the library, she opened the window and a damp breeze blew in.

Violet lit the oil lamp, settled in, and began reading. She became so lost in the book that it wasn't until the clock chimed eight that she looked up.

The breeze had grown heavier with moisture, and cooler. Violet got up to close the window, wondering if she should have a bite to eat before tomorrow's breakfast.

She paused in the act of closing the window. Lights blazed in Drew's laboratory building. As she watched, she saw movement through the window. He was striding to the table nearest the window. He lifted a book from there, then stood turning pages. He must have found what he wanted, because he walked to the back of the room and disappeared from her sight.

She felt her heart move, as if stretching toward him. She knew instinctively that he was upset, missing his brother.

Without thinking, she placed her book down on a table and hurried toward the back of the house. Passing the green room, she noted Patricia was no longer sitting there.

She let herself out the back door. As she hurried down the path toward the laboratory, a brisk wind chilled her. She should have gone upstairs and gotten her shawl, but she didn't want to stop now. Reaching the building, she pulled open the door.

Quite a few oil lamps glowed.

"Mr. Cov—Drew?" she called out, moving down the room.

"Violet? I'm in here." His voice came from his study.

She walked swiftly to his study, pausing in the doorway.

Drew sat at his desk. The book he must have taken from the table lay open, a paperweight holding it open to a specific page. But he wasn't reading it at the moment. His chin was propped on his right hand, and his left hand held the photograph of his brother.

She must have made a sound, because he looked up and met her eyes. "I managed to have a good time at the festival, but once I got home, I couldn't stop thinking of Charles. He always enjoyed the Apple Festival a great deal. I want so much to contact him." He sighed heavily.

"I know," she whispered. Impulsively she moved forward and, daringly, rested her hand lightly on the shoulder of the arm which held the photograph.

Drew stared at her. Abruptly he stood up, and she dropped her hand.

"Violet—" His voice was hoarse.

"Yes?"

He stared down at her. Then he said, his voice low, "I somehow manage to forget about Charles when I'm with you. You—you're like a breath of fresh air."

Warmth suffused Violet and her heartbeat accelerated. "Thank you." Her voice was faint as she looked up at him.

He reached out and gently touched a curl that lay against her cheek.

Violet caught her breath at the intimate gesture.

"I want—" He stopped, his face close to hers.

And then he placed his hands on either side of her face, tilted his face to hers, and kissed her.

The moment his lips touched hers, fire flowed through her veins, from her face through her body and down to the soles of her feet.

It was a gentle kiss, but oh so delicious! His lips pressed lightly against hers, and after a moment or two, harder.

And suddenly she was engulfed in his embrace, clinging to his arms as they slid around her waist and pulled her ever closer.

They stood, and she was conscious only of being held close to him, pressed against him, his lips suddenly hard on her own. The fire he'd ignited within her burned brightly, threatening to consume her with a wondrous longing she'd never felt before.

Sudden wind blew through the half-opened window, gusting around them. Drew loosened his hold, but as he pulled back slightly, he studied Violet's face.

"Violet." He should say he was sorry, he supposed, but he didn't. He wasn't sorry. For in that moment when he couldn't resist and he'd kissed her, he had felt more alive than he had since any time after Charles' death.

"Y-yes?" Her voice squeaked. She looked up at him, her face flushed with what he recognized was the beginning of passion.

He gripped her arms. He was quite sure she was an innocent, and he usually only shared a kiss on the hand or a quick peck on the cheek with a member of that group. But somehow, he'd been drawn to Violet from the beginning. It wasn't just that she was lovely. Nor was it that she was intelligent and warm. There was a certain chemistry, something that drew him to her as surely as a magnet was drawn to metal.

"I—I should apologize," he began, his voice rather gruff. "But—I'm not sorry I kissed you."

She smiled suddenly, and there was laughter in her

eyes.

"I'm not sorry either." Her voice still sounded breathless.

He didn't want to take advantage of this young woman—his assistant, for Christ sakes!—so he stepped back.

But he did want to spend time with her, and in that moment he remembered the perfect opportunity was coming up.

"Violet, my sister—Mary—is hosting a ball two weeks from tonight. Would you like to attend with me?"

"I would love to," she answered.

Still under the spell of their intense kiss, he stepped back another few inches. "We will travel there the day before and stay that night and the night of the ball. My aunt and my cousin Betsey will accompany us. Mary lives near Basking Ridge, so it is easier to stay at her home. Her neighbors and friends and some of our relatives will be present.'

"I should like it very much," Violet said, her mouth still upturned.

"Good. That is settled then." Wind gusted again, and the oil lamp flickered.

"Perhaps you should not work further tonight," Violet said, laying her small hand on his arm. "Why don't you relax?"

She might be right. It had been a long, exciting week, and he'd worked hard both on the job and with his research and the séances. Taking time for a break might be a good thing.

He covered her hand with his own.

Lightning suddenly lit the sky outside, followed

rapidly by a clap of thunder.

"I believe you are right—" he started, when the wind blew again, and the two candles flickered, then went out.

Tension filled the air, as if energy was a living thing.

And at that moment, in the dark, he heard his brother's voice, as if from a very great distance:

"Drew…"

Chapter Seven

At the whispery voice, Violet and Drew both jumped.

"Charles?" Drew's hoarse voice was eager. "Is that you?"

Violet held her breath as they waited in the dark.

The very air surrounding them seemed to spark with the static of lightning and—something else.

Silence.

"Charles?" Drew repeated, hopefully.

There was no voice, no sound. Outside, the wind blew loudly, and a tree branch snapped. Violet started again.

She knew instinctively that Charles was gone.

"Charles?" This time Drew sounded pleading.

They stood in the dark for a few minutes. Lightning flashed a second time. A cold gust of air swept through the window, and Violet shivered. After another minute she exhaled, and she could hear Drew's breaths, shorter and quicker than usual.

Finally he fumbled for the tinderbox and lit a match, then ignited an oil lamp.

She observed that his hands were shaking.

"I think he was here," Drew said. "That was his voice! But he's gone now." He sighed heavily. "I want so badly to see him."

Violet's heart went out to him. "I know," she said

sympathetically. "After my parents died, I felt the same. But it's worse for you—your brother was cut down in the prime of life." She tilted her head to regard him.

The pain on his face pulled at her. "Yes," he answered. "He was—so young." He swallowed. "And—murdered." The anguish was in his voice, his face.

Her heart stretched toward him.

"Has that—ever happened before?" she asked. "Where suddenly you could hear his voice—when you weren't even sitting in the séance room or trying to contact him?"

"Never." Drew met her eyes. "But—it gives me hope that we will be able to contact him again—and for a longer period!" His voice rose.

"It is highly unusual," Violet agreed. "I believe he is trying to contact us, but is experiencing difficulty. But the fact that he got through, without a séance, even for a few seconds..." She paused, thinking. "If that could happen, then perhaps we will have more success with our future séances."

He stared at her, hope shining in his eyes. "Yes!"

"We should write down our notes on what occurred," Violet pointed out.

"Yes, immediately." He opened a drawer and pulled out some papers. "Let us do so."

He closed the window, put out the lamp in his office, and they went into the main room where they sat for several minutes, writing. They compared notes, and Violet offered to copy them immediately. Intermittent lightning lit the sky outside, accompanied by wind and thunder which sounded fainter as it moved away.

"It is late, and Sunday is the day of rest," Drew

said. "You may do this on Monday."

Violet covered a yawn with her hand. Besides being out in the fresh air for a good part of the day, the evening had held its share of exciting moments— between being asked to the ball by Drew and the ghostly whisper from his brother. And his kiss! She felt herself sagging with fatigue.

"Come, let us return to the house," Drew suggested. "I am tired too."

A fine rain had begun falling while they were in the laboratory. Drew locked up. And without an umbrella—he said his was in the house—they scurried back. The house was dark, except for a candle burning in the hallway and a small light in the kitchen. It seemed the entire household had gone to sleep.

They walked up the stairs and down the hall. Violet felt a warmth as they walked, a friendly feeling. It was as if she and Drew were on the same wavelength.

Perhaps they were.

"Goodnight," he said, somewhat formally, as they came to the junction of the corridor where her room was.

"Goodnight," she said, and walked down the hall.

She felt he was watching her as she walked toward her bedroom.

****

Monday dawned clear and bright, but the temperature had dropped.

Violet got to work right after breakfast, copying the notes regarding the incident late Saturday night.

Sunday had been a quiet day. Violet had observed many people yawning during the church service— especially during the minister's rambling sermon. After lunch, she had read the book Drew had given her, in the library, with Patricia reading a mystery novel there as well. Drew had joined them later, absorbed in a book about séances in England. Later he had switched to reading a mystery too.

Patricia had been astounded but excited that they had heard Charles' voice the night before, and seemed eager for their next séance, which was scheduled for Tuesday with Mrs. O'Grady.

Sunday evening Violet wrote a long letter to her sister, describing the Covingtons and their house, the Apple Festival, and telling her they'd had some minor success in their séances. She also mentioned how she enjoyed the company of Mr. Covington.

"Of course," she finished, "I know he is above me in social rank, so nothing will come of this but a friendly employer-employee relationship." With a sigh, she signed the letter.

Right after lunch on Monday, Drew sent word that he would be at the factory until later than usual, due to a problem they were trying to solve with one of the machines. Violet took the time to finish reading the book he'd loaned her, then hunted up another which looked interesting from his study in the house.

When Drew arrived home late in the afternoon, he seemed harried. "We finally got the machine fixed," he said to Violet and Patricia," but it was quite frustrating. I believe I am going to have to tinker with it further until I can get a new one. It is on its last legs."

He pored over Violet's notes but had nothing to add. He did, however, announce that he wanted to try another séance tonight, even without Mrs. O'Grady, since they'd had moderate success without her—and the big event of hearing Charles' voice.

So shortly before eight o'clock, Violet and Patricia, wrapped in shawls, walked over to the laboratory.

"Cousin Betsey will be arriving on Wednesday," Patricia said. "She wants to attend Mary's ball with us." She gave Violet a sidelong glance. "I understand you will be escorted by Drew."

"Yes." Violet looked at his aunt. Would she object to his bringing along a research assistant? Especially since she did not come from a family as wealthy and esteemed as his?

His aunt beamed. "I am so happy! I believe you are just what Drew needs to pull him out of this terrible sadness over Charles' death."

Violet felt her cheeks growing warm. "I..." She wasn't sure what to say. "I am flattered to be asked and to be joining you all."

"And what do you think of my nephew?" Patricia asked boldly as they neared the building.

"I like him—very much," she answered. She paused. *He is handsome, and I am drawn to him*, she thought. But she didn't voice her opinion. She was simply not bold enough to declare *that* aloud. "He has treated me very well."

Patricia nodded, a smile on her face. "That is wonderful." As they drew close to the laboratory, she switched topics. "You will like Cousin Betsey. She is only a few months younger than Drew, and they have always gotten along famously. More like brother and sister than cousins. They were always so lively when they were together. Drew's sister Mary is much quieter." She sighed as they reached the door. "When you see Betsey, you will see what Drew was like before

Charles' death—and what he might be like again." She gave Violet an appraising look. "Charles was even more happy go lucky—Drew and Betsey both have a serious side—but Drew has changed so since Charles' death."

"Perhaps, if we can contact Charles, it will bring peace to Drew, and he can return to his old self," Violet said, and pulled open the door.

When they entered the laboratory, they discovered Drew had been taking notes from a book at his desk.

"I didn't realize the time," he said, running his hand through his dark blond hair.

"I will help set up the room," Violet volunteered.

They were soon ready to conduct the séance and sat by candlelight in the room.

"We will try without holding hands again," Drew said. "Then, if we meet with no success, we will hold hands."

"In the same session?" queried Violet.

He shrugged. "Why not? I have found nothing in my research to say people have or have not tried this way of doing things."

They sat in the near dark. The window was open slightly, and a cool breeze blew in every so often. Violet heard the breathing of the three of them, the occasional movement of a foot or hand.

After fifteen minutes or so, Drew spoke, "Let us try holding hands."

He grasped Violet's hand with his own warm one. Patricia's hand, in Violet's left hand, was smaller and cooler. She had to stretch to grasp both.

They sat quietly. They had only to wait a few minutes, when she heard the lilting voice of an

Irishman.

"Good evenin' to you all!"

Violet hesitated, since Drew usually liked to take the lead in speaking to the spirits.

"Eddie?" Drew asked.

"It is I," the spirit answered. The chair in between Violet and Drew scraped back, and she felt the familiar heaviness beside her, as if Eddie had truly taken the seat. She made a mental note that tonight he had spoken before sitting down.

She found herself leaning forward eagerly. "Good evening, Eddie. How are you?" The greeting came automatically.

"It's grand over here, just grand," Eddie told them in his jovial tone.

Violet peered through the darkness. Was that her imagination, or was there a certain fogginess beside her?

Would Eddie materialize?

Her heart beat rapidly with hope.

Drew and Patricia were staring at the spot where Eddie's voice had come from. Did they see the mistiness too?

"Have you a message for us?" Drew asked. His calm voice belied excitement, Violet surmised. He was leaning forward too, and his hand gripped hers tightly.

"No, sorry, my friends." She could imagine Eddie's face, looking perhaps a trifle disappointed. The mist near her seemed to curl. It became more solid as she watched. "I tried to contact Charles Covington, I did…but I couldna' reach him."

"I thank you for trying," Drew said, and Violet heard the disappointed note in his voice.

She spoke to her former neighbor. "Is there something we can do to help him come through?"

There was a momentary pause. "I donna know," Eddie said, his Irish lilt thick. He paused again. "Perhaps—" He stopped.

"Perhaps?" It was the first time Patricia had spoken.

"If you try something different."

Well, that was a vague answer, Violet thought.

"For example…" Drew urged.

There was another silence. The chair scraped again. "I believe he is trying to get through, truly." The mist began to recede, and when Eddie spoke again, his voice seemed farther away. "I canna reach him. Try something…different…"

"Yes?" Violet urged, hoping Eddie wouldn't leave yet. "Eddie?"

The heaviness lifted beside her. She hadn't even noticed it receding, she'd been so focused on his voice, and the mist in the air.

"Beware…" Eddie's voice was barely audible.

There was a small popping sound.

The room was still.

****

It took them longer than usual to write their notes, since so much had occurred. By nine thirty Patricia stood and said she had finished, was tired, and wanted to go to bed. Violet returned with her to the house, while Drew stayed behind to finish his notes and to continue some research.

Violet sat in the library and added a few more comments to her notes. She was just finishing when she heard the clock strike ten.

She started, then laid down her pen.

Going to the window, she looked out. Lights still shone from the laboratory, although she couldn't see Drew in the main room. Perhaps he was in his study there.

The household was quiet, the servants recently retired. As Violet gazed outside, she observed the flicker of candlelight from the laboratory.

She sighed. Poor Drew. He wanted so badly to contact his brother. And other people kept coming through.

From a scientific perspective, she knew they were achieving some wonderful successes. They had contacted Eddie and Samuel Murray; they had heard Charles' voice one time.

But the desire Drew had to reach his brother, to hear him speak and perhaps see him; and above all, to find out who had murdered Charles, was as yet unfulfilled.

She could only hope that they would achieve the success he so yearned for.

As she regarded the laboratory, she saw him pass by the window. He held a book in his hand.

Would he find the peace he so much wanted?

Suddenly weary herself, Violet doused the light in the library and headed for the stairs. Leaving the oil lamp that was lit in the hall to guide Drew, she went to her room and placed her papers on her desk.

She did not fall asleep immediately. Instead she lay on her comfortable bed, thinking of Drew, and how much he wanted to contact his brother.

And then thinking of the kiss they'd shared over the weekend. Something she kept reliving every night, when she was alone, in her dark room…

****

Tuesday dawned clear and cool again. Patricia was bustling about with the housekeeper, directing the two young serving girls as they prepared for Betsey's visit. Violet volunteered to help after she finished copying her notes, and Patricia put her to work arranging flowers in a vase for Betsey's room.

The postman brought a letter that interrupted them for a few minutes. Patricia scanned it, then smiled.

"Our cousins Harvey and Henrietta are joining us at Mary's ball," Patricia said happily, folding the letter and putting it in the pocket of the apron she wore. "They will then come to Twin Bridges and stay here for two weeks or so. They will be staying at the Twin Bridges Inn. Of course we have room for them here, but they prefer to stay on their own when they travel."

"How are they related to you?" Violet asked, moving the mums slightly and placing two daisies in the vase.

"Harvey and his sister Henrietta are the children of John's cousin Simon Covington and his wife Celeste. Their parents died several years ago of a fever that was going around London at the time. That makes them— second cousins, I believe?"

"Yes," Violet affirmed.

"They like America very much and come to visit often. They have been renting a home in New York for a month now and will probably stay for several months before returning to England. It will be good to see them. Oh—and Harvey is the Earl of Wethersgate. He likes people to use his title, so call him 'my lord' until he gives you permission to address him by his given name."

Violet, like most Americans she knew, did not believe in titles and the English system of aristocracy. But of course she would never offend her employer or his family. "All right," she agreed.

They finished getting Betsey's room ready, then had lunch.

Drew returned to the house at the usual time, and he pored over Violet's notes.

"Very good," he said, and Violet was pleased by his words.

He looked up. "Can you join me in my laboratory? I want to go over some things about tonight's séance, and tell you about some plans I have for upcoming sessions."

"Certainly," Violet said. "Let me get my shawl."

She hurried up to her room to get the shawl. Drew was waiting for her by the back door when she returned downstairs, and they proceeded to the laboratory, the wind whipping at Violet's skirts.

Once inside the laboratory, he asked her to take a seat at one of the large tables. He had cleared whatever was on it, except for several papers with notes.

"This is how I would like to proceed," he began. "We have tried séances with note-taking during the séance and without; it seems to go better when you take the notes afterward."

Violet nodded.

"And we have tried both holding hands and with no hands," he continued. "The séances seem sharper, with better results, when we are all holding hands."

"I agree," Violet said.

"So, from now on let us use those variables—hand

holding and no notes until the session is finished." At her murmur of agreement, he went on. "There is something else I'd like to add."

"What is that?" Violet questioned.

He picked up three books, all with leather strips marking different pages, and opened each with a flourish. He placed them on the table, then sat across from Violet.

"Several mediums and séance organizers have had success using rocks and crystals during their séances. The crystals, they claim, help focus the spirits' energy, or the medium's. Perhaps both." He pointed to the first book. "Paulette, a medium in upstate New York, has been using them for years."

Violet noted the passage he pointed to and quickly read it. Drew's voice had risen with excitement.

He showed her the second book. "Antonelli, an Italian medium doing most of his work in England, has had much success since incorporating crystals into the séances he leads."

Violet skimmed the passages Drew indicated. "Most interesting," she said.

"And," he added, pulling forth the last book, "look at this." He sounded even more excited. "Smithson, in Canada, has had astounding results with a rock that many believe was part of a meteor from outer space—a meteorite!"

Violet read the passages, then met Drew's shining eyes. "And the rock you bought on Saturday—"

"Yes!" he exclaimed. "Is a meteorite!"

She stared at him, feeling rising excitement herself. Could this rock help them in their quest?

"We must try using it," she said, her heart beating

rapidly. "We've gotten fairly good results so far; this could be a breakthrough to wonderful results—to reaching your brother!"

"That's right!" he said, and pulled Violet to her feet. "We must try this soon!'

"Tonight?" Violet asked, feeling almost dizzy with hope.

He stopped, shook his head, and put her away from him by several inches. "No, we have too many variables. First, we must again try holding of hands with Mrs. O'Grady. Then later this week we will try adding Cousin Betsey; and then, another night, using the rock." His eyes gleamed. "It will be extremely hard *not* to use it right away. I was tempted last night but wanted to discuss it with you first. And the scientist within me wants to do this strictly in a scientific manner, with very few variables changing—one at a time, in fact."

"We should write out a schedule," Violet suggested.

His eyes widened. "Yes, and add all the variables we will use each time. Good thinking!" His voice rose with enthusiasm.

Violet suggested a calendar, which Drew produced from his office. Together they sat, poring over it, and she made notes of the dates of the séances for the next two weeks.

"Billy can't join us this week," he informed her. "He sent me a message saying he is very busy traveling and selling our shoes, but he will let me know when he returns to Twin Bridges again."

"Tuesday we are with Mrs. O'Grady, and perhaps Thursday?" she asked. "Friday, we leave for your sister's home."

"Yes, damn—ugh, pardon," he said hastily. She smiled to herself. Obviously, he was about to swear, preferring a séance to a grand ball. She wondered what his sister would say if she knew.

They worked out the schedule for the following week, wrapping up with a séance on a Friday, which would include Cousin Betsy's last appearance since she was headed home after that. That would be the night they used the mysterious meteor rock.

"And," Violet added excitedly, "look, Drew." She pointed to the calendar. "That is the night of a full moon!" Meeting his eyes, she saw understanding dawning in them. "Mediums in New York State have written in essays that during a full moon, more spirits have come through. I know I read that in the book I borrowed recently—"

"Yes, and Haversham in London said the same in his essays!" Drew looked at her with growing respect—and dare she believe—admiration? He stood suddenly, pulled her to her feet, and whirled her around. The shelves of his laboratory and their contents sped by her eyes in a dizzying whirl. Violet gasped.

"Brilliant, my dear Violet, brilliant!" He laughed for a moment, then set her on her feet and held her, steadying her. Her head spun, but with his hands on her arms, the world returned to upright. She looked up into his eyes.

Suddenly, he was no longer smiling. His lips moved toward hers, lower, lower...

They touched hers, lightly. Then, with growing urgency.

She clung to his shoulders, and without thinking,

kissed him back.

They stood that way, and Violet lost all track of time. It could have been a minute, or ten.

Slowly Drew pulled back.

She gazed up at him, dazed by the intensity of the kiss.

He stared down at her. "I…" He cleared his throat. "I hope—you don't mind—"

"Ah…no," she responded, breathlessly.

And quite suddenly he said, "Hang it… I want to kiss you again, Violet." And leaning forward, he did.

This kiss was swifter. Just as Violet was beginning to melt again, he pulled back.

"We must—remember—we are doing research." His voice was gruff, and as Violet stared at him, bemused, it seemed like he was trying to gather his thoughts. Drew gave a slight shake of his head. "I don't want to take advantage in the exhilaration of the moment."

"You did not take advantage," she reassured him. Her voice was whispery thin.

I wanted that too, she thought.

He ran his hand through his hair, and Violet guessed he had been affected by this kiss—perhaps not as deeply as she had been, but affected nonetheless.

She reached out and placed her hand on his cheek. "I mean it."

Instantly, he covered her hand with his own. They stared into each other's eyes before he broke the contact. Dropping his hand, he moved back.

"We must return to our scientific research." His voice remained hoarse.

Disappointed, Violet wondered if the kiss

embarrassed him—or perhaps it hadn't been as significant to him as it was to her.

She forced herself to withhold a sigh.

Drew had stepped back far enough to view the calendar they had created. "Can you make another copy of this so we can each have one?"

"Certainly." Her voice still didn't sound quite normal. She coughed, then continued, "I'll do that straight away."

"I am going to re-read those passages in Haversham," Drew said. He began rummaging in one bookcase for the book. "Of course, a full moon is another variable—but comes only monthly."

"I was reading the book yesterday. and it is in my room; I will get it," Violet said, and hastily left for the main house, glad to get away for a few moments.

She hurried to the house. She was grateful for the outside air, which cooled her hot cheeks. In fact, her whole body felt warm.

Drew had seemed to enjoy the kiss they'd shared. She knew she had.

Why had he backed away? Did he feel it was unseemly of a gentleman to kiss his assistant? Did he regret it?

She did not understand men and wished Rose was here so she could discuss the situation with her sister.

And—a sudden feeling of guilt flooded her. Drew did not know the secret she kept, the other reason she had come here.

She shook her head.

No. She would not speak of them to Drew. Not yet.

****

Drew stared after Violet as she left the room.

He deserved a thrashing, he knew, and if Violet had a male relative nearby, he would have gotten one.

Her ideas had been intelligent and worthy of respect.

But instead of respect, he had let his impetuous side come to the forefront and without thinking had whisked her off her feet in a show of excitement.

And then he'd kissed her enthusiastically in a show of—what? Delight with her ideas? Hardly. Simple pleasure, more like.

Violet was a young woman, well brought up, of a decent family if not an upper-class, nobly-related one such as the Covington clan. One didn't go about kissing young, gentle women out of the blue.

Especially a young, innocent, gentle woman.

He swallowed hard. The last thing he wanted was to take advantage of a young woman such as Violet. It was unseemly.

But he did want to kiss her again.

He steeled himself. He must resist the temptation! She was here to do research with him, nothing else.

But for the first time in over a year, he found himself drawn to a woman—both physically and on an emotional level.

He stared at the front door where Violet had exited. Did he imagine it, or was there still a trace of a floral soap scent that lingered on the air from Violet?

He glanced around the room, looking for he knew not what.

His eyes rested on the four books piled haphazardly on the middle table. Then he let his glance sweep around the rest of the room.

Books leaned haphazardly against each other on

the shelves. He knew that, in his office, more were piled on the desk and on shelves there.

He had originally intended for Violet to catalog his large collection of science books and those on the occult. It would certainly help him find books when he didn't remember where he had placed them, or what he had. Several times he had bought copies of something which turned out to be a duplicate; or bought a book he couldn't find, only to find the original with the week.

Yes, he would get her started on that, so she would be busy and he would have fewer opportunities to take advantage of her.

****

The night was surprisingly foggy, with a thick blanket of white that hung over the Covington house and land, even though it sat on a hill. It seemed to mute the atmosphere as they sat and waited, holding hands.

Once again Violet held Drew's hand to the right and Patricia's to the left, with Harriet O'Grady sitting between Patricia and Drew.

They waited in silence. Violet could hear the clock in the main room ticking faintly in the background.

Harriet O'Grady slipped into a slight doze. Her breathing slowed, and through the almost-darkness Violet observed her eyes were closed.

After about fifteen minutes of their sitting peacefully, Mrs. O'Grady started.

Violet watched, tightening her hand in Drew's and on Patricia's.

Harriet made a muffled sound, then went silent again.

The candle on the sideboard flickered, releasing a wisp of smoke that was visible in the almost dark room.

They waited, and after a few minutes, Harriet moved. Her mouth opened.

"Drew…" she groaned. The voice was a woman's, unfamiliar to Violet.

But Drew sat up straighter, and Patricia gave a small gasp.

"Pa…Trish…a…" The voice coming from Harriet's mouth seemed far away, strained, as if struggling to get through.

"Claire?" Patricia queried softly.

A shiver moved up Violet's spine.

There was silence, and then Drew asked, his voice equally subdued, "Mother?"

Another silence fell. Harriet opened her mouth, as if struggling. At first nothing came out.

After another minute, she spoke. "Can't…get… through." There was a pause, then the voice added, "danger…" and faded away once again.

Danger? There was that word again.

They waited. Violet realized she'd been holding her breath for the last minute and let it out in a soft whoosh.

Suddenly the trumpet—which had never moved during any of their séances—flew off the sideboard and across the room. It landed with a thump somewhere near Drew's feet.

Drew's hand tightened on Violet's.

Mrs. O'Grady continued to breathe deeply, still in a trance. Then she shuddered.

They waited. The clock ticked, the sounds of their breathing was muted.

"Hmmph," Harriet O'Grady muttered. After a moment she raised her head.

The woman looked at the other sitters.

"I believe it is over," Drew said, and sighed.

"Did someone come through?" Harriet asked. "I feel—tired, as if someone did take over." She had told Violet she often felt tired after the séances, especially when someone had come through, although she rarely remembered the details. "However, I sense that this presence was weak."

"Yes." Drew's tone was cautious, but Violet caught the note of excitement it held. "Someone did. My mother!'

Harriet let out a soft gasp. "Claire?"

"Yes," Patricia chimed in. "There is no question that it was Claire's voice."

"And…" Drew got up and raised the candle. "The trumpet moved." He pointed to where it rested on the floor.

They all stood up to look.

Violet peered at the trumpet, which lay close to Drew's chair. "That is the first time that has happened in my presence," she said.

"It has not moved for many months," Drew observed.

"Claire was obviously having trouble getting through," Patricia said, her voice pitched higher than usual, and Violet turned to look at Drew's aunt. She had never heard her so excited. "She could barely speak. So perhaps she moved the trumpet to tell us she was here!"

"Did it make a noise?" Harriet O'Grady asked.

"No, but it moved quite suddenly, as if someone had thrown it." Drew sounded excited, too. "As if my mother was frustrated by her lack of communication and had thrown it as a way to let us know she was here."

Harriett nodded. "The spirits do that sometimes. I wish I could remember something." She ended with a yawn.

"Come, I'll walk you home," Drew said.

After they departed, Patricia and Violet sat down to write out their observations.

Patricia finished first, as she usually did. Her notes were accurate but not usually as detailed as Violet's.

She was yawning too. "I am going to turn in. Cousin Betsey will be here tomorrow."

Violet stood up. "I'll walk back to the house with you and finish my notes in my room."

When she finished them less than fifteen minutes later, she looked out the window. The fog was still thick, and she couldn't see the laboratory building from her room, so she hurried to the conservatory. As she peered out the window, she saw Drew striding toward the building, walking confidently despite the fog.

She had to squash a strong impulse to run downstairs and follow him back to the laboratory.

****

Violet awoke at the usual time on Wednesday, but remembering instantly that Betsey was arriving today, she hurried to dress and eat breakfast.

Patricia was in the morning room already, spreading jam on toast.

The rich aroma of coffee greeted Violet as she poured a cup of the liquid and added sugar. Then she took a roll and butter and joined Patricia.

"You'll like Betsey," Patricia said, wiping some crumbs from her fingers. "She and Drew are of an age and they are so alike—both full of life—well," she said, her smile fading, "they were. When you meet Betsey you'll see what Drew was like before Charles' death. He and Betsey—and Charles too—were so full of vitality. Charles was a little more mischievous, it's true, but the three of them got along famously."

"Perhaps Drew will be like that again, one day," Violet suggested.

Patricia regarded her over her teacup. "Yes, I certainly hope so. But I am afraid it will not happen until Charles' killer is caught."

"And we are trying to accomplish that," Violet said. "So, let us hope Drew will soon be back to his normal self."

Patricia eyed her. "He does seem closer to his normal self when he is around you."

"Oh." Violet was not sure how to respond. "I am glad." She smiled.

Patricia smiled back.

After breakfast she took her notes, Patricia's, and the notes Drew had left for her in the library and copied them all neatly into her notebook. Between the three of them, they had a good solid summary of last evening's events.

Betsey was expected on the train that would come in early in the afternoon, and Drew would be meeting her with a couple of the footmen and a carriage and wagon.

When Violet finished, she left the notes for Drew in his study in the house and then went to see if Patricia needed any help. She didn't, so Violet spent the hours before lunch reading the book on séances she was currently reading, and like she had with the book before that, took a few notes.

She ate lunch with Patricia, then they retired to the green salon to read and wait for Betsey.

It was not long after two when they heard the rumble of wheels, and Violet followed Patricia into the hall.

The butler had already opened the door, and they could see the carriage climbing up the approach to the house.

Once the carriage stopped, Drew helped his cousin alight from the vehicle.

"Aunt Patricia!" Violet knew it was a courtesy title, since Betsey was a cousin on Drew's mother's side, but she appeared close to Patricia Covington anyway.

She turned to Violet, and Violet curtsied.

Betsey wore a dark blue traveling outfit and appeared elegant and fashionable in a modest way.

"No need to be so formal. You must be Violet Moore," Betsey greeted her, and Violet got her first good look at Betsey.

Betsey was a short woman. Her blonde hair was a little lighter than Drew's and her eyes a paler blue than Drew's. But something about her mouth and smile reminded Violet of Drew. Her face was rounder than his, her nose pert, but Violet thought they definitely looked related.

"A pleasure to meet you," Violet murmured as Betsey unexpectedly clasped her hand.

Betsey peered at Violet's face, then smiled again. "I have heard so much about you from Drew. Once I unpack we must chat. I want to hear all about these séances you are having with my cousin and aunt."

The two footmen were bringing in her luggage.

Betsey chatted about the trip and how the train had

improved in the last year. Her maid, who had ridden in the wagon, hurried upstairs behind her to help.

"We will have tea and biscuits in the green salon when you are ready," Patricia called after her.

Betsey paused and turned back. "Perfect. I will be downstairs in less than a half hour."

Several of the servants had come forward to help and greet Betsey. Patricia now ordered one of the housemaids to tell Cook to serve the refreshments in fifteen minutes. The housekeeper went upstairs to see if anything more was needed.

Apparently, everything was well in hand, and the household had the routine of Betsey's visits down pat. Violet turned to go into the green salon when Drew reached out and touched her arm.

"Can we discuss last night's séance before Betsey comes downstairs?"

"Certainly," she responded.

He led the way into his study. Violet noticed he seemed more relaxed and happier than he usually did. He seemed at ease, the way he had been at the festival on Saturday. His cousin appeared to be a good influence.

She paused to pick up the notes from the library and then sat in a chair across from Drew's desk.

He perused the notes, then looked up. "As usual, your notes are meticulous. You have been a great help these past weeks, Violet."

She found herself blushing. "Thank you."

"In fact"—he leaned forward as he spoke—"I have something else I hope you can help me with. I mentioned it in my letters but forgot to discuss it with you until recently."

"Yes?" she asked, puzzled.

"I had hoped you might help me catalog my books, at least the ones on psychic topics and the scientific tomes."

"Of course," Violet said. "It was part of your requirements for the job. That will be no problem."

He looked relieved. Had he been afraid she would protest? To be truthful, the séances and note-taking was not enough to justify her generous salary. Even with this assignment, she was probably overpaid. But at least she would be useful.

"I believe it is a much needed task," she said, letting her eyes sweep over the bookshelves where books stood at odd angles, and then to the desk, which had five books piled haphazardly on it.

He grinned. "Much needed."

"I shall begin at once," she started, but Drew waved his hand.

"Tomorrow will be soon enough," he said. "Let us visit with Betsey, and have our séance tonight."

"That is fine," Violet said, when they heard steps in the hall.

"Drew?" Betsey called out.

He got up and leaned out the doorway to the hall. Waving to Violet, he said, "We were just about to move to the green salon."

"I am most eager to hear how the séances are going since you last wrote two weeks ago," Betsey said, pausing to wait for them. They all proceeded into the green salon where Patricia was already pouring tea.

"I will be happy to tell you what has transpired." Drew took a seat after Violet and Betsey and reached for a scone.

He described, with comments from both Patricia and Violet, the séances they had held since Violet's arrival. Betsey listened attentively, her eyes growing round as they described some of the encounters, especially with people she knew like Charles' voice and Claire's.

"My goodness," she breathed, finishing off a lemon cookie. "That is fascinating, and certainly you have had far better results than you ever had while I was present." She turned to Violet. "The best we did was once hearing a knocking on the table. The spirit knocked 'yes' with two knocks to the question of whether he was male, but we could never identify him."

Violet nodded. "I have been to séances also where we have had rapping, but voices have only spoken briefly, with no materializations."

Betsey turned back to Drew. "Can we try tonight?"

"You won't be too fatigued from your journey?" Patricia inquired.

Betsey shook her head. "Nonsense. I am most eager to attempt to contact the spirits!"

She sounded quite enthusiastic, Violet thought, taking another cookie for herself.

"Mrs. O'Grady will not be here tonight," Drew said, lifting his teacup. "But we can certainly attempt it ourselves. Let us meet at eight o'clock."

Shortly after that they dispersed, Patricia to rest before dinner, Drew to go over his notes, Betsey to check the unpacking her maid had done, and Violet to read.

Dinner was a rather festive affair, with Betsey entertaining them with stories of her two nephews—her older brother's sons—and her trip here from New York

City.

Cook had made a special effort to serve a sumptuous meal in honor of Betsey. There was creamed corn soup, roast chicken with a side of roasted parsnips and carrots, and freshly made rolls. For dessert there was an apple pie from the festival with a slab of cheddar cheese on the side.

After dinner, they scattered again. Shortly before eight Violet walked to the laboratory to help Drew set up. As she lit the candle and checked the placement of the trumpet on the sideboard, Violet felt a cozy feeling descend on the room. It was almost as if she and Drew had worked together like this before, getting ready, double checking that they had all they needed.

"I believe we have everything well in hand," he commented.

"Yes." She smoothed her hands over her light green skirt.

The sound of voices alerted her to the fact that Betsey and Patricia were here.

The air had grown chill when the sun went down, and Drew had left the window in the room only partially ajar.

As Patricia and Betsey entered, Betsey said, "I declare, it is always colder out here than it is in New York City." She had taken off the jacket of her traveling dress but now was wrapped in an expensive-looking gray shawl.

"Well, tomorrow is the first of October, and it is always cooler then," Patricia observed, taking a seat. She too was wrapped in a shawl, although hers was older and more worn than Betsey's.

Drew lowered the oil lamps in the main room, until

only one shone dimly. "Tonight," he announced, "Mrs. O'Grady is not with us, but Betsey is. We will take no notes until afterward. Tonight, we do not hold hands; we shall try that next time and see if there is a difference in the responses we get."

He sat down, and they fell silent.

Several minutes passed.

Air gusted through the window, cool and holding a damp note.

There was another silence. Violet could hear Drew's even breathing, Patricia's soft breaths, and Betsey's more rapid ones.

Then Violet caught a whiff of something. Smoke…from a cigar?

She peered through the dim light. There—there was a wisp of smoke, curling, near Drew's left shoulder.

The smoke grew thicker, and longer, as if someone had breathed more smoke into the room.

"Charles?" Drew's question was quiet.

The smoke lingered on the air. Definitely a cigar smell, Violet decided. Would they see the man smoking it?

The smoke suddenly dissipated, and for just a moment, Violet thought she saw the outline of the cigar.

Someone—Patricia or Betsey—drew in a sharp breath.

Then the cigar, too, was gone.

They waited. A quarter hour must have passed, but nothing further occurred.

Betsey coughed delicately. They waited again, until Drew said, "I believe we will see—and smell—no more tonight." He stood and went to the sideboard, reaching for the oil lamp and lighting it so the room grew brighter.

Betsey's expression was awed. Patricia looked disappointed, and Drew—

Violet thought Drew looked pleased.

"Has that ever happened before?" she asked.

He shook his head. "Never. This is amazing!" His sudden smile revealed his excitement over the events of the night. "We had a partial materialization, complete with a smell!"

****

Traveling to Mary's home in Basking Ridge took the better part of the day.

Drew, Patricia, Betsey, and Violet took the carriage, while several servants followed in a wagon with their luggage. The trip was pleasant, and the October weather was cool but sunny. During the ride over, they discussed the séance on Wednesday once again. It was the topic which had been on their minds so much.

Drew was convinced that his brother's spirit had visited them. "It was the cigar he favored," he repeated a number of times. "I recognized the smell. It is from Havana."

Betsey shook her head. "He did like a cigar every evening—but I certainly would not recognize his favorite from among other kinds of cigars. Could it have been another entity?"

"I don't know how you can tell," Patricia said, sighing. She'd expressed the belief that cigars all smelled the same, and it could be anyone who had appeared.

"But even so," Betsey pointed out, "to have materialization of any kind is extraordinary."

Violet found herself nodding along with Drew.

When they arrived at Billings House, Violet liked Mary right away. She had light brown hair and kind blue eyes. There was a definite resemblance between her and Drew, although she was shorter and plumper. She had a quieter demeanor than her brother and a sweet smile.

"Please come in," she greeted them. "I'm so happy you could join us too," she added to Violet.

She introduced her husband Theodore and said she would meet their two boys later. Betsey and Patricia were greeted with big hugs, and for a moment, Violet wished she could be part of this warm family. A twinge of envy knotted her insides.

She had little family left. Her sister Rose, and her husband. Her elderly aunt Minnie. And her brother who was out west. She sighed inwardly.

Their belongings were brought inside, and Mrs. Hawkins, the housekeeper, directed footmen to bring them upstairs.

Mary herself showed them to their rooms. Drew, Betsey, and Patricia all seemed to know to which rooms they would be assigned. Mary then led Violet to a wing in the back of the house. They took a step down into a narrower hallway.

"I apologize," she said quietly. "Between Drew's family, the cousins from England who are coming, and my husband's brother and sister-in-law, our other rooms are all filled. I hope you won't mind being back here. This used to be the governess' room."

"Not at all," Violet replied. "I appreciate your

inviting me." When Mary opened the door, she observed the small but clean room with a few pieces of furniture. Much smaller than the room she had at Covington house, it was still tidy and had a window which overlooked some trees in the back of the house.

"We'll have tea and snacks shortly," Mary said. "So if you'd like to wash up..." She pointed out the water closet down the hall.

Violet thanked Mary, and she left. Violet made use of the water closet, combed her hair, and freshened up. By then a footman had delivered her suitcase.

Since they were only staying two days, she didn't want to unpack completely, so she only took out a few items and hung up her good gown, the sky blue one she was going to wear to the ball on Saturday evening.

She went downstairs, and voices led her to the others who were gathered in a parlor at the back of the house.

Patricia and Drew were there already with Mary and her husband and their two sons, who must have been around six and eight. Violet was introduced and then sat beside Patricia as Mary poured tea.

After the introductions, the boys left to return to playing, obviously thinking the adult company would not be as much fun as running around outside.

Betsey entered the room, and Mary asked about their success with the séances.

"If you could only contact Charles," Mary said with a deep sigh.

As usual Violet felt that tightening deep inside her, that pull of regret at the thought of Charles. Could she have done something to warn him? To prevent the tragedy?

"We have tried numerous times," Drew said, a hand on the fireplace mantel. He gazed at a photograph there, what appeared to be a family portrait. Even from this distance, she recognized Drew and Charles and Mary in back of two adults sitting on chairs—probably their parents.

"And we had some success the other night!" Betsey said spiritedly. "We smelled cigar smoke—" She paused.

Violet waited for her to admit that on Thursday—last night—they had had no success at all. No smells. No voices. No materializations.

"Really!" Mary gasped.

"I recognized it as Charles' favorite kind," Drew stated.

"We couldn't hear anything, if he was trying to speak," Patricia added.

"But how wonderful you got some kind of response!" Mary said excitedly.

Her husband looked decidedly skeptical.

"Yes," Drew said, "although..." He straightened and sighed. "Thursday night was the worst of the séances since—well, since Violet arrived." He cast her a glance. "We've been having so much success. But last night, we had no visitation, no voices at all. Simply—nothing. And although that has happened often in the past, I was so hopeful since we'd had so much success recently—well, let's just say I was very disappointed."

Seeing him last night after the séance and their note-taking on the lack of success, Violet had wanted to go to him, hug and comfort him. His disappointment had been so stark.

There was a commotion at the front of the house,

and voices. Mary rose.

"Perhaps that is our cousins Harvey and Henrietta," she said, and left the room.

Drew looked as if he was relieved by the interruption. Perhaps, Violet thought, it was hard for him to admit that they'd had an unsuccessful evening.

Voices grew louder, and a few footmen rushed to help the guests.

Two figures appeared in the doorway. Violet stood along with the others.

One was a rather short, thin man with nondescript brown hair, a small mustache, and nice blue eyes like Drew's.

The other was a somewhat plump woman with creamy skin, dark blonde hair in careful curls, and a decidedly British look to her features with an aquiline nose and small mouth. Her eyes, a bluish-gray, narrowed as they swept the room.

"Hello Harvey, Henrietta," Patricia said, and moved to greet them.

Henrietta's gaze swept over Violet as if she was unimportant, rested on Patricia, then Betsey, and alighted on Drew.

"Drew!" she practically cooed and moved toward him, her hands outstretched.

Drew looked decidedly unimpressed, Violet observed, and Patricia's expression was carefully neutral.

Betsey, on the other hand, looked almost annoyed.

"How nice to see you again, Cousin Henrietta," Drew said somewhat formally. He bowed over her hands, then turned to shake Harvey's. His smile for Harvey was wider.

Henrietta turned and gave Patricia a brief smile. "Aunt Patricia." The two hugged loosely, and then she turned to Betsey. "Cousin Betsey, it's always a pleasure," she said, in a rather gushing voice, as Mary and Theodore re-entered the room.

"May I present Miss Violet Moore, my research assistant?" Drew said, taking Violet's elbow and leading her to the brother and sister.

Henrietta's eyes met Violet's as Violet gave her a smile. For a moment, Henrietta's eyes narrowed and her lips thinned, as if she was displeased. Then her expression smoothed out. "How nice to meet you, Miss Moore," Henrietta said coolly.

Violet gave a brief curtsey. "I am happy to meet you," Violet said. She observed that Harvey's glance was lingering and felt herself flush. He was studying her.

He gave her a brief smile. "A pleasure, Miss Moore."

"Likewise," she responded.

"Please, have some tea," Mary was saying.

Harvey and Henrietta sat as cookies were passed around, and Mary poured more tea. The conversation returned to séances as Betsey told her cousins that Drew was experiencing some successes.

"Really?" Henrietta said, sounding disbelieving. "What kind?" She sipped from her china teacup.

Violet sipped her own tea as Betsey described the cigar odor which had permeated the room several nights ago.

"That hardly means you were able to contact Charles," Henrietta said waspishly.

Drew sat up straighter.

Henrietta cast a glance his way, then softened her voice as she added, "But I know you have been trying very hard."

"We certainly have," Patricia said, her voice rather tight and vehement.

"And we have had other successes," Violet said. "For instance, only a week ago, we were able to contact Samuel, an employee of Drew's who passed on last year—"

"Fascinating, old boy," Harvey said, sounding much more interested than his sister. "Do tell us more."

Drew launched into a description of that encounter while Harvey listened avidly. His sister, on the other hand, listened with a neutral expression on her face, similar to Theodore's now placid one.

"And we also contacted a former neighbor of mine," Violet said.

Harvey stared at her, although Henrietta looked unimpressed. "Did he have anything interesting to say?" Harvey asked.

"No," Drew admitted," but it shows we're doing things the right way. I believe in time we will be able to contact Charles. With any luck, he'll give us information about his killer or killers—"

"Oh!" Henrietta started, her teacup clinking against its saucer. Tea sloshed over the rim.

Mary snatched up a napkin and leaned over, dabbing at the spot of tea, which had landed on the side table.

"Do you really think you could find out his killer?'" Henrietta asked.

Harvey's eyebrows shot up. "Thought you just wanted to say goodbye to your brother, old man,"

Harvey said. "I had no idea you hoped to learn who his killer was."

"I do indeed," Drew said. "I intend to question his spirit when we finally make contact and learn all I can."

"It sounds—frightening," Henrietta said. She shuddered.

Indeed, she did look pale, Violet thought. She knew the very thought of séances scared some people. Henrietta hadn't seemed scared at first. Perhaps the idea of talking to the ghost of a departed cousin, someone she had known well in life, was frightening her.

Violet glanced around the room. Harvey was leaning back in his chair, looking intrigued. Drew was now standing straight and tall by the fireplace, not leaning against it. Mary and her husband exchanged a long look. Patricia was staring at Henrietta, the slightest frown on her face. But as Violet watched, it disappeared.

Violet wondered if there were some family undercurrents she was unaware of.

"Fascinating, fascinating," Harvey said. He sipped his tea. "May I join you one evening?"

"Of course," Drew responded. "I will be happy to include you."

"And me," Henrietta spoke up, giving Drew a winning smile.

But something about that smile rubbed Violet the wrong way.

"Yes, we should all like to join you," Theodore said. "Will it make a difference if it is here rather than at your home?"

"Perhaps," Drew admitted. "Charles was here infrequently, so he wouldn't have a significant connection with this house. We can try here, and again in Twin Bridges, when you visit," he said, looking at Harvey.

Harvey nodded. "Yes, let us try both."

Henrietta sent him a look that Violet could not interpret.

"Yes, why not?" Patricia murmured, picking up her teacup and sipping the tea.

"A splendid idea," Betsey said, clasping her hands.

"We will, of course, not have our usual medium here," Violet pointed out. "Although we have had some success without her." She reached for a cookie.

Henrietta turned and scrutinized Violet. Violet held the cookie tightly in her fingers.

"I—" Henrietta's voice was faint. She swallowed, and when she spoke again it came out stronger. "I fear the spirits who come through, but I am willing to try for your sake." She turned and directed her gaze at Drew.

Violet could have sworn that Henrietta batted her eyelids at her distant cousin.

"Of course," Patricia said crisply, "we all want Drew to succeed. I would certainly enjoy a visit with my nephew Charles. And if we could find out what really happened to him—well, that would be a real coup."

"I intend to." Drew's voice sounded grim.

"I know how much you want this," Mary said softly. She stood and approached her brother. Reaching him, she laid a hand on his arm. "We all do."

He nodded.

"Well, when shall we make the attempt?" Harvey asked.

"Tomorrow is the ball. Tonight?" Drew asked,

looking at Mary.

She turned to Theodore. "Theo?"

"It's fine with me." He sounded slightly bored. He too stood. "After dinner, we'll gather in the library. I used to smoke my cigars with Charles and Drew there when they visited."

"A good idea," Drew said.

He gave some instructions to Theodore for setting up the room, and Theodore and Mary left them to see to the arrangements. Later Theodore's brother and his family arrived, and then everyone dispersed to their rooms to rest before dinner and the evening's event.

During dinner, gray clouds skittered across the sky and it was obvious, looking out the window, that rain was imminent. Violet enjoyed the conversation, which revolved around the latest musical and theatrical productions in New York and New Jersey; and a discussion about who might be the next president. The food was simple but plentiful, ending with apple tarts which were delicious.

The men retired to the library to smoke, and the women to the parlor they'd sat in this afternoon. After being lively at dinner, Henrietta became withdrawn, and Violet wondered if she was frightened of the séance.

Theodore invited them into the library, without the children of course, and his brother and sister-in-law begged off, saying they wanted to retire early.

One window in the room was open. It appeared to be raining lightly outside, and a gust of damp air blew into the room as they sat down. Violet was on Drew's left, with Patricia to her left and Harvey next to her. Mary, Betsey, and Henrietta were across the oval table from Violet.

There were no trumpets in the house, but Mary had borrowed a toy drum from one of her sons, and it rested on another table near the window.

Theodore doused several candles so only two were lit. Taking his seat with the rest of them, on Drew's right, they waited.

A stiff breeze blew in, and Violet noted that Mary shivered. Violet drew her own, new shawl more closely around her shoulders, noting that both Mary and Henrietta's shawls appeared to be very expensive-looking, fashionable, and new.

They sat in silence for perhaps ten minutes. Nothing occurred. Twice, Violet heard Henrietta sigh, as if impatient. Then Drew asked, "Why don't we try holding hands?"

He grasped hers and Theodore's. Violet's hand felt small and fragile in Drew's grasp, but his hand was warm, and she felt the heat sink into her. On her other side, Patricia's hand was smoother but also cool. Patricia gripped Violet's fingers closely.

They sat. A clock in the hall ticked loudly. Then wind gusted again, and the candles began to flicker.

The temperature in the room dropped. Violet felt a chill skim up her left arm.

And something else—a presence.

Drew must have felt it too, because he announced suddenly, "Someone is here."

"Yes," Violet concurred. "Near you, Betsey." She felt and saw a displacement of air; the slightest shimmer.

"My dears..." It was the faintest of whispers. A woman's voice.

Henrietta let out a shriek.

"Silence!" Betsey commanded her.

"Shh," Drew said at the same moment.

They were silent again, and Drew leaned forward slightly. He tightened his hold on Violet's hand so she could feel the pulse racing in his thumb.

"Who do we have the honor of addressing?" he asked.

"Drew...Mary...my darlings..." The air near Betsey shimmered again.

"Mother!" Mary exclaimed. Even in the dim light Violet could see she'd gone completely white.

Henrietta moaned and slumped to the side of her chair in a dead faint.

Claire? Their mother? Violet's heart began to race. Would she say something? This time, would she expose Violet as a woman who hadn't warned her sons when she had the chance?

Chapter Eight

Harvey began to stand as he looked at his sister, slumped in her chair.

"Sit down!" Drew's urgent whisper was like the crack of a whip.

Harvey sat.

"Mother?" This time Drew's voice was soft, appealing, reaching out into the silence blanketing them all.

More silence.

And then: "...can't...get...through." The voice seemed to push against the very air.

She sounded exhausted, but Violet recognized it as the same voice from when she'd visited them at Drew's home.

Patricia sat up straight and rigid. Her hand gripped Violet's tightly.

Violet's heart was beating rapidly.

Mary leaned forward, as if straining to hear.

"Mother?" Mary whispered, and the shimmer of tears gleamed in her eyes.

A cold breeze swept around them. There was silence again. Violet thought the air nearby was tightening, then all of a sudden, there was that strange popping sound.

And the air around them lightened.

The candles flickered, the flames brightening.

It—she—was gone.

"She's gone." Drew's sad tone echoed Violet's thoughts. His shoulders slumped.

"But she was here!" Betsey said, her voice rising excitedly. "Aunt Claire was here!"

"I believe she was," he concurred.

Harvey stood. "I must tend to Henrietta."

Patricia rose too and swiftly moved beside the young woman. "Smelling salts?" she asked, looking at Mary.

"I'll get them." Mary hurried from the room.

Patricia tapped on Henrietta's hand as Harvey spoke in a low tone. "Wake up, Henrietta. Whatever—whoever it was—is gone."

Mary returned and held the smelling salts to Henrietta's nose. The woman flinched, then coughed and sat up.

"What—" she gasped.

"You fainted," Patricia said, her voice gentle. "You must have been very frightened."

"I—was. Was that...?" Her voice shook as her eyes met Drew's. She looked young, scared, and rather appealing.

Violet wondered if Drew would embrace the fair-haired woman. Instead, he stared at her. "You made a lot of noise," he said, his tone nearly accusing.

Her eyes widened. "I was so frightened!" she cried.

"It's all right, sister dear," Harvey said. "Whoever it was is gone now."

Henrietta shivered, casting Drew an entreating glance.

"Along with our chance to speak to her," Drew said resignedly. "I do believe that was my mother."

"It was her voice, though faint," Mary agreed. "Oh, Mother!" She began to cry.

Her husband rushed to her side and handed her a handkerchief.

Drew paced. "It was Mother." His voice was strained, as if he was holding back emotions. He crossed to the bar and poured himself a brandy from the decanter on a side table. "Harvey? Theodore?" at their positive replies he poured two more, then handed one to each man.

"I certainly did not expect that," he admitted. He picked up his glass and took a hearty swallow of the brandy.

"If only she could have stayed, could have gotten through better!" Mary exclaimed.

"What—what do you think she wanted?" Henrietta asked, clutching her shawl.

"To greet us," Drew replied promptly.

"Perhaps to give us information!" Betsey declared. "Maybe she has the same information as Charles!"

A silence fell upon the group. For a moment Violet held her breath, and it appeared that everyone else did, too.

"I am so frightened!" Henrietta clutched at her brother's arm, but her face turned to look at Drew beseechingly.

"There is nothing to be frightened about," Drew reassured her. "You have met my mother on numerous occasions. She was a gentle soul and would wish no harm to anyone."

"That is true," Patricia stated. "If you are so frightened, Henrietta, perhaps you should stay away from the séance next time."

Heads turned to look at Patricia. Her expression was bland, unreadable.

But there had been a decided edge to her voice. And Violet thought: Patricia does not care much for Henrietta.

She did not care overmuch for her, either.

"Come, I will take you to your room," Mary offered, rallying herself. She took Henrietta's arm and led her to the doorway.

Henrietta shot one more glance at Drew. He seemed unaware of it, staring at the place near where his mother's voice had seemed to emanate.

Mary and Henrietta left the room, closely followed by Harvey, who was murmuring to his sister.

"That was...most interesting," Betsey said.

"Yes," Drew said. "I shall make some notes." His gaze swept to Violet's.

"I shall, too," she said. She'd brought paper and pen with her; she moved over to another table and seated herself.

"I will check on Henrietta in a few minutes," Patricia said, sounding reluctant. "But, really, there was nothing particularly frightening about that visitation."

"Some people frighten easily," Betsey pointed out. "And Henrietta seemed scared about the idea of ghosts."

"She should not attend the next séance," Drew said. "I believe you are correct in that, Aunt."

"I doubt she will want to stay away," Patricia said.

Violet began making her notes, and she was aware when Patricia and Theodore left the room a few minutes later. Drew was making notes, and Betsey fidgeted a bit, then left too, with a quiet "goodnight."

When she finished, Violet looked up to find herself alone with Drew in the library.

She became aware that rain was tapping at the window, which someone had closed. The room was warm and cozy, with the candles flickering in a faint draft.

"Would you like to see my notes now, or later?" she asked quietly.

Drew looked up. "I am almost finished…why don't we review them in a few minutes?"

Violet agreed, then went to look at some of the books on the shelves, curious about her hosts' reading materials.

She found the usual popular novels, some classics, Shakespeare plays, and even two books on spirits and séances. Perhaps Mary was interested in learning about her brother's pursuits.

"There." Drew stood and stretched. He smiled at Violet. "I am ready to review our notes."

They sat at the large table where they had conducted the séance and went over their notes together.

When they were finished, Drew gave her a long look. "You are doing a splendid job, Violet."

"Thank you." Was it her imagination, or was that admiration in his expression?

"I'll turn in now," she said, standing.

"I'll walk you upstairs." He said it rather formally, but she was glad of his presence as they moved through the silent house. Glad to be with him, and looking forward—more than she should perhaps—to tomorrow night's ball.

Would he ask her to dance? She had daydreamed

of it many times since she had been asked to attend.

They paused at the top of the stairs.

"Goodnight," he said solemnly.

"Goodnight," she whispered.

She proceeded to her room. She felt him watching her, and paused to look back when she reached her door.

He still stood in the main hall, watching her.

As she regarded him, he gave a little wave of his hand, then turned, and went the opposite way to the other wing of the house.

She pushed the door open and entered her room, shutting the door quietly behind her.

And leaned against it.

Even a look from Drew had her heart fluttering.

She could not wait until tomorrow!

****

Saturday dawned bright and warmer than the preceding day. Mary's household was bustling with activity, and Violet admired the way she calmly had things under control as she directed the housekeeper, servants, and extra servants who were brought in to help prepare and run the ball.

Most of the overnight guests tried to stay out of the way and kept to themselves, except for breakfast and a short lunch, which were both served buffet style in the morning room. Violet sat over coffee with Betsey and Patricia for a while after breakfast. But after lunch, she went to her room. Harvey had challenged Theodore and Drew to a game of cards in the library, and they had retired there to play.

Henrietta did not appear at breakfast, and when she did appear at lunch, she looked wan and was subdued.

It seemed that the events of last night had disturbed her.

Mary had declared that the family would have a simple meal together in the dining room just prior to the ball, and they should dress in their finery.

As she slipped on her dress—she had declined the need for a serving girl to help her since she was quite capable of dressing herself—Violet hoped once again that she would have the opportunity to dance with Drew. It would be wonderful to be in his arms, moving to sweet music!

She turned to regard herself in the mirror.

Her best party gown was a beautiful shade of sky blue, and she thought it was flattering. With a few flounces and ribbons in white, it had a low—but not too low—neckline and showed off her small waist.

She had smoothed her hair back but left a few curls, and now she added the simple locket necklace her mother had left to her. The metal felt cold against her neck. Another look in the mirror, and she pinched her cheeks to give them more color.

She thought—she hoped—she looked attractive.

She smiled.

She heard voices in the hall and peeked out.

Patricia and Betsey stood in front of Patricia's door. Betsey looked lovely in a green and cream striped gown. Patricia wore a lemon yellow gown and looked elegant.

She moved to join them.

"You look lovely," Betsey said, catching sight of her.

"Thank you, so do you both!" Violet replied.

They walked together downstairs and went into the dining room.

Drew, Theodore, and Harvey were standing in the room, chatting. As soon as she saw how devastatingly handsome Drew looked in his formal black eveningwear, Violet felt herself melting inside. He looked dashing, tall, and handsome—and when he turned to look at them, a pleased smile lit his face.

She hoped it was for her, too, and not just his relatives.

"Ladies, you all look beautiful," he said gallantly, coming forward. He kissed his aunt on the cheek, and she smiled back. He took Betsey's hand and kissed it, grinning at his cousin. Then he turned to Violet, and taking her hand, kissed it as well.

Heat swept up from her hand, and up her arm, and she felt her cheeks warm as his lips touched her fingers. He straightened and smiled again at her.

"Yes, beautiful," Theodore echoed.

"Indeed!" Harvey declared, smiling.

He appeared to be studying them. Violet was surprised at how good Harvey looked dressed up. He might not be as good looking or tall as the other two men, but dressed in his elegant evening attire, Harvey did cut a dashing figure. She suspected some of the ladies present at the ball would find his English accent and Continental looks very appealing.

Harvey moved forward too and bowed over each of their hands. But when he did, Violet felt no special warmth. Just the usual gladness at being appreciated by a man.

Betsey asked if anyone else they knew would be there, and Theodore mentioned some long time friends the others knew, as well as some other very distant cousins from Connecticut who were staying at a nearby hotel. Harvey had met these cousins only once and inquired about them.

"Walter shares a great-grandfather with us all," Drew told them. "His wife Elaine is originally from Boston, and we've only met a few times."

Violet heard a throat clearing and looked up to see Henrietta standing in the doorway. She appeared to be waiting for everyone to turn to her.

"You look ravishing as usual, sister dear," Harvey said, moving toward her.

She smiled and regarded the others in the room. "Thank you, dear brother." Her gaze rested on Drew, and her smile became coquettish. "And may I say that all you gentlemen look wonderful? You will surely turn the heads of the local girls."

Drew smiled at her but didn't look overly impressed.

Mary entered the room. "Please sit down; dinner is ready to be served."

Conversation was gay as they spoke of the ball and seeing old friends. The Covingtons reminisced about similar balls when their parents were alive, and both Henrietta and Harvey told amusing stories of balls and masquerades they had attended in London.

"Everything in London is the epitome of elegance," Henrietta declared.

An expression of annoyance crossed Mary's face.

Violet stared down at her roast beef. Was Henrietta implying that Mary's party would not be elegant? It sounded so, and Violet shared Mary's annoyance.

As they were finishing, the musicians arrived, and Mary and Theodore went to supervise them and the other servants.

Shortly afterward, coaches and buggies began to arrive, as well as a few neighbors on foot. Violet caught a glimpse of Mary's sons peering down from upstairs at the arriving guests. Now she stood with Patricia, Betsey, and Drew as people entered the ballroom. The room was soon filled with women in beautiful silk and satin gowns and men in formal black attire. Glasses clinked, there was laughter and talking, and the musicians warmed up in the background. A woman near her wore a heavy perfume, and Violet stepped closer to Betsey, trying to avoid the overwhelming scent.

The musicians began a lively dance.

"May I have the pleasure?" Drew asked Betsey, bowing.

They moved toward the dance floor. Mary and Theodore began the dancing, and as she watched, Violet saw Harvey guide his sister out on the floor.

"You look truly lovely, my dear," Patricia said warmly as she moved closer to Violet.

"Thank you," Violet said.

An older couple came over to greet Patricia, and she introduced Violet to them. They were soon surrounded by several neighbors, all laughing and talking, with the music providing a lively accompaniment.

When the dance ended, Drew then asked Mary to dance, followed by Patricia. He was doing everything correctly, but Violet wished he would ask her.

Theodore asked her to dance, and she enjoyed dancing with him. Then, surprisingly, Harvey asked her.

"So how are you enjoying the séances with Drew

and his family?" he asked as they moved in time to the music. He was a good dancer, keeping time with the music well.

"I am enjoying them very much," she answered. "Drew is very scientific in his approach so we can repeat what is working and eliminate what does not."

"Do you truly believe he can contact Charles?" he asked her, his eyebrows raised, as they moved together across the floor.

"I hope so," Violet said. "He would feel so much better if he could—even if it was just a few words, an appearance…"

"Ahh." Harvey nodded. "Do you think Drew will be satisfied with only a voice or a brief materialization? He seems to want to have an entire conversation with Charles' spirit."

"That is his hope," she admitted. "But even if he got some sign—something in his brother's voice or perhaps a materialization—I believe Drew would be very, very happy."

"Then let us hope that Charles can get through to him," Harvey said as they turned. His voice was light, but his eyes looked more serious, almost—wary.

Perhaps he was skeptical of séances in general, Violet thought. Yet—he had been there last night, when something had definitely happened. They had all heard the voice—

"Is your sister not a fan of the occult?" Violet probed.

Harvey shrugged, even while dancing. "My sister, like many gently-bred gentlewomen, is interested but frightened as well. Last night completely scared her."

"I can understand that," Violet said carefully. She

did not wish to criticize his sister, although she didn't care for the woman. "Especially if one has not attended such a—gathering—before."

"Yes, and the shock of hearing the voice of her—I suppose she was a great aunt?—second cousin?—certainly was unnerving." Harvey continued, "English women are more delicate, you see, not hearty as you American women are." He smiled, as though he thought it was a great compliment to be "hearty."

"I'm sure," Violet murmured, wincing inside.

The dance ended, and people applauded.

"May I get you a refreshment?" he asked.

"A lemonade would be wonderful," Violet said.

He gave a brief bow. "I will return." Then he set out toward the dining room, which Violet knew would be stocked with drinks and food.

She glanced around. Patricia and Betsey were talking to Theodore's brother and his wife, and another couple. On the dance floor, she caught sight of Mary and one of the neighbors; and Drew, with Henrietta.

Henrietta was looking up at her tall partner, smiling and laughing prettily.

Violet's stomach clenched. Did Drew find his very distant cousin appealing as a woman? Henrietta was a distant enough relative to be considered a potential mate. She certainly seemed interested in Drew. But Violet could not read his expression.

They turned so Drew was looking at her face on, and his eyes met hers.

He winked.

Her heart once more did that peculiar little fluttering. She swallowed. Was he perhaps dancing with Henrietta only because it was the polite thing to do, dancing with one's cousin?

They turned in the dance again, and she could no longer see his expression.

But inside she felt warm.

Several minutes later, after her lemonade, Theodore asked her to dance. After that, she danced with the son of a neighbor, a young man probably a little younger than she was. They stood and talked with some others following their dance.

And then suddenly Drew appeared before her.

"May I have this dance?" he asked with a slight bow. "I have been waiting to dance with you since the ball began, but I felt obliged to dance with my relations first."

"I would be honored," she said, and let him lead her onto the dance floor.

The moment he put his hand on her waist and swung her into the waltz, every nerve in her body felt heightened, and a tingling swept through her. Drew was a good dancer, but it was much more than that. Touching him, her hand in his, one on his shoulder, close enough to breathe in the soapy and masculine sent of him, hear his breathing—her heart hammered.

She was in his arms, just where she had dreamed of being. And it was heavenly. More than she had dreamed. Whirling away on the clouds of music, she felt as if she was dancing on air with him.

He smiled down at her, and her heart tripled its speed as happiness burst through her like sunshine.

She knew she was smiling widely. And he gazed down at her, smiling too, and despite the crush of people around them, she felt like they were alone, isolated on their own cloud on this magical evening.

****

Gazing down at Violet's upturned face, her beautiful smile, and glowing eyes, Drew felt happiness deep within his chest.

He'd wanted to dance with her immediately. But he knew he was obligated to dance first with his aunt, his sister and then, several cousins. He'd done so rather impatiently, counting the dances until he could ask Violet.

Now she was in his arms, and as they stepped to the music in perfect synchronicity, he imagined that they were alone in the room.

He knew it was silly. They were probably among nearly a hundred people. But for him, at this moment, he was with the only woman who mattered.

He didn't stop to analyze the thought. Just let it linger in his mind, like a fine wine.

Dancing with his aunt and sister and cousin Betsey had not been difficult. But he had felt compelled to dance with Henrietta too. And as the woman had looked up at him, beaming and flirting no-too-subtly, he'd tried to appear merely polite and distantly friendly.

He didn't dislike Henrietta. He just found her and her brother overbearing. Harvey was constantly showing off and bragging about being one of the English aristocracy. And Henrietta usually played the helpless female, flirting and leaning on any men who were nearby. She acted as if she and Drew were a lot closer than they really were, and that, too, annoyed him.

It used to annoy Charles too, when she acted that way.

"I do believe she wants to marry one of us," Charles had remarked to Drew on more than one occasion.

"Really? But she's our second—no third—cousin," Drew had protested.

Charles had shrugged. "According to Harvey, it is not uncommon in England, especially since the connection is distant."

Drew had found the idea unappealing, to say the least, and so had Charles.

But he didn't want to think of Henrietta now.

The only one he wanted to concentrate on was Violet.

Violet. She looked so lovely in her blue dress. Like a shining star amid duller ones in the galaxy on a clear night.

He wanted badly to whisk her away outside so that they truly could dance by themselves under a canopy of stars.

Perhaps it was possible. The French doors to the terrace were open, so that the room could be cooled off. Surely there weren't too many people out there. They might garner a few moments of privacy.

He steered them gradually toward the French doors.

"You dance well," he told Violet.

"It's easy with you leading me," she answered, her eyes sparkling.

The music ended, and people applauded. The musicians immediately struck up another tune.

"Shall we go outside for a few minutes?" he asked, indicating the doors. "It is quite warm in here."

"Yes," she answered.

Society in this part of New Jersey was not so strict that he couldn't stroll outside for a few moments with

Violet. Unlike some cities where Violet would be more heavily chaperoned. As they stepped onto the terrace, he saw three other couples there, apparently with the same idea—get outside where it was cooler and they could get a little privacy to talk. Two of the couples were engaged in quiet conversation. The third couple was stepping off the terrace, to a path that wound around the gardens.

"My sister's gardens are beautiful," he said, daring to make a suggestion. "Shall we take a brief walk?"

"I'd like that," she said, and slipped her hand into the crook of his arm.

He knew his way around the small maze, and they stepped down into the shrubbery, passing a fourth young couple who were laughing loudly at something. They walked forward, then turned left.

It was quieter here, and Drew was happy to be alone with Violet.

He led her forward, then they turned right.

"I'll show you the statue in the middle," he said.

****

Violet tightened her hold on Drew's arm as he led her deeper into the maze, away from the crowd.

Her heart beat hard as she realized they truly were alone now and protected from staring eyes.

Would he try to kiss her, as many men might when alone with a woman in a garden maze?

They reached an opening with a statue in the middle of a small pool.

They stopped, and for a moment gazed together at the small statue of an angel.

"This is lovely," Violet said. Should she speak about the statue, the greenery, séances, or something else? For a moment she was at a loss for words.

"Violet." Drew spoke softly. He moved to stand in front of her, and cupped her face. "I have wanted to be alone with you all evening. I danced with my family members because I felt obligated to do so. But all I wanted was to dance with you, to spend time with you, to have a few moments with you alone—"

He kissed her.

She felt streamers of sheer joy unfurl inside of her. Lightning seemed to flow along her veins, from their lips straight to her heart.

"Drew," she whispered against his mouth.

And then his lips pressed harder, and he drew her closer to him, until she was pressed against him. Her arms went around his neck, feeling the beat of his pulse there, feeling the fiery streams of pleasure as he kissed her and held her tight.

"Violet, Violet..." he murmured, his lips leaving her mouth to kiss her forehead, her cheeks, her hair. And then they returned to her mouth, and he groaned. "Violet...I've wanted to kiss you again since our first kiss...so much..."

"I've—I've wanted to kiss you again too," she whispered, clutching at his shoulders as he moved back slightly to gaze at her.

He brought a hand to her cheek and stroked it gently. Smiling, he said, "You are beautiful and bewitching and the most wonderful woman I have ever met."

Her heart leaped into the sky, and excitement raced through her.

"Drew, you are...you are the most wonderful man *I* have ever met," she said.

144

They gazed at each other for long moments.

And then laughter erupted nearby.

"Do you think anyone followed us here?" a female voice said from beyond the bushes.

"No," was the answer in an unknown male voice. There was a muffled giggle, and footsteps drew near.

Drew stepped back.

A young couple came around the bend in the shrubbery and stopped, obviously surprised to see another couple taking advantage of the privacy in the middle of the maze.

"Oh, sorry, didn't mean to interrupt," the young man said hastily.

Violet recognized the oldest daughter of Mary's immediate neighbor. Even in the dark, the young woman appeared to be blushing.

"It's all right," she told her hastily.

"We better head back," Drew said, and took Violet's hand firmly in his. He led her away.

They walked in silence for a minute, punctuated only by the young woman's giggle.

"I'm certain they will not say anything about finding us," Drew whispered. "I don't think she will want us talking about seeing *them*."

"I am sure you're correct," Violet responded. The young woman couldn't be a day over seventeen, and the man only a year or two older. They had obviously sneaked off for a few minutes of privacy.

Drew stopped and pulled Violet to him.

She gazed up at his face, and he gently placed his hand on hers.

With the stars shining in the sky, the partial moon glowing and casting a magical light, Violet felt enchanted. Like she and Drew were on a magical adventure in this garden, just the two of them, wrapped in…

Love.

She loved him.

Oh, my word! She was in love with Drew!

Chapter Nine

Violet gasped inwardly and fought not to let out a sound. They gazed at each other, and then Drew tipped his head down and captured her lips again.

She reveled in his kiss, as the world seemed to spin joyfully around them. Every nerve in her body leaped to attention, and she wanted to remain there forever.

Voices nearby again penetrated the haze of their embrace. Drew stepped back.

"Violet…" he said, his gaze still locked on hers.

She smiled.

"We better go back," he said, reluctantly.

"Yes," she whispered.

This time the laughter was closer.

He led her back to the terrace. Several couples were standing there, and Violet hoped her cheeks were not too flushed as they joined a group of four other young people, and Drew introduced her to more of Mary's friends.

They spoke about travels, and one of the young men, Tobias, talked about his recent trip all the way to Spain. When one of the young women began to shiver, they decided to go inside.

Going inside with the group meant their absence would not be overly remarked on, Violet knew. Still, when they entered the warm and crowded ballroom, she felt eyes on all of them.

She found Mary smiling at her. But behind her, Henrietta, who stood with a quite handsome man, was regarding them carefully, and frowning.

Theodore approached them, and asked Violet to dance. She accepted, leaving Drew discussing with Tobias the sites the young man had visited in Spain.

Theodore was a good dancer. "I hope you are enjoying yourself," he said to Violet.

"Very much so!" she exclaimed. "Thank you so much for including me in the invitation."

"Not at all. Patricia wrote how much you have helped Drew, and how good you have been for him. She believes Drew has been much happier since you came to work for him."

"Thank you," Violet murmured. Patricia had said she was good for Drew; she had wondered if she meant for the experiments alone. It seemed Patricia thought that Violet had been good for Drew's spirits.

"And I believe she is right," Theodore continued. "Seeing Drew after not seeing him for several months—I have observed a change in him. He's more positive and outgoing, not brooding as he has been since Charles' death. You have been excellent for him, my dear. I hope—I hope you will continue your association with him and this family."

She felt herself blushing. Did he mean what she thought he did? That Drew cared for her and that the family was happy with a potential relationship? They must know she was not from a wealthy family like theirs; but her family was intelligent and hard-working and certainly not low-class.

"I like your family, very much, as well," she said. "And Drew—not only is he a fair and nice employer—

he is a wonderful man. Very much so."

"I agree." His face took on a more serious expression. "Mary and I would very much like to see him happily settled down."

And that, she thought, sounded like the family was considering that she could fill a permanent role.

At a loss for words, she merely smiled.

He smiled back.

The song ended. Theodore gave a little bow, and they returned to Drew and the other people they'd been talking with. Mary, Harvey, and the other cousins from Connecticut soon joined them.

"Of course, balls in England go on until the wee hours," Harvey boasted to the young woman beside him. "And are extraordinarily lavish."

Talk turned to England and then to European travels. Of course Mary was frightened of the idea of traveling in Italy since her parents had died there.

"I assure you it is safer now," Tobias' brother declared. "I was in Italy, Switzerland, and Austria only a year ago, and I found it a delightful trip and perfectly safe."

"There are train accidents even here in America," the young woman, Anna, who stood beside Tobias pointed out. "My cousin perished in one out in Missouri."

"That is true," Mary said, "but I am still scared to go to Europe."

"Perhaps one day when the boys are older," Theodore suggested. "There will be even more improvements by then."

"Speaking of the boys—I will go check on them," she said.

When Mary left the group, Anna said she was stepping out for a moment. Violet guessed she was going to the retiring room and decided to accompany her.

Anna was friendly, chatting while they walked to the back of the house. A room had been set up near a water closet just for the ladies. Several women were there, combing their hair.

The refined but loud tones of Henrietta's English accent reached her ears the minute Violet entered the room behind Anna.

"...and while Mary and Theodore's home is quite nice, I wouldn't exactly call it a manor house," she was saying to the woman beside her. "Why, Covington Manor in England is easily four times the size of this home! Our morning room is twice as large. We have three formal parlors and a library that makes the one here seem miniature..."

Violet could not believe the disparaging comments falling from Henrietta's mouth. She tried to ignore her strident tones as she followed Anna toward the water closet. She waited until Anna had finished, listening to Henrietta's praises for her own home and others like it in the London area.

One woman interrupted Henrietta, saying that Mary and Theodore's home was one of the finest in the area.

"And furthermore," the older woman went on, "I do not believe you would find a nicer, kinder family in the whole state of New Jersey."

"Oh, yes, of course," Henrietta said hastily, as if realizing she had been reprimanded. "But still, if you were to visit England..."

Anna left the water closet, and Violet entered as Henrietta droned on. When she left it and re-entered the ladies' retiring room, Henrietta's complaints had turned to the "rustic condition" of American roads and the poor state of travel in the Americas. She was moving toward the door, speaking to two young women as they left the room.

Violet seated herself beside Anna and combed her hair.

The door shut.

"She certainly is not going to make many friends here in America if she keeps talking that way," Anna observed.

"That is true." Violet sighed. "I wish she would not be so critical of her host and hostess…they have been nothing but kind. And they are her distant cousins."

"Yes. I have met her once before, and this appears to be the way she talks about many," Anna said. "There! My hair looks better now. I do love dancing, but it messes my hair dreadfully."

"Mine too," Violet said as they walked together back to the ballroom.

The rest of the evening sped by, and it was more than pleasant. Violet had talked with Drew and Mary and Theodore, and they ate some of the snacks that were placed in the dining room. Later the cousins from Connecticut joined them, recounting some tales of when they had all been young, and mischief they had gotten into, along with Charles. She enjoyed hearing their stories and got a better picture of the fun-loving, cheerful lad Charles had been.

And, sadly, recognized how very much they all missed him.

A sudden stab of pain struck her. If only she had listened at that séance, if only she had gotten others to believe her, if she had believed more herself...

"Are you all right, Violet?" Mary asked. "You've gotten so pale."

Drew was regarding her solicitously. "I believe the heat is getting to me," Violet said, her voice somewhat scratchy. "Perhaps I will find a quiet room to sit in for a few minutes."

"I will accompany you," Patricia said, as Drew said "I will come with you" too.

In the end, Patricia professed that she was hot also and led Violet into a small lounge. Drew brought them additional lemonade and then left them to cool off, saying he was going to speak with Mary's neighbor who had recently returned from a trip to Canada. He was very interested in the séances performed there.

They sat for perhaps fifteen minutes.

"You have been very good for Drew," Patricia said again, sipping the cool drink.

"Thank you." She felt a lovely satisfied glow within her. She was in love with Drew...and his aunt thought she was good for him. So did his brother-in-law.

"Mary noticed it too. He has been much more positive, not gloomy, since you began working for him."

And his sister.

"He is a good employer...and a most... wonderful...man." She felt daring saying even that.

"I have always thought so." Patricia smiled at her. "You have been so good for him, child... I hope you will be here for a long, long time."

Perhaps...forever? Violet couldn't help the thought.

The idea of marrying Drew bloomed like a flower, blossoming all of a sudden in her mind and holding on tightly with vine-like strength.

She smiled at Patricia. "I enjoy working...and spending time with him...very much," Violet said.

Patricia beamed.

The door opened, and Cousin Matilda joined them. "You are right; it is quite warm in there."

They spoke for a few minutes about Mary and her family and neighbors, then they returned to the ball.

The ballroom was not quite as warm, though the party was still in full swing. Violet danced again with Theodore, and then with Drew. Dancing with him was like dancing upon the very air, it was so wonderful!

Within an hour people began to depart, and the party wound down. Everyone proclaimed it was one of the best parties Theodore and Mary had ever hosted.

"I am quite fatigued," Patricia declared. "I am ready to go to my room."

Drew escorted his aunt to the stairs and then returned. After a few minutes, Violet excused herself, and he walked her to the stairs, too.

"I have not enjoyed myself so much in ages," he said in a low voice as they walked.

"Myself, as well," Violet said. "This was a spectacular party."

"I especially enjoyed every moment I spent with you." He paused by the stairs and bent to kiss her hand.

Even that light touch sent thrills up and down her spine.

"Goodnight, Violet."

"Goodnight, Drew," she responded, smiling. Then she quickly went up the stairs.

She was rather wound up and found after undressing that she was not quite ready to sleep. She lay on the bed, reviewing in her mind her dances with Drew, their private moments in the garden, and his kisses. Oh, those kisses! Had any kiss ever been so grand?

She finally fell asleep, happy and satisfied, and dreamed of dancing with Drew.

****

The following morning the family gathered for breakfast, then departed. Mary and Theodore looked tired and had decided to forego church today. Drew was eager to get back so that they could set up for the next séance. "Perhaps there will be time for a nap prior to that," he told his aunt.

Henrietta begged to go in the carriage with "the other ladies, so we can talk girl talk," she said. So she sat with Patricia, Betsey, and Violet, and they discussed hats and the latest Parisian fashions for most of the trip back. Drew rode with Harvey. Harvey and Henrietta had decided to stay at Covington House after all instead of at the hotel in town.

When they reached Covington House and the servants were bringing their luggage inside, Harvey surprised them.

"I wish to stay in Charles' rooms," he stated.

There was a moment of silence.

"No one has stayed there since Charles—since Charles…" Patricia began but looked unable to finish.

"No, I don't think it's a good idea," Drew said firmly, watching his distressed aunt.

"Why not? Perhaps it will make me feel closer to him and help with tonight's séances and any others," Harvey said.

"Well, if that is true, then I will stay there," Drew told him. "I do not feel comfortable having anyone else stay in my brother's quarters."

For a moment they stared at each other. Then Harvey shrugged.

"Fine, old man," he said easily. "I simply thought it would be a good idea."

"Henrietta, you're in the main wing, near Betsey," Patricia said to her. "The pale blue room."

Henrietta cast her brother a sideways look, then moved forward smoothly. "Of course. I've had that room before."

Violet proceeded to her room, where she took some time unpacking, then washed up. She was too keyed up to nap, so she decided to go over her notes from the last few séances.

But now that she was back "home," the excitement of the ball and the sparkle of her love for Drew began to wear off. Oh, she loved him. But memories crept forward, sapping her of excitement. Memories of that séance in Morristown, her hesitancy to believe the truth of the spirit's warning, her inability to get people to believe her when she did take it more seriously, and the warning she'd penned too late.

Much too late.

She slumped in the desk chair, a wave of guilt washing over her.

Could she have done something to prevent Charles' death?

Chapter Ten

Shortly before dinner time, Violet went down the corridor, intending to sit in the green parlor until dinner was announced. Perhaps Patricia or Betsey would be present, and surely company would dispel some of the guilt and gloom that seemed to have surrounded her like a cloak since arriving back in Drew's home.

As she passed by the room she supposed was Henrietta's, she heard raised voices. She would have continued past except that she heard her name, and froze.

"Violet, a nobody!" It was Henrietta's voice, and she sounded angry. "What can he possibly see in her? I am prettier, am I not?"

"Of course." Violet recognized Harvey's voice. "By far, sister. Prettier than anyone else at last night's party."

"And what can she offer him? I am sure she has little money. Her parents were in trade, by all accounts."

"That doesn't seem to bother people here in America," Harvey responded. "It's different than it is in England."

"Well, I do not see what he sees in her." Henrietta sounded annoyed now. "Did you see how he gazed at her last night after they returned with the others from the terrace? Like he was—was moonstruck."

"I'm not sure he is," Harvey said. "He has said nothing to me, or anyone else, about caring for her, or anything more than that she is a good employee and takes fastidious notes."

Violet swallowed. Henrietta sounded jealous, and spiteful. She did not want to get on the bad side of these two distant cousins. She had done nothing but—

They seemed to think Drew cared.

He must, if he had kissed her like he did.

She took another step, reminding herself of the saying that eavesdroppers rarely hear good of themselves. She felt her cheeks grow warm.

"You will have to redouble your efforts to attract him," Harvey declared. It sounded as if he was pacing the room. "You must do a better job—"

"I am doing my best," she wailed.

His voice dropped, and Violet could not hear what Harvey was saying.

She did not want to be caught listening. She swiftly continued down the hall, stepping carefully on the carpet so that she made no sound.

When she reached the stairs, she hurried down them, anxious to get away from the cousins she disliked.

Walking into the green parlor, she clutched her shawl closer about her shoulders, warding off a sudden chill.

She found Patricia sitting there, knitting quietly.

"I'm making a scarf for Betsey," she said. "She requested another one for a new dress she just bought— the one she was wearing today."

"These are nice colors," Violet remarked.

Patricia was working in autumn tones of gold, red,

and brown. The scarf would go nicely with Betsey's gold-colored dress.

She seated herself near Patricia, in a comfortable chair.

"I am so pleased," Patricia began," to see how happy Drew is lately. Your coming here has made a big difference in his attitude."

"Really?" Violet asked. Theodore had said as much, but it was different hearing it from Patricia, someone older and wiser, who lived with Drew. And hearing her say so again.

"Yes." She clicked her knitting needles but glanced at Violet. "He is much happier and has found his positive outlook once again. You don't know—he was very dejected for months after Charles died, especially when he got it into his head that he could reach him with a séance—and then was unable to."

"Oh. Well, I am glad," Violet said. She smiled at Patricia. "I like your nephew very much."

"I hope it will be more than that." Patricia stopped knitting, reached over, and clasped one of Violet's hands. "I hope you will come to care for—come to love him. I think he cares a great deal for you already. You have been good for him, Violet, and I don't mean just because of your work with him."

Sudden tears gathered in Violet's eyes. "Thank you," she said. "I do—care—for him a great deal—" She was not quite ready to admit she loved Drew; it was too new, too exciting an emotion to speak about just yet.

Patricia squeezed her hand, and smiled, as if she knew what Violet was too shy to say.

She returned to her knitting, and Violet remarked

on the wonderful time she'd had at Mary's ball.

"What do you think of our distant cousins Harvey and Henrietta?" Patricia asked suddenly.

Violet hesitated. She wanted to be truthful; yet she was unsure how far to go in criticizing members of the family. She settled on, "I hardly know Harvey, although he seems to be a genial man. Henrietta is—is—rather critical, I would say, although I hardly know her either."

"That is a tactful way of putting it," Patricia said as her needles clicked. "I have always found her to be self-centered and critical of others—"

The door was open, and the sound of people farther down the hall reached them suddenly. Harvey's voice, saying something about horses, and then Betsey saying that women in New York did not ride as much as women in the country.

Violet and Patricia fell silent.

"Ah, but in London every genteel woman rides," Henrietta said as they all approached the doorway.

Patricia looked at Violet, her eyebrows raised.

The group came into the room and sat down with Patricia and Violet. Two minutes later, Drew entered the room, and the discussion of horses and riding continued for several minutes.

"Do you ride?" Henrietta asked Violet suddenly.

"Yes, I do, though not exceedingly well," Violet admitted. "My brother, who now lives out west, says it is essential that all people there ride."

"That is true," Drew said. "But here, of course, we do have so many modes of transportation—"

A serving girl came in to announce that dinner was ready, and they filed into the dining room.

Violet found she didn't have much appetite. Between her confused feelings—guilt, a slight worry about how the séance would go, and overhearing the unpleasant conversation between Harvey and Henrietta, she picked at her food.

Most of the conversation was lively, with Betsey and Harvey conjecturing about who they might contact tonight. Henrietta was unusually quiet, and Betsey challenged her.

"Are you not eager to see who we might hear from tonight?" she asked her cousin.

Henrietta put down her fork. "I will not be there."

"Why not?" Betsey asked.

"She does not feel comfortable," Harvey put in, "after what happened last time."

"You're frightened?" Drew asked, his expression one of astonishment.

"Please understand," Henrietta said, turning to him with teary eyes, "I was so scared. I sensed a—spirit. We thought we heard your mother. There was something— bad there—"

"My mother was *never* evil," Drew said, his voice grim.

"No, of course not!" Henrietta protested. "It was just—it was just—" She leaned toward Drew across the table, looking beseeching and innocent. "I was so— very frightened. There may have been another presence there—I sensed something evil—I am afraid!" She clutched her cloth napkin and brought it to her lips, looking terrified.

Perhaps, Violet thought cynically, she thought the helpless role would appeal to Drew. But she found it hard to believe that Henrietta was so frightened.

Drew seemed unimpressed. "I did not sense anything evil. Did any of you?" He glanced around the table.

Violet, Patricia, and Betsey shook their heads no.

Only Harvey came to his sister's defense.

"There was something, old man," he said calmly. "Something—strange. I sensed it before your mother came through—if that was indeed her."

"It was her," Patricia affirmed as Drew began to object.

"Of course it was her. Do you think I wouldn't know my own mother?"

"It is said sometimes entities—evil entities— masquerade as others," Harvey said quite calmly, helping himself to more roasted potatoes.

"I don't believe that was the case here," Drew said.

"So, will we be doing everything the same?" Betsey asked, obviously trying to steer the conversation to less controversial territory.

"Yes...except that I am going to add the crystals I bought recently." Briefly, Drew explained his research findings that some people were having more success at séances when they had crystal rocks present in the room or on the table.

"How fascinating," Betsey said.

"I wish it was a full moon," Drew said, sighing. "And Mrs. O'Grady will not be able to join us tonight. I sent word, but she already had plans with her family. That is disappointing."

"Perhaps she is becoming scared too," Henrietta said.

"No, she has done this often," Drew said, meeting Henrietta's eyes.

"And I haven't." Henrietta pouted. "Really, try to be understanding, Drew. I had never before attended a séance, and I was frightened nearly out of my wits! Most gently-bred Englishwomen would be!"

"I was not. Neither, I may point out, was Aunt Patricia nor Violet," Betsey said.

Violet had a sneaking suspicion that Betsey was enjoying baiting Henrietta.

Henrietta frowned. "They are not delicate English ladies. Neither are you," she said.

"Well." Betsey coughed and grinned at Henrietta. "Perhaps there is something good to be said about being a modern American woman."

Henrietta's cheeks flamed.

"It may be natural to have some fear," Violet said, trying to placate Drew's irate cousin. "But I assure you nothing bad has happened to us. With all of us there, I don't believe anything bad would happen."

Henrietta turned and positively glared at Violet.

"We will watch out for you, *if* you do decide to come," Patricia said. She was smiling, and Violet suspected she did not want Henrietta to attend. "But I believe it would be best if you did not attend." Patricia looked like a stern teacher at the moment.

"I will not put myself at risk." Henrietta glanced around the room. Only Harvey looked slightly sympathetic. Henrietta turned to Drew. "You should not risk yourself, either, Drew. All this to try to have a conversation with your brother's spirit—is it worth it?" Her tone was skeptical.

"It is to me." His voice and look were cold as steel. "Even if it were dangerous—which I do not believe—I would be attempting to contact him."

Henrietta flinched at his words. Then, as Violet watched, her face took on a neutral expression, as if she was considering. Her eyes narrowed cunningly, and then smoothly—too smoothly, she said, "Of course. I admire your dedication, Drew. Even if it is dangerous, you will attempt to contact Charles. You are truly a devoted brother."

He shook his head. "Not devoted enough. If I had only known, if I could have somehow stopped the deadly deed—"

Violet felt as if she'd been punched in the stomach. She had suspected. If only *she* could have stopped the deadly deed.

She tightly gripped the thick cloth napkin lying in her lap. The smooth material bunched in her fingers.

Patricia gave the serving girl the signal to begin clearing dishes, and another started bringing in dessert, which was an apple tart. Violet could smell the apples baked with cinnamon.

The smell of the apple tart and spices was reviving. She slowly relaxed her fingers, forcing herself to relax her shoulders which had tensed as well.

"There was nothing you could have done," Patricia said to her nephew. "Even if you had a warning, you would not have known when, or where...was Charles to live his life in fear, afraid of anything and everything?"

"He might have been more careful." Drew's voice was anguished.

"Perhaps he was careful," Harvey said. "But he was jumped by thugs. It's hard to expect that kind of thing, or know how to react."

But Drew continued to stare glumly at his plate.

Patricia leaned over and patted Drew's hand. "You

are doing all you can now, Drew, to contact him, and to learn about his killer or killers."

"That's all I can do," Drew said, raising his head and glancing around the table.

Violet spoke up. "That's all anyone can do." She swallowed, as guilt continued to pound her.

He gave her a brief smile.

The rest of the conversation during dessert turned to the weather. Once Violet sensed Henrietta staring at her, but when she met the woman's eyes, Henrietta swerved her head and studied Patricia.

After dinner, they disbursed. Henrietta claimed she needed a quiet night to calm her nerves after "the excitement of the ball and the fright of the séance." Her brother escorted her upstairs, promising to be back downstairs at seven thirty for the séance.

Patricia and Betsey went to the green parlor, and Violet joined them for a few minutes, then left to go to her room to prepare her notes.

She passed by Drew's study and saw him sitting in a chair, a brandy or another similar drink in his hand, a book open on his lap.

"Violet?" he called out as she passed.

She stopped. "Yes?"

He stood and strode over. "Can you come in?"

She entered the room, and he closed the door.

"Are you frightened of the séances?" he asked.

"No," she answered honestly. "I find them exciting—but not frightening. At least, nothing has frightened me yet."

He ran his hand through his hair. "That is good. I do not want you frightened as Henrietta appears to be." He frowned suddenly. "Although I don't know if she is truly frightened; or just thinks, perhaps, that a lady *should* be scared."

"That may be so," Violet said, not wanting to malign his cousin although she also thought there was a possibility Henrietta was play-acting.

He nodded. "That is all I wanted to ask you."

"Then I will see you soon in your studio," Violet said, and looking up at him, smiled.

The smile he gave her sent a wave of pleasure shooting down her body to her toes.

He reached out and cupped her face with both hands.

"After the séance..." he began. He hesitated, then added, "afterward...we can talk and compare notes."

And you can kiss me, she thought.

It was as if he read her thoughts. "And we...can spend time together." His voice dropped to a husky note, and bending his head, he gave her a swift kiss on the lips.

Even that quick kiss was enough to send shimmers of sensation throughout her body.

She smiled up at him.

A door shut somewhere down the hall.

Violet moved toward the study door. "I'll see you in your séance room shortly."

"I'll see you soon," he responded.

She left, walking rapidly. But in truth she felt like skipping.

****

Drew gazed after Violet when she left.

He could not wait for the séance...and yet even more, he found himself thinking he couldn't wait until they were alone again.

To have her in his arms, crushed against him, smelling the light floral scent of her hair, her warm and sweet lips pressed to his—

Patricia appeared in the doorway.

She smiled at him. "I see Violet just left."

"Yes." He wondered why she was mentioning it.

"She is a very nice young woman. And she is good for you." His aunt tilted her head, as if studying him.

"I agree." He wondered again what his aunt was getting at.

She just smiled, and he considered if she knew he had feelings for Violet. Feelings that, well, kept him thinking about her at night. Feelings that had him thinking about her at the most unexpected times. Feelings that...had gradually grown stronger, taking hold in a way he'd never experienced before.

Patricia simply continued to smile, then cleared her throat. "I guess I will get ready for the séance." And just like that, she left the room.

Was she humming as she walked down the hall?

****

As Violet stepped outside and went toward Drew's laboratory, she was struck by a chill in the air that was considerably cooler than last night's mild breeze. Light rain spattered her, and she drew her shawl closer and hurried up the path.

She glanced up at the moon. It was shrouded in a haze, and she knew that meant rain for the morrow. It was almost full, and she hoped that Mrs. O'Grady would join them on the night of the full moon, Wednesday.

She opened the door and went inside.

The building was warm and almost cozy. The small

fireplace had a fire burning in it, sending waves of warmth into the main room. A glance at Drew's office showed him standing at the desk, rifling through a drawer.

"It's here somewhere," Drew was saying aloud. Then, "Ah..." He looked up, caught her eye, and smiled. She smiled back.

Violet entered the séance room. Patricia was already in the séance room, looking out the window, which was only opened slightly to let in a breeze. Harvey stood at the side table, idly examining the trumpet.

"Betsey will be here in a minute," Patricia said. "She returned to her room to get a shawl."

"It is rather chilly this evening," Violet said.

Drew entered.

"Interesting trumpet," Harvey said, placing it back on the table. "Was this the one cousin Bertram used to play?"

"Yes," Drew concurred.

"Who is Cousin Bertram?" Violet asked.

"Our grandfather's first cousin, who settled in the Boston area," Drew said. "He was a good musician and played a number of instruments. He left me his trumpet, a violin for Mary, and a clarinet for Charles. I believe the clarinet is in the attic."

"Yes," Patricia said. "It is still there. I do believe Bertram would be most pleased we are using the trumpet."

"He came through once, back in May," Drew told them all. "He played a few notes, and we distinctly heard his laugh."

"How exciting!" Betsey said as she hurried in. "I

did not know that you had reached Bertram."

"Yes, it was quite a successful séance," Patricia said.

Drew began lighting a few candles, placed the crystal in the center of the table, and doused the oil lamp. When they were in semi-darkness, he took his seat, with Patricia to his right and Violet to the left. Harvey sat on Patricia's right, and Betsey sat between Violet and Harvey.

"Let us think of Charles," Drew said, "and hold hands."

They connected and fell silent.

A stiff wind blew through the window, damp with rain.

It was quiet except for the beat of rain lightly hitting the window. The air seemed hushed, waiting.

As Violet sat, she sensed something, a heaviness in the air, again.

"Someone is here," Betsey said suddenly. "I feel...something."

Harvey gave her a sharp look.

"I feel it too," Violet whispered.

They waited.

There was a muffled cough.

"Please identify yourself," Drew invited.

"Drew..." the voice was faint, very faint. A man's voice.

Drew sat up straighter. "Charles?"

Violet's heart started to beat, hard.

"Is that you, old man?" Harvey whispered, sounding awestruck.

The trumpet suddenly moved from the table and went crashing to the ground, making an unpleasant sound.

Harvey almost jumped in his seat.

"Charles?" Patricia asked.

"He can't get through." It was another voice now, also masculine, but stronger and older. "He is trying…"

Harvey's face had turned white.

"Whom are we addressing?" Drew asked, but Violet thought she recognized the voice of Samuel from previous séances—the voice of their employee who had passed.

"Samuel," was the answer. "Charles is trying…he can't get through. He is trying to signal you…"

Samuel stopped speaking abruptly.

The trumpet moved on the floor with a screech.

Betsey gasped.

"Charles?" Drew asked.

There was silence.

The trumpet rocked, as if pushed by a hand.

Patricia tightened her hold on Violet's hand as Violet's pulse raced.

"Charles?" Drew repeated. He waited a moment, then asked "Samuel?"

There was silence.

A gust of wind blew into the room with a whistling sound.

Violet couldn't help shivering.

They remained silent, and Violet felt as if they were all straining, waiting to hear Charles' or another's voice, hoping for something. Another sign.

But there was nothing. Until they heard the strange popping sound.

Violet looked at each person in turn. Betsey was pale, but her expression was thoughtful. Patricia looked hopeful, almost smiling. Drew looked determined, his mouth in a firm line, not frowning but not smiling either. Serious. Harvey looked shaken but still his expression was a far cry from his sister's frightened look the other night.

No one spoke for several minutes.

Then Drew sighed. "I'm afraid we've lost him—them."

"Yes." Betsey sighed as well. "I thought for a minute—when the trumpet moved—that Charles had joined us. He did so love listening to music—and Drew, I remember he used to go into your room and blow that trumpet occasionally to tease us."

"And he would say Uncle Bertram was doing it, that he was signaling us," Drew finished.

"Yes." Patricia smiled fondly. "He did like to joke about that. It would be so like him to use a trumpet now that he's crossed over."

"Do you really think it was him?" Harvey sounded skeptical. "Perhaps it was Bertram. Or Samuel."

"I think Samuel was there to guide the way—to show us that Charles was trying to get through," Violet said. "We have had visitations when one told us another one was trying to get through, such as Charles."

Drew nodded. "Yes. I think—I think he was trying." He sighed again. "We need to repeat this, with Mrs. O'Grady, and on the night of the full moon."

"Does the moon make a difference?" Harvey asked.

"Supposedly the spirits find it easier to reach us then," Violet told him.

"Oh." He appeared to mull that over. "Then, by all means, we must try on the full moon...when is that?"

"Wednesday night." Drew turned to look fully at his cousin. "You will still be here then? I believe you are not heading back to New York until Friday?"

"Yes," Harvey said.

"Well, I guess we'll go make our notes," Drew said.

"I thought Violet was here to write your notes," Harvey said.

"She does a very thorough job; but Aunt Patricia and I jot down some notes and then we compare them all," Drew said, pushing his chair back and standing up. "It is always beneficial to have the observations of other participants."

"I will make some notes too," Betsey volunteered.

Violet stood, and they soon were going their separate ways. Patricia told Harvey she preferred to make her notes in her room. Betsey said she would walk back with her. They left Violet and Drew with Harvey.

"Do you want me to write notes too?" Harvey said, sounding as if the thought annoyed him.

"Only if you want to," Drew said.

Harvey stood, looking at his cousin, as if he was reluctant to leave.

"I, ah, do you mind if I take a turn around your main room?" he asked. "I'm curious to see what you have there, what books. I've never really looked before."

Drew sounded uninterested as he replied, "Help yourself if there's anything you'd like to borrow."

"Thanks, old man."

Violet began making her notes as Drew went into his office. She immersed herself in remembering the sights and sounds of the séance, and for a while lost track of time. When she finished and looked up, rain was still hitting the window rhythmically, coming down harder now. The wind blowing in was stronger, and she went to shut the window.

She peeked into the main room. She didn't see Harvey. Perhaps he had left quietly, and she hadn't heard him. Still, she couldn't assume he was not about. She walked through the room but did not see him. Looking into Drew's office, she saw Drew studying a book, papers and a pen before him. He must be done with his notes.

Harvey was nowhere in the building. He must have exited very quietly.

"Goodnight, Drew," Violet said quietly, not wishing to startle him.

"Oh, goodnight, Violet." He glanced up at her, for a moment looking almost confused, as if he'd forgotten she was in the building. Then his expression softened.

He stood and came over to the doorway where she stood. "Goodnight, my dear." Leaning forward, he gave her a chaste kiss. When he pulled back, his eyes seemed to smolder, as if he was deliberately suppressing himself from anything more. "I am reading up on the significance of trumpets and other musical instruments," he confided.

"Oh, I see." Obviously, he was in the middle of his research. "I shan't interrupt you. Goodnight."

He was watching as she left the building.

She hurried through the rain—which was coming down harder now—and let herself into the house.

Lights had been dimmed by now. It was nearly ten o'clock and the house was quiet, with only the tick tock of the grandfather clock in the hall echoing through the downstairs rooms. Violet hurried up the stairs. The hallway was shadowy with the dimmed oil lamps burning.

As she walked down the main corridor, a door opened behind her with a creak. She felt a shimmer of uneasiness.

She glanced behind to see Harvey standing in the doorway to his room.

"Goodnight, Violet," he called out.

"Goodnight," she replied, and continued on her way. She heard the door click shut.

Had he been waiting to see her come upstairs? Or—waiting for someone else?

Drew?

Still uneasy, she hurried to her room. Once inside, she lit the oil lamp, shut the door, and locked it, something she rarely did here.

She perched on her bed, wondering why Harvey made her feel uneasy. He could simply have been waiting to have a word with Drew. Hearing someone coming upstairs, he had looked to see if it was his cousin.

She waited 'til the hammering of her heart had slowed. Then she got up, used the water closet, and returned to her room, once again locking the door. She prepared for bed, and once she lay down, tried not to think of Harvey or Henrietta or anyone else but Drew.

And dancing in his arms...

****

She slept deeply and awoke later than usual. Hurrying to dress, Violet finished and went to breakfast.

173

Henrietta and Betsey both sat in the breakfast room. Drew, Patricia, and Harvey must have eaten earlier, Violet guessed.

Violet poured herself coffee and selected toast and jam before seating herself at the round table.

"I was just filling in Henrietta on the events of last night," Betsey declared. "She had not yet seen Drew or Harvey."

"My brother rises earlier than I do," Henrietta said. "So, Miss Moore, what did you think of last night's séance?"

With anyone else, Violet would have said it was fine to call her by her given name. But she did not ask Henrietta to do so. She stirred her coffee. "I believe Charles did try but was unable to get through."

Henrietta gave a shudder.

"I would have been frightened to death," she stated, picking up her coffee cup.

"Charles would not want you to be frightened," Betsey said in a calm voice. "He would do nothing to scare you, I am certain."

"Nevertheless, I am glad I didn't go." Henrietta made a face. She speared a piece of ham. "My constitution is so delicate. I am sure I would have fainted again."

Betsey simply nodded, as did Violet.

"Well." Henrietta stood. "I believe I will find my brother and go for a walk. I understand there is quite a good milliner in town, and I would like a new hat."

"Yes, there is," Betsey agreed.

Henrietta asked, "Would you like to join me, Cousin?"

She did not invite Violet.

Violet swallowed her coffee, as hurt welled up inside her. It was obvious Henrietta did not consider her good enough even for a simple visit to the milliner.

Betsey sent her a quick glance. "No, I must write to my mother today and tell her of the ball and the events of the weekend. I may go into town later to post the note." She smiled at Violet. "Perhaps you will accompany me, Violet."

"I would enjoy that," Violet responded. "I must write to my sister today as well."

Betsey stood too. "After lunch then?"

Violet nodded and bit into her toast.

Henrietta sent her a sour look. But then she turned to Betsey and smiled. "If I give you a letter later, can you post it? I must write to my dear friend Arabella."

"Of course," Betsey said.

Henrietta left the room. Betsey hesitated, looking at Violet. "I am sorry she is being rude. She normally isn't, but I do believe she is jealous of you."

"Jealous?" Surprise shot through Violet.

"Yes." Betsey moved to sit down right beside her. "It seems obvious that Drew is quite taken with you, Violet."

Violet stared at Betsey. "It is?" She hoped—was fairly certain—that Drew liked her. That he also liked kissing her. But—taken with her? She did not know how far his feelings extended.

She voiced that thought. "Dear Betsey, I do not know how far his—feelings—extend."

"Betsey grinned. "Oh, I think he cares for you—a lot. I saw the way he was looking at you at the ball. As if he were—mesmerized. I think—Aunt Patricia and Mary and I all think—that he is falling in love with you,

Violet."

Violet started, clattering her cup against its china saucer.

"You do?" Her voice squeaked, as a wave of great hopefulness rushed through her. "That would be—that would be so extraordinarily—wonderful."

"Because you love him too," Betsey observed.

Violet swallowed. "I—I haven't—have tried not to think about it too much, but I know I care for him, and hoped he cared for me—" All the while, the thought was humming inside her.

I love Drew. I'm in love with Drew Covington.

"I understand," Betsey said simply. "You care but didn't want to give voice to the thought until you knew how he felt."

"Yes. I—I don't come from such a famed and esteemed family as Drew, nor as wealthy—"

Betsey waved her hand. "That is no matter. Drew would never marry for money or prestige, I am convinced of it. He is not that sort."

"Others are, and may tell him not to—to—" she paused, as her deep fear spilled forth. That others would consider her inferior to Drew, convince him she was just someone to pass some time with, not take seriously. "Like Henrietta and Harvey."

"Believe me, he would never listen to their opinions on such matters." Betsey grinned again. "Besides, I don't think he likes them overly much. Which irks them terribly. Aunt Patricia confided—" Betsey paused.

"Yes?" Violet asked eagerly as she buttered another slice of toast.

"Well, he was neutral about Harvey, until last year.

Harvey asked Drew for money. It apparently was not the first time—he'd given him some the year before, which he was supposed to pay back promptly and never did—and so Drew said no. Then Harvey went to Charles." Betsey sighed. "Fortunately, Drew had warned Charles that Harvey does not pay his debts, and Charles refused him, too. Drew was angry that he was attempting to play the two brothers against each other."

"Oh dear." She was beginning to dislike Harvey. She took a bite of the crispy bread.

"That's why I think he is back in America now," Betsey said as she spread jam on some toast. "It is my theory that he is looking for a rich American wife to bring back to England and enrich the family coffers."

"I see." Violet was unsure what to say. "Well, I won't have to worry," she added lightly, "about his flirting with me. I have no fortune."

"You have other attributes—you are intelligent, and personable," Betsey said. "Alas, that is not what Harvey wants in a wife. But better for you," she continued. "Really, he is too self-centered to make a good husband. If he finds a shallow New York woman who simply wants to marry a man with a title and has the money to do so—well, I wish them well. They will deserve each other." She chuckled.

Violet grinned at Betsey's words.

Betsey got up, walked to the long table, and poured herself another cup of tea. Sitting beside Violet once more, she sipped it. "As far as Henrietta—well, you know she wants Drew for herself."

Just what Mary's husband Theodore has said. "But she is a cousin, although a distant one," Violet pointed out.

"Yes, but there is no law against it, and apparently from what I have heard very distant cousins marrying is not unusual, in England," Betsey said. "Henrietta tells all the time about her friend Lydia who married her third—or fourth cousin—an earl."

"Harvey is an earl, not Drew," Violet said. "It is not as if she would gain an English title."

"Well, my cousin is handsome," Betsey observed, smiling.

"And very personable and intelligent and charming—" Violet began.

Betsey laughed. "See? You cannot say enough good things about him—you do care!"

Violet smiled back. "Yes, I do." She sighed. "But I do not know how he feels—"

"Give him time," Betsey said sagely. "I am not engaged or married, of course, but I have spoken to many men... I don't believe they realize this sort of thing as quickly as women do." She sipped her tea. "And, back to Henrietta—I believe Drew's money is a *big* attraction for her." She wrinkled her nose. "Even if he wasn't handsome and charming she would probably want him."

"I have met women like that," Violet said, dropping her voice.

"Yes, I see many in New York society," Betsey agreed. "Grasping, money-hungry—like vultures!"

They both laughed, and Violet felt a lot lighter when she returned to her room.

There would be no séance tonight, or Tuesday, because they were going to hold one on Wednesday. She hoped to review her notes with Drew, however, tonight. She penned a short note to him suggesting that and asked one of the footmen to give it to him when he returned in the afternoon.

Then she went over her notes, finding nothing new to add. She wrote to her sister and then read the séance book she had been reading since last week.

This book had no notes on trumpets or other instruments so she decided to ask Drew if there was another that he could suggest that made mention of that topic.

Lunch was actually fun, with Harvey relating some stories of his travels throughout the British Isles and the beautiful scenery he'd encountered. He'd also done a "tour" of the continent, as he called it, and spoke of museums in Italy and France and the countryside he had traveled through in both areas.

"Germany was beautiful too," he told them, and went on to speak of some of the castles he had visited, and the nobility he'd met.

His sister remained quiet, a rather bored look on her face. Perhaps she had heard all these stories before.

"Have you traveled to the same countries?" Violet asked, turning to Henrietta.

"Of course not," she fairly snapped. "In English society, a young man makes the Grand Tour of Europe...not a young woman. My father would never dream of letting me go." Her lip curled, but Violet thought she detected a note of jealousy in Henrietta's speech.

"That would probably not happen amidst New York high society," Betsey said. "Why, many parents take their sons *and* their daughters to visit Europe, and other parts of America. My best friend visited the South recently."

"How fortunate," Henrietta said stiffly. "And didn't you say you visited Spain?" She asked Betsey.

"Indeed I did," Betsey said, smiling. "Five years ago. It was a memorable trip. We visited London, too, Henrietta, although I believe your family was visiting friends in—Cornwall, was it?—when we were there, so we were not able to see you."

"In Devon, actually," Harvey said. "Our dear friends the Baron and Baroness Clavendish and their family."

"It was a boring trip," Henrietta said churlishly.

Harvey sent her a glance—almost a warning. Perhaps he was getting tired of his sister's sour attitude.

Betsey asked about Scotland, which she said she would love to visit someday, and Harvey talked for a little while about that country, which he had seen while visiting a schoolmate.

After lunch, Violet went upstairs to get her shawl and bonnet. Going into town with Betsey was fun. They walked, and though it was sunny, the air had a faint chill which made brisk walking pleasant.

At the milliner's Betsey purchased a blue hat with wine-colored ribbons. Violet admired several but didn't purchase any, knowing she did not have the luxury of too much spending money. Instead, they went into the general store, and she found some cologne she liked, with a light floral scent. She splurged and bought a small bottle since it was inexpensive.

"Let me smell," Betsey said. After taking a sniff, she said "I approve. I think Drew will like it too." She winked.

Violet felt her cheeks warm.

Betsey bought some periodicals and offered to

share them with Violet. They looked at ribbons and materials for dresses, then moved on to examine some boots made by the family's manufacturing company that were on display.

Finally Betsey suggested walking back.

The walk was less than a mile but mostly uphill. They spoke a little, and Betsey admitted she was having fun but missed her mother and brothers.

The walk was not too strenuous, and the cool breezes made it comfortable. Halfway home, they heard their names called and found Drew striding up to them.

"Were you doing some shopping in town?" he asked, noting their packages.

"Yes! We had fun," Betsey declared.

Violet nodded. "There are such nice stores here."

"I'm glad you enjoyed yourself. I'm on my way home now to do some reading before tomorrow's séance." He looked at Violet.

"I left a note for you," she said. "I was hoping to go over our notes this afternoon."

"Excellent. We'll do that first," he said.

They reached his home and parted ways, Betsey and Violet to put away their purchases and Drew to go to his laboratory. Violet joined him there shortly afterward, her notes in hand.

They reviewed their notes companionably. Afterward Drew sat down to do research, and Violet began reading the book he recommended.

Supper was rather lively, with Harvey continuing to speak about his travels and Patricia talking about some places in the United States she had visited like Boston and Baltimore. After dinner, they gathered in the large red and gold parlor in the front of the house.

Betsey sang—she had a wonderful voice—and also played the piano well. After a few songs, Patricia joined her, and then they all sang along to some popular songs. Even Henrietta joined in and acted as if she was having a good time.

Drew left to get the trumpet, and then played a few songs. They ended with singing "Camptown Ladies" while Betsey played.

By that time it was nine o'clock, and Patricia said she was getting tired and they dispersed.

Violet was not tired so she sat and read in her bedroom. She heard Drew's door open and shut, and suspected that he, too, was reading in preparation for Wednesday's séance.

Tuesday passed quietly, with nothing notable.

The following morning Violet woke at the usual time, ate breakfast with Patricia and Betsey and Harvey who informed them Henrietta was still abed.

"She is most uneasy about this séance tonight," he told them as he heaped bacon on his plate. "But I think I have convinced her to join us."

Violet was not sure she was happy about this.

Betsey turned to Violet. "If someone is present who is reluctant, will it adversely affect the results?"

"I have no idea," she replied honestly. "We should ask Drew."

Drew had left early for the factory, but Patricia offered to send a note.

Harvey looked annoyed.

After breakfast, Violet went to continue further research, and Patricia sat down to knit. Betsey had borrowed a book yesterday from Drew, and they all sat in the green parlor. Violet found it soothing to read alongside Betsey while the knitting needles clicked rhythmically in the background.

Henrietta joined them at lunch, looking rather pale, and Violet guessed she was worried about the séance. She did not broach the subject.

Dinner was again lively, with discussion of past séances. Once again Henrietta was quiet, but Harvey asked a lot of questions.

"And we even reached one of my neighbors who passed on," Violet told him, reaching for her water glass. "Eddie, a very congenial man."

"Yes, and he was quite amusing, too!" Patricia declared as she passed a platter of roasted squash to Harvey.

"How interesting," Harvey said.

Henrietta shivered. "Were you not scared?" she asked Violet.

"No, I was glad to hear his voice," Violet said.

Henrietta looked unsure—something different for her, Violet mused.

"Look, if you really want to come to the séance, you can sit between me and your brother," Drew said. Violet thought she caught a reluctant note in his voice. "However, you must be very quiet. I don't want you screaming or disrupting." He gave her a stern look.

Henrietta swallowed. "All right," she said meekly.

Harvey sent her a smile. "That's my brave sister."

She smiled back, a wavering smile.

They went their separate ways after dinner, agreeing to meet before eight.

By seven-thirty Violet donned her shawl and picked up pen and paper. She went downstairs and found Patricia by the back door, putting on her shawl.

They walked together down the path to the laboratory in companionable silence. The evening was beautiful, with a clear sky and only a few wispy clouds. The moon was large and white and seemed closer to the earth than usual. Violet could see the darker spots and ridges visible on its surface.

"It's a harvest moon," Patricia told her as they walked. "The moon that's closest to earth in a year."

"How fascinating!" Violet said. The air was chilly, typical for an October evening, with a breeze.

They found Drew in the building already, moving some things about in the séance room. He carefully placed the trumpet on the side table.

The door opened, and Mrs. O'Grady entered. She called goodbye to her son who had walked her over, then came into the room, taking off the scarf from around her head. "It's a beauteous night," she observed. "A good night for contacting spirits."

"That's wonderful," Betsey said, appearing in the doorway. She smiled widely. "I hope we are able to contact many!"

Drew pointed out seats for them to take. A few minutes later Harvey and Henrietta joined them.

Drew was seated in his usual seat, with Henrietta to his right and Harvey after her. Then came Betsey, Violet, Mrs. O'Grady, and Patricia and back to Drew again.

Drew lowered the gas lamps, and Patricia lit several candles. They all sat down and joined hands.

In the middle of the table where Drew had placed it, the meteorite twinkled, reflecting the candle light.

"Let us begin," Drew announced.

They were quiet. Violet could hear quiet breathing,

although Henrietta's was more rapid than many of the other's. Still nervous, she guessed.

Violet felt that peculiar heaviness she usually recognized as a spirit joining them. Mrs. O'Grady's eyes were now closed, her breathing having gradually gotten deep and heavier. Her hand appeared to be resting in Violet's.

"Good evening, friends." The rather stiff cadence—as if it was not his first language—and deep voice of Mrs. O'Grady's Indian guide was clear in the quiet room.

"Do we have the honor of addressing Red Feather?" Drew asked quietly.

"Yes, you do."

"Welcome, Red Feather."

"Welcome," Patricia murmured, and they all followed suit.

There were a good two minutes of silence. Then Drew asked pleasantly, "Have you news for us? Perhaps a message from my brother?"

"He is one who is trying valiantly to come through," Red Feather responded. "He is having difficulty." He fell silent. Then he added, "He wishes to speak."

A candle flickered wildly although there was no breeze. Violet found herself holding her breath, and Betsey gripped her hand hard.

A low groan sounded form near Drew. Henrietta flinched.

"Charles?" Drew whispered.

They were silent, hands clasped, waiting.

All three candle flames danced.

"Drew…" it was the faintest of whispers, barely

audible. But definitely a man's voice.

"Can you help him, Red Feather?" Drew asked.

Red Feather answered, "I have tried. This he must do himself."

They waited again. Henrietta was very pale. Harvey looked fascinated, and Betsey excited.

"Charles? Anyone?" Drew asked after several minutes.

The candle flame bent, then danced again.

"Bet...sey..." a low voice ground out.

"Charles?" Betsey whispered, tightening her hold on Violet's hand.

Violet grasped hers back. Her heart hammered with excitement. Was he truly going to get through?

Henrietta gasped suddenly.

Violet felt a whoosh of air at the back of her head, and a sudden tingling moved up her spine. Something—someone was here, and something was happening.

To her amazement, the trumpet moved into her line of vision, slowly drifting through the air to her right. It stopped, wavered, and then suddenly, as if thrown, sprang through the air and shot in between Drew and Henrietta, slamming against the wall behind them with a honking sound.

Henrietta slumped forward. Only Drew's and Harvey's grips on her hands kept her from hitting her head on the table as they braced to hold her.

Her head bowed over her chest.

"Charles?" Drew asked, his voice uncertain. "Did you move that—trumpet?"

There was no answer. Only...silence.

Then Red Feather spoke once more. "He did."

"Can he speak?" Drew asked.

"He has tried. He is fatigued." Red Feather paused. "He is...fading away."

The heaviness nearby seemed to be dissipating, and Violet thought Charles must be leaving them.

"Charles, please don't go," Betsey entreated.

Wind whooshed through the room, and the candles flickered madly.

"He is trying to stay," Red Feather declared. "He is...very weak."

The popping noise—one they'd heard before— sounded loudly, almost crackling near Mrs. O'Grady.

He must have left, Violet thought, disappointment spiraling down through her body.

"He has retreated," Red Feather said.

"Can we get him back?" Drew asked.

"Another day," was the answer. Red Feather was sounding weary too. "Now, friends, I must depart."

"Thank you, Red Feather," Drew said solemnly.

"Thank you," Violet said, and Betsey and the others murmured their thanks too.

All except Henrietta, who still appeared to be unconscious.

Mrs. O'Grady started, and the candles wavered as more air blew through the room.

Mrs. O'Grady sat straighter and opened her eyes. "I sense Red Feather was here," she stated. "But he is gone now."

"Yes," Drew said, nodding.

"Well." Harvey gave a brief smile. "That was— quite a show, eh?"

"Not a show," Drew objected.

"Just a figure of speech," Harvey said. "It was—

quite an evening."

"Did anyone else come through?" Mrs. O'Grady asked.

"We thought Charles was trying," Drew said. "But all we heard were a few words. Red Feather said he was having trouble. Even, apparently," he said, with a glance at the meteorite," with the help of the meteorite, and the full moon."

"The important thing is you made some contact!" Betsey said, her voice excited.

Patricia let go of Mrs. O'Grady's and Drew's hands, took out a handkerchief, and dabbed her eyes. "That was Charles, struggling to get through," she said. "I am sure of it."

"Yes, but I wonder why he was having such trouble," Drew said. "And why did he fling the trumpet at me?"

"To get your attention perhaps?" Betsey guessed.

"To tell you something?" Violet asked. "He knows the trumpet is a family heirloom. Perhaps that is his way of letting you know he, your family, is here."

Harvey stared at her.

"That is possible," Drew said. "But—why throw it? Why not play it?"

"Sometimes, the spirits have trouble breaking through the veil," Mrs. O'Grady said, her voice solemn and mysterious. "Perhaps that was the only thing he was able to do tonight."

"Well." Drew stood, dropping Henrietta's hand on the table. "We should make our notes." He looked at Violet.

"Of course." She stood also.

"I will make my notes too," Betsey said

enthusiastically, rising.

"And I as well," Patricia said. "Oh my, this is our most exciting encounter yet!"

Harvey placed a hand on Henrietta's shoulder and shook her lightly. "Wake up, sister. We are done for the night."

"Mmph?" Henrietta moaned and raised her head. She looked around, unfocused, then sat up abruptly. "What—what happened?"

"Are you all right, dear?" Patricia asked solicitously.

"Y-yes." She looked shaken, though.

"Come, I will tell you all as we walk back to the house." Harvey extended a hand, and she placed hers in her brother's, allowing him to pull her up.

"See that she is all right," Drew said.

"Perhaps a glass of water will help her," Patricia suggested.

"I believe a stiff brandy would help more," Harvey said. "I will take her to her room and fetch some." He pulled his sister along. "And I will stay with her until I am assured she is fine."

He departed, tugging his silent sister with him.

"We will have our next séance on Friday," Drew announced. "I am hopeful we will contact Charles soon. We seem to get closer each time."

"Yes," Patricia said. "We do." After a moment Patricia gathered her shawl and said, "I will check on Henrietta," and left too.

"I will walk Mrs. O'Grady home," Drew said. He turned to Violet. "I will meet you back here in half an hour, tops."

"I will be making notes," she said.

"I will stay here too," Betsey said, "until you return."

He left with Mrs. O'Grady, who looked tired. Violet immediately sat down at the table and began writing.

Betsey had brought pen and paper, too, and they were soon scribbling in silence, immersed in their observations. Only the scratching of their pens interrupted the supreme quiet. Even the wind seemed to have died down.

The sound of the door opening and shutting startled Violet. She looked up to see Drew striding into the room.

"Quite an exciting night!" He declared, setting his hat on the side table. "Mrs. O'Grady was quite weary; she observed that it must have been a powerful séance to make her that tired." He went to grab paper and pen from his office, returning at once. Sitting down, he began to write rapidly.

Betsey put her pen down. "I'm finished."

"I am nearly done," Violet said, as she wrote about Red Feather's last comments.

"We can compare our notes after I write mine," Drew said, looking up. "Unless, of course, you are tired and want to leave."

"I can wait," Betsey said with a big smile. "This is so exciting!"

She left to wander around the main room, pulling out a few books to look at. Violet finished her notes, then joined Betsey. They whispered about the séance, about Henrietta's fear and the excitement of possibly making contact with Charles.

Betsey dismissed Henrietta's faint. "She may be

play-acting," she said. "She probably thinks it's feminine to swoon at the slightest fearsome occurrence."

"Do you think so?" Violet nibbled her lip. "Her fear seems genuine."

"It may be—but I find her swooning to be very melodramatic and unconvincing," Betsey stated. "It seems to occur just at the most dramatic of our moments!"

"Yes," Violet agreed. "But perhaps she is easily frightened."

Betsey shrugged. "I am simply suspicious of her. I guess it is my dislike showing." She giggled.

Violet glanced at the séance room, where Drew had his head bent over the paper, busily writing. "We should be quiet."

"You're right, of course," Betsey whispered. She linked arms with Violet and drew her closer to the front door. "I am being mean, perhaps, but I have never cared for Henrietta. I find her mean and selfish."

Violet nodded. "Me too," she whispered.

They spoke in low tones for a few more minutes about the séance.

Then they heard the scraping of a chair, and Drew strode into the room.

"You are whispering like schoolgirls," he said. But the fond look he sent them both warmed Violet and took the sting out of his words.

"Well, this was one of the most exciting evenings of my life!" Betsey declared.

"It was certainly one of our most exciting séances," Drew said. He sent a sideways glance at Violet.

Was he thinking the same thing she was thinking,

she wondered? That perhaps, the most exciting night was the ball where they'd danced together—and kissed?

But with Betsey nearby, they couldn't mention it.

They sat down at one of the long tables and meticulously reviewed their notes, comparing them. Betsey had forgotten something Red Feather said, and Drew had forgotten Mrs. O'Grady's deep breathing—not that that was very important, but Violet had noted it. She gathered her notes when they finished, including Betsey's and Drew's, to copy on the morrow.

"Well," Betsey said, with a glance at the small clock on a shelf, "It is after eleven. I am growing tired."

"I am too," Violet admitted.

Drew returned. "Thank you, ladies, for doing this tonight and not waiting until tomorrow. I wanted to capture all the details of this important evening." He looked pleased. "Although we did not make a great contact with Charles, I still sensed he was there, trying to reach us…and it's the closest to him we've gotten."

"Yes," Violet said. "Tonight was an achievement." She smiled up at Drew. "I feel Charles was there, but we did not establish true contact for whatever reason. Something was blocking him."

"Yes," Betsey said eagerly. "Maybe something was preventing him from coming through."

"Interesting idea," Drew mused. "What could be blocking him? I thought perhaps he didn't have enough strength, but Violet, you may be right. Something may be preventing him. Well," he said, with a glance at the small black clock. "I better walk you girls home. It is quite late."

Betsey yawned, quickly covering her mouth with a

delicate hand.

Drew doused the remaining candles and oil lamps, then shut the door and locked it. They strolled toward the house, which was dark in the moonlight.

"Everyone must be abed," Betsey said quietly.

When they reached the house, he escorted them to the staircase. "I think I will have a brandy," Drew said. "Goodnight, ladies, and thank you." With a smile he turned and strode toward his study.

Violet and Betsey climbed the stairs. The house was quiet, shadowy with only a few dim wall sconces to light the way in the hall. When they reached Betsey's room, she whispered goodnight. Violet continued to her own, where she rapidly got ready for bed. Fatigue was beginning to overtake her, and her excitement was fading beneath it.

She slipped under the blankets.

Sleep came quickly. But she had an odd dream that awakened her early.

Charles was there, reaching out to her.

"I'm trying," he said. "I'm trying to get through."

Violet stretched out her hand to him. "Take my hand. I'll help you!"

He grasped it, and it felt so warm, so alive, she gasped.

She tried to pull him, but he was big and weighed too much. She tried again, but nothing happened.

There was a shadow nearby, lurking.

He tilted his head toward it. "It's in the way... I can't get around..."

"What is it?" she asked, frantically.

But he was fading away, his very being dissipating like a cloud, coming apart and scattering to the wind.

"Help...me...please."

"I'm trying!"

She sat up and blinked.

It was dawn. She could tell from the pale light peeking around her curtains.

She got out of bed. The room was chilly, but she padded to look out the window.

It was too early to get up. She sighed. The dream had been so realistic, so very...real.

She got back into bed and pulled the covers up, attempting to get a little more sleep. She must have dozed off for a short time, because she suddenly awoke as usual at half past seven.

She was eager to get down to breakfast. She found Drew, Patricia, and Betsey there.

They were discussing last night's séance. Drew was hopeful that they were getting nearer to solid contact with his brother.

"Last night was the closest we've come," Patricia said.

"And we seem to be getting more positive results each time!" Drew said, his voice excited. He gave his boyish smile and looked at each one of them in turn.

Harvey entered the room. "Morning, all," he said.

"How is Henrietta?" Patricia asked.

"I have not yet seen her this morning." Harvey poured himself coffee. "I had to calm her down last night. She was quite—agitated." His tone was rather annoyed. Over his coffee cup, he stared at Drew.

"She should not come to any more séances then," Drew said firmly. "We don't want her getting so upset."

"I agree," Patricia added.

Harvey nodded, putting his coffee down on the

table. He returned to the sideboard, picked up a plate, and began piling it with food. For a thin man, Violet thought, he certainly could eat a lot.

"It was our best séance yet," Betsey told her cousin. "It's a shame she fainted and missed some of it."

"I think she is glad she fainted," Harvey said, seating himself in between Drew and Patricia. "She was scared out of her wits." His tone was sardonic.

Drew frowned. "I doubt any ghost would try to harm her. I have never seen that happen."

"Someone threw the trumpet," Harvey pointed out, lifting a forkful of eggs.

"True," Drew conceded, "but I believe that was to get our attention, not to harm anyone."

Harvey shrugged.

They continued to speak of the séance, and then Drew stood.

"Can you meet me in my laboratory office at two?" he asked, looking at Violet. "I want to discuss the séance for Friday, and possibly making a few changes."

"Certainly," she answered.

"Good. I am off to the factory. I will see you all later." He left the room.

"Well, he seems cheerful," Harvey said, sipping more coffee.

"He is well pleased with how the séance went," Betsey remarked and pushed aside her plate. "I am going to do more reading on séances. This is fascinating, just fascinating." She too left the room.

"And you, Violet, do you find it fascinating as well?" Harvey asked her.

"Yes, I do," she replied.

She finished her breakfast quickly, finding herself uncomfortable with the way he was scrutinizing her. Patricia stood at the same time, and they said goodbye and left him to finish his breakfast alone.

Violet went to her room and spent several hours reading and copying yesterday evening's notes. She saw no one until lunch. Drew usually ate a quick lunch at the factory, but everyone else was there, including Henrietta, who looked pale and tired. When Patricia tried speaking to her, she answered in monosyllables and avoided eye contact most of the time. She looked totally glum.

Was she embarrassed by her childish behavior? Violet wondered. But Henrietta did not seem the type to be embarrassed easily.

Betsey began chatting with Violet about some of the styles of ball gowns they'd seen at Mary's ball, and Patricia joined in. Harvey appeared bored and Henrietta disinterested, even in the fashion comments. Lunch passed quickly.

Violet left to continue reading, with Betsey right behind her. Patricia was speaking in a low voice to Henrietta and Harvey about the home they were renting in New York when Violet left the room.

She was immersed in her reading when she glanced at the clock and saw it was ten of two. She hurried to comb her hair, then grabbed her notes, and went downstairs to meet with Drew.

As she got near the laboratory building, she noted the day had turned gray and chilly. She wrapped her shawl closer as wind struck her body. She suspected they would get a storm later.

She was nearly at the building when she saw a

shadow form the corner of her eye.

"Watch out!" the voice seemed to burst in her head. A male voice—Charles?

She gasped and turned away from the dark shadow. Just as something struck the side of her head.

For a moment, she saw stars. Then her vision dimmed, and she felt herself sliding downward.

"Help!" It was her voice, feeble.

It was the last thing she was conscious of.

****

"Get out of the way!"

Violet heard Drew's voice, anxious and brusque.

She was being carried, she felt it. Opening her eyes, she realized Drew was carrying her up the stairs. "Call the doctor!" he barked at someone. "She's hurt."

Her head throbbed. She closed her eyes, and the next thing she knew she was being lain gently on her bed.

"Are you all right, my dear?" Patricia was bending over her. "We've sent for the doctor. What hurts?'

"My...head." Violet reached up and gingerly touched the side of her head which was smarting.

"How did this happen?" Drew asked.

"I was going to meet you—" She started to sit up, but her head throbbed, and she could not help a moan escaping.

Drew's hand had been on her arm, and it tightened.

She laid her head back against pillows that Patricia was placing behind her. She was conscious of Drew, Betsey, and—was that Harvey hovering nearby?

"I saw something near the corner of the building," she said. "And something—seemed to warn me." Caution warned her about saying anything to all of them about the voice that sounded like Charles. She would tell Drew later, perhaps Betsey and Patricia as well. "I started to move out of the way, and something hit me."

"You were attacked?" Betsey exclaimed, aghast.

"Something hit me," Violet repeated.

"There was a tree branch right nearby Violet," Drew said. His face was grim. "After the doctor arrives, I will send for the constable."

"Let's make her comfortable," Patricia said. She called to a housemaid outside the door, asking for cold water and compresses.

The doctor arrived shortly. Violet guessed Drew's family was prominent enough for him to respond quickly. He said her injury was not too bad and prescribed some laudanum for the evening and rest for three days.

"No excitement," he cautioned.

Mrs. White appeared at the doorway. "Mr. Covington, the constable is here to see you."

"Excuse me," he told them and disappeared.

Patricia and Betsey helped Violet wash up and slip into comfortable night attire. She was becoming sleepy from the draught of laudanum the doctor had given her. He told her to sleep and left. The pain in her head was rapidly diminishing from the effects of the laudanum.

She slipped into bed. Drew reappeared with an older man who had a weathered face and a gray mustache. Briefly, she described to him what had happened. He told her he was going to examine the area where she had been hit and see if he could find any clues.

Drew paused bedside her bed. "You get some rest

now." His voice was kind, and his eyes showed concern. He followed the inspector out.

Violet caught sight of Patricia, Betsey, Henrietta, and Harvey hovering by the door. Henrietta looked scared.

"Do you think someone is lurking about, trying to hurt us?" Henrietta gasped.

"Nonsense," Patricia said briskly. "Perhaps someone meant Violet harm, or is trying to stop Drew's research." She cast Henrietta an annoyed look.

"I'll stay with her while she dozes off," Patricia told Betsey.

"Thank you," Violet murmured and closed her eyes.

She heard Betsey leave the room and shut the door. Patricia seemed to be pulling the drapes shut, and she drifted off to sleep, comforted by Patricia's presence.

When she woke, it was dark. A single candle was lit in the room ,and Drew sat in a chair pulled up to the bed.

"How are you feeling?" he asked quietly when she moved.

She gingerly felt her head. "It aches...but not as much as it did before."

"That's good." He hesitated. "Mr. Smith, the police constable, found the tree branch you were probably struck with. If you hadn't seen something and moved, it might have been worse."

"Does he—does he have any idea who did this?" she asked, pushing herself to a sitting position.

"Unfortunately not. But he and I are determined to get to the bottom of this." His mouth tightened. "No one should be attacked in my home. Everyone should be safe. We will find the culprit!"

She smiled. "I hope you do, soon. I would hate for something like this to happen again."

"We will all be on the lookout for any strangers, anything unusual," he said.

"What if..." she stopped.

"What if...?"

"It was not...a stranger?" She waited for his response.

"I have thought of that." His voice was grim. "Although I don't know who in the household would attempt to harm you—or why." He ran his hand through his hair. "I simply have no idea."

"I don't either." But she had an uneasy feeling. She decided to tell him both about her dream and the voice that sounded like Charles.

He listened intently as she described the dream and the incident that afternoon.

He sat back, reflecting. "Hmm...perhaps Charles was trying to tell you something in the dream about what is preventing him from getting through. I don't know what it is. Do you?"

She started to shake her head and winced. "No. I am not sure."

"As far as the warning"—he regarded her—"I believe Charles *was* trying to warn you. Perhaps he saved your life."

She shivered. "Perhaps he did...it was as if I heard him in my head. I'm sure it helped me to turn away from that—shadow."

"Well, we will try and reach him tomorrow. Maybe we can ask him about both," Drew added.

"I would like to be there—"

He stopped her. "No," he declared. "The doctor said specifically, no excitement! You are to rest for three days—tomorrow, Saturday and Sunday. Then, if you feel up to it, you can resume your activities." He stood. "Mrs. White has prepared some nourishing chicken soup for you. It is amazing what her chicken soup can do to make one feel better. I will have her bring it up. Then, the doctor wants you to have more laudanum and get more rest."

"Soup sounds delicious." To tell the truth, Violet did feel fatigued and still in pain, but she wanted to eat the soup before going back to sleep.

"I will have her bring it at once." He paused, then bent and kissed her gently. "Get some rest, Violet. I will check on you later."

Mrs. White brought up the soup herself and sat with her while she ate, chatting a little about Drew and his brother when they were young.

When she left, Betsey came in, helped her prepare for sleep and gave her another dose of laudanum.

"Who could have struck me?" Violet asked her friend as she snuggled beneath the blankets.

Betsey stirred the fire, then closed the grate and put the poker down. "We don't know as yet...but Drew is determined to find out." She sat at the foot of the bed. "He really cares about you, Violet."

"Thank you." Violet smiled and closed her eyes as the drowsiness from the medicine crept through her.

Rain tapped her window musically, and a breeze stirred the curtains. She opened her eyes to see Betsey regarding her.

"We will keep you safe," Betsey said, repeating Drew's words.

"I know," Violet said, trusting the truth of Betsey's words. She snuggled farther into the blankets, feeling warm and cozy despite what had happened that afternoon.

She lay there for a few minutes, then heard Betsey whisper "goodnight" and quietly leave the room.

She slept deeply, not waking until the maid came in the morning with a breakfast tray, followed by Patricia.

"Good morning," Patricia said. "I'm sorry to disturb you, but the doctor wanted us to check on you. He will be by later. In the meantime, we have some nourishing oatmeal and coffee for you."

The smell of brewed coffee was invigorating. Violet had breakfast while Patricia sat nearby, talking about plans for the séance tonight.

"I promise I will come by afterward and tell you all about it," she said.

"I want so much to be there," Violet said, adding a little extra sugar to her coffee. The breakfast made her feel better, and her headache had turned to a dull annoyance rather than a sharp pain.

"I know, but you must listen to the physician," Patricia told her. "You must get rest the next few days. There is no sense in making your injury worse."

Josephine, one of the maids, came in and helped Violet get dressed. Then she lay on the bed with the book she was reading.

Because of her head, it was hard to concentrate on the words. She kept looking out the window at the gray, overcast day. And wishing she could be present at the séance tonight. Although the moon was no longer full, it would be nearly so. She wondered if the clouds blocking the moon would have an adverse effect on the spirits they were trying to contact.

Betsey, Harvey, and Henrietta came to see her mid-morning. She was actually surprised to see Harvey and his sister.

"Do you have any idea who could have done this terrible thing?" Harvey asked.

Henrietta looked disturbed, her face pinched.

"No," Violet replied.

"I can't imagine, either," Betsey said. "Perhaps some vagrant who is living in the woods hereabouts?"

"Drew has not heard of anyone," Harvey said. "I asked him about that last night. Neither have the police. But it is always possible there is someone new to the area, camped out hereabouts."

Henrietta shivered. "We may all be in peril."

Betsey staunchly defended her family. "Drew is doing all he can to see that nothing like this happens again! I understand he has the footmen patrolling the grounds and is hiring two more employees."

"Well, he certainly is taking this thing seriously," Harvey remarked.

Henrietta still looked unconvinced.

They left after a few minutes, and later Violet had lunch in her room with Patricia. She determined to go down for meals by tomorrow. "I really don't want everyone making such a fuss," she told Drew's aunt.

"It is no trouble," Patricia said. "We want to be sure you heal quickly."

The afternoon dragged. Once again, she had trouble concentrating on her book. Looking out the window, she saw it was raining again. Bored, Violet walked up and down the upstairs corridor a few times, then returned to her room to attempt to finish reading the mystery she had started last week. She'd been so busy reading Drew's books on occult research that she had put it aside. But now she found it entertaining.

Betsey came to visit with her again and amused her with stories of when she visited Drew, Charles, and Mary as a child.

By dinner, Violet was growing restless, although she still felt tired from the medicine and from the dull headache. She ate alone, and then Betsey and Patricia came to see her before the séance.

"We'll be by to tell you how it went," Patricia promised. "And Harvey and Henrietta have decided not to go back to New York City yet."

"Please do come by," Violet urged.

It was seven thirty, and they persuaded her to slip into her nightgown and robe. Sighing, she complied, with their help. The two left, and she was alone again, wishing she could be with them. But she knew the doctor was correct—the séance was sure to be exciting, and she wanted to get well.

Betsey had told her Harvey would be in attendance, but Henrietta wasn't going, since Drew was in favor of her staying out of anything she was scared of.

"She would only interfere," Betsey said dismissively.

From her window, Violet saw Mrs. O'Grady's son walking her over, and then him going home a few minutes later. She sat back on the bed and tried to read, but she was too restless.

"I might as well be there," she grumbled to herself. "I'm excited anyway."

But knowing the others would object, she stayed

put.

She could hear sounds of the household, as she had all day. Two maids talking as they put some things away in a linen closet. One stopped to ask if she'd like some hot cocoa or cookies. She accepted the hot drink, and soon had it in front of her, smelling divine and comforting. She sipped it slowly, enjoying the sweet taste as it slid down her throat and warmed her insides.

A footman came back to make sure her fire was lit and hearty. She heard him moving along the hall and assumed he was lighting fires in Betsey's and the other bedrooms. The day had grown chilly, and it promised to been a cold night for October.

Rain still struck the windows intermittently.

The house became more quiet, and she guessed the servants were retiring. Then a door opened and closed loudly. She wondered if it was Henrietta.

She went to her door and opened it slightly, peering out. Nothing.

She heard movement in the main corridor, then another door opening and closing. Had Henrietta left her room and returned? Was she in another room, or was something else going on?

She did not want to simply be a nosy, annoying guest, so Violet stayed in her room. When she couldn't concentrate on her book, she decided to walk the hall. It was eight forty, and the house was already quiet.

Both her corridor and the main one were dim, with only a few wall sconces flickering. The door to Henrietta's room was shut, and she heard no noise from there or anywhere else.

Violet walked to the back of her hall, to the solarium.

The lush plants greeted her with a sweet fragrance. Even in the autumn months, there were a few blooms present—mums, she thought. She moved to the back window, overlooking the back yard. She could clearly see Drew's laboratory from here.

There was no light in the front room. She could see a faint flicker from beyond...the corner séance room. Probably the single candle. The room was at the right side in the back, so only the faintest light could be seen through the front window.

What was happening there, she wondered? What were they seeing, hearing?

"I can't get through."

The voice seemed to spring from the very night air.

Violet jumped back.

The motion caused her head to throb. She put a hand on a nearby chair, steadying herself.

"Charles?" she whispered. For just a second, she sensed a presence.

It had certainly sounded like his voice. Was he trying to get through, and unable to?

Excitement coursed through her, and just a little fear. She was alone...with a spirit, without Drew or anyone else in the family.

She clutched at her throat. "Charles?" she whispered.

There was no sound. Not a thing.

She heard herself breathing, felt her rapid heartbeat.

Still, nothing. She waited a few minutes, then edged closer to the window.

She looked at the laboratory building. The same dim light shone through the window. There appeared to be no change.

"Can you go there? Get to Drew?" she asked.

But there was no answer.

The presence she had sensed seemed to be gone. She reached out mentally, extended her hands, even.

There was nothing there.

But she asked again anyway. "Charles? Are you here?"

There was no sound.

She sighed, frustrated. How could they help him to come through?

And why was he reaching out to her instead of those seated at the table in the séance room?

She continued to gaze at the building from the solarium window. After a few minutes, the light grew brighter, as if Drew had turned on an oil lamp.

The séance must be over.

She gripped her hands. Had they had any success reaching Charles? She wondered.

She began to see shadows moving about in the main room. Then the door opened, and Patricia and Betsey came out, followed by Harvey. Lastly Drew escorted Mrs. O'Grady.

Patricia and Betsey would be mad if they found her out of bed and not resting. She scurried back to her room, climbed into bed, and willed her heart to slow down. Taking up her book again, she rested against the pillows.

A few minutes later, she heard voices down the corridor. The voices grew closer and then a tapping sounded on her door.

"Come in," Violet invited.

Betsey and Patricia entered. Patricia looked

serious, Betsey disappointed.

"What happened?" Violet asked eagerly.

Betsey sat at the foot of the bed. "Nothing. Not a thing."

"Nothing?"

"No," Patricia added, taking the chair near the bed. "We waited. Mrs. O'Grady appeared to fall into her trance state, but...no one came through. Not our employee Samuel, not your old neighbor...no one."

"Drew asked if Red Feather was present," Betsey said. "We heard not a word from him. No one responded to his inquiry."

"Oh. How disappointing!" Although Violet was not completely surprised—why would she hear Charles' voice if he could get through to the others?—she nevertheless shared their disappointment.

Down the hall, they heard a sharp exclamation. "Henrietta? Let me in." Loud, impatient tones carried, even though Henrietta's room was around the corner and farther down the hall.

A door opened and closed. Betsey made a face.

"Harvey tried asking for Charles, and Red Feather, too," she said. "Nothing worked. Afterward we all agreed we did not sense a presence among us."

"I'm sorry nothing worked tonight," Violet said. If she had been there, she couldn't help wondering, would things have been different?

It was on the tip of her tongue to speak about her experience, but then she decided to share it only with Drew. She wanted to hear what he had to say.

"Well..." Patricia stood up. "We should let you get some sleep." She glanced at Betsey. "We have had a few séances with no results...it's just not the usual for us lately. Don't be disappointed, dear. We will make contact again."

"I hope so," Betsey said, standing too. "Goodnight, Violet."

"Thank you for telling me what happened," Violet said.

They left, and she got ready for sleep. Peeking out the window, she wondered if Drew had returned. She didn't see him, but a few minutes later, she did hear someone moving down the main hall; and then the sound of a door, coming from the corner, opening and shutting.

She imagined he was in his room, making notes, perhaps staying up late to read. She drifted to sleep, thinking of Drew Covington.

****

Violet got dressed without help and was at breakfast only a little later than normal.

"Should you be downstairs? You need rest," Patricia said as she entered the room.

"I am getting quite bored in my room, all alone," Violet said, and stepped over to the sideboard to get coffee. "Not that you haven't all been good about visiting me—but I am feeling better, truly I am, and I want to rejoin everyone." The dull ache now came and went; it was no longer constant.

Drew stood and walked over. "Are you sure you feel all right?" he asked in a low voice.

"Yes," she answered, feeling her cheeks warm at his solicitousness.

Betsey and Harvey were seated at the table. Again, Henrietta was absent.

"You missed a rather tedious séance last night,"

Harvey drawled. "No one appeared."

"So I heard," Violet said, stirring sugar into her coffee, then adding cream.

"Betsey and I went back and told her how nothing occurred," Patricia said.

"I told Henrietta the same. She was curious about what was happening, even though she is scared to be present," Harvey said. He cut a piece of ham.

Violet took some toast and bacon and sat down in between Patricia and Drew.

She breathed in the scent of the coffee. The rich aroma served to wake her further even before she sipped the bracing liquid.

She wanted to ask to speak with him alone and tell him of her experience yesterday, but she didn't even want to request time alone in front of the watchful eyes of Harvey. She had caught him studying her several times of late, and it made her uncomfortable. Henrietta had a habit of doing this too, but she was not yet present.

Just as she thought of the woman, Henrietta walked into the room. "Good morning," she greeted them all. She moved to the sideboard and took up a cup and saucer. "Ahh, the coffee here is always excellent, Drew." She shot him a smile, then poured some.

"Mrs. White does make the best coffee," Patricia agreed.

Henrietta helped herself to breakfast, then sat beside her brother on Drew's other side.

"I hear tell there was no contact made at yesterday's séance," she said, and Violet noticed the almost smug note in her voice. "Why do you think that was, Drew?"

"I'm not sure," he replied slowly. "I have been thinking of little else."

Over her teacup, she sent him a winning smile. "I would like to join you the next time you have a séance."

Drew's mouth tightened into a frown. "I do not believe that is a good idea," he said somewhat formally.

"Why not?" Innocence rang in her voice.

"You have an unfortunate habit of fainting," he said, his words surprisingly harsh.

"I am very much afraid that it disturbs the spirits when it happens while they are in the midst of contacting us."

"I can't help fainting!" she almost shrieked. "'Tis not my fault! I get—so afraid!"

"It could happen again," he went on. "If you are afraid, it is best if you stay away from the séance."

There was a moment of silence.

"You don't want me to—attend?" The sad note in her voice was, Violet was certain, much exaggerated.

"I do not want the proceedings interrupted." Drew's voice was firm.

She blinked at him. "I was not there yesterday, yet you made no contact."

Drew's posture and voice were both stiff. "That may have been an exception. We have had much success lately. I don't want to chance having our sessions disrupted."

Henrietta sniffed audibly and wiped a tearless eye.

"Perhaps," he added, his voice not as stringent, "you can join us in the future, if you feel you can be brave enough to remain quiet, and not faint."

She stood suddenly, and without a word flounced out of the room.

The minute she left, Harvey threw down his napkin. "Now you've done it," he accused. "She will be beside herself today."

"I did not mean to upset her," Drew said coldly. "Only to make sure she does not harm our sittings. We will do better if she is not there to disrupt them."

Harvey said nothing, just stalked out of the room. They heard his footsteps running up the stairs.

"Well," Patricia said, and reached for her tea cup. "Perhaps you were a trifle harsh, Drew."

He stared at his aunt. "Only because I find her irritating, and her fainting has come at the worst times. I cannot risk having her disrupt our séances."

"She is a guest," Patricia pointed out. "Although I know you want to contact Charles desperately, I don't think having her at one or two séances will hurt. She does not come to most."

Drew sighed. "You are right about her being a guest. And as they will be leaving in a week or so, I guess I can let her attend another one or two." He drank some coffee. "All right, Aunt Patricia. I will go speak to her and see if I can make peace." With a sigh he left the room.

"I think she is disruptive," Betsey said after he exited. "And I don't blame him. Plus—did you see her? She was only pretending to cry."

"I know," Patricia said. She turned to Violet. "Harvey and Henrietta have decided to extend their stay here by at least a week, perhaps two."

"I am surprised she wants to attend," Violet said mildly. "She seemed so—frightened—previously."

"She's moody. She goes from one mood to another quickly," Betsey said. "I get along with her, but I find her a difficult person to like."

Patricia nodded. "I know. Even Mary, who is so patient, has found herself annoyed with Henrietta many times."

Betsey nodded vigorously. "This is true."

They finished breakfast, switching to talking about Mary and her lovely home and family. Drew returned and sat down to have more coffee, telling them he had spoken to Harvey and Henrietta, and Henrietta seemed mollified when he'd said she could attend another séance next week.

"But I warned her to try not to faint or disrupt our proceedings," he said, his expression still rather dark.

When they finished up, he announced he was going over to the laboratory.

"May I accompany you?" Violet asked. "I'd like to look for another book." It was an excuse, but she could think of no other. And she needed to speak to him alone.

"Of course."

"Let me just get my shawl," she said. Her head still ached slightly, and it looked cold and damp outside. She didn't want to take a chill.

****

Drew was waiting in the hall when she returned downstairs, and together they strolled to the laboratory. The day was chilly, and she wrapped her shawl around her closely.

"I'll light the fire in here," he told her as they entered the building.

The woodstove in the corner was soon burning merrily and chasing the chill away. They sat together at the largest table.

"I want to tell you what happened last night while you were holding the séance," Violet began.

She was sitting at the table. He perched beside her, and reaching out, grasped her hands. His were warm and calloused but enclosed hers in a way that made her feel safe and secure.

"I got out of bed and went into the solarium to look at the building where you were all sitting." At his tsking sound, she added, "I was restless and needed to walk around. The doctor said I could be up and about, as long as I didn't walk too far, yesterday." She paused, then continued, "I heard what sounded like Charles' voice as I was watching. He said 'I can't get through'."

Drew stared. "Incredible. He—was trying to get through to us and couldn't—yet he must have found a pathway to you, some way to get through to you last night." He stood abruptly and began to pace. "This is amazing. He couldn't get through to us—" He whirled to regard Violet. "You must have an extraordinary ability—something about you that helps spirits come through."

At his excited tone and hopeful look, she found herself shivering. "No, I'm a normal woman, I don't think I have any special ability—"

"Don't you see?" Drew's eyes were shining. He moved back to her and grasped her hands again. "He managed to get through to you, somehow. And without you—our séance was dismal. No one was able to get through!"

Violet sat back, stunned. Was she the conduit, some sort of essential person to help the spirits with getting through?

"You are as important to our séances as Mrs.

O'Grady!" he continued excitedly. "You are a vehicle—a conduit—for spirits making themselves heard."

"But I—but you have had some success without me," she protested.

"Perhaps I am a vehicle too," he said. "But we have had much more success since you joined us, Violet!" He was beaming. "Perhaps you and I together—"

"Oh." She was unsure what to say to that.

He smiled at her, and then suddenly his expression shifted. He tilted his head.

Violet was in danger. He knew it instinctively. If she was the one having the most success, and people found out—well, whoever had killed Charles very likely would not want Charles' spirit coming through. They might take steps—

He gasped.

"What is it?" she questioned.

"My God, I know why you were attacked." He ran his hand though his hair. "Violet, someone does not want you getting through to Charles. Someone must be afraid you will find out the secret to his murder."

For a moment, she stared.

"Oh." It was a whisper.

He clutched her hands hard. They were soft and delicate within his. "They are trying to harm you. I vow I will do everything, everything in my power to protect you."

"Do you have any idea…?" her voice faded.

He shook his head. "No. I just know I have always been suspicious of Charles' friend Louis LeBlanc…he used to try to tempt Charles into troublesome ventures, deals I thought were shady. Charles lost money twice, then refused to do more. But Louis kept trying to get him to invest. A few months before Charles died, they had a falling out. That's all I know. Louis seemed saddened at Charles' funeral, but who knows how much is true and how much fake?"

"Do you really think Charles' friend would kill him?" she asked in a subdued voice.

He stood and resumed pacing around the room. "I don't know. Louis could be very congenial, and I never sensed anything violent about him. But…he did have a dark, moody side. Sometimes he and Charles would start drinking…" He paused, remembering coming upon them at the local pub here in town, both deep in their cups. Louis began raving about some girl who had used him, and how life was horrible, and wanted Charles to agree.

"He sometimes got Charles drinking more than he should," Drew admitted. "But—to murder someone? I believe Louis thought of Charles as a friend…yet his was the first name to come to mind when I was wondering who could possibly want to harm Charles."

"Perhaps that means something," Violet stated. "Perhaps your subconscious is telling you something."

"Still…would Louis be so base as to murder a friend? He had many, but still…" Drew shook his head. He had wondered, idly, once or twice if there was something darker to Louis' nature…but was he capable of…?

He should investigate. "I will send a note to Donaldson, the private investigator I told you of. I will ask him to do some quiet investigating about Louis, to see if there is anything…unusual. Any debts, any suspicious activities."

"That is a good idea," Violet said, as if measuring her thoughts.

"In the meantime, you are to go nowhere alone," he told Violet. "I want to guard you, make sure you are safe at all a times."

"I feel very safe in your house," Violet said.

"In my home, yes, but—you were attacked right outside of it." Worry for Violet spiked through him. "And what if—" No. It was too horrific.

"What if?"

"What if it was someone—from my household?" he whispered. How much, after all, did he know about his servants? Suppose one was bribed? He didn't want to voice the idea, let alone even think that way.

"The thought that Patricia or Betsey could possibly want to harm me is ridiculous," Violet said with spirit.

"No, of course not... Aunt Patricia doesn't have a mean bone in her body, and Betsey loves you already as a dear friend."

"Unless..." her eyes widened suddenly.

"What?" It came out sharper than he'd intended.

"Harvey," she whispered. "Sometimes I feel—uncomfortable—around Harvey."

He stared at her.

Harvey? His second—no third—cousin?

But even as he looked at Violet's pretty face, memories began to rush at him.

Harvey asking him for money. Harvey asking Charles for money.

"What if...he asked Charles again for money..." Drew wondered aloud.

"And Charles turned him down?" she asked.

He looked at her. She wore a frown of concern, and her brow furrowed.

Suddenly he did not want to see the anxiety on her face.

"I do not want you to worry," he began.

"I am not worried. I want to help you solve this crime," she said, with surprising vehemence. "Your dear brother was killed; we must get to the bottom of this."

"I do not want you taking any risks," he said. "Violet, I will pen a note immediately to Donaldson, and let you know what I find out. I will ask him to investigate Louis, and any other friends who may have known Charles…and also ask him to check on Harvey, nose around, see what he's been doing since he returned to America. Or at any time he's been here in the last few years. He has an associate who will help him, and I will pay, so we should get some useful information." He paused and studied her beautiful face. "And you must promise to be careful." He went back to lean against the table and captured her face in his hands. "Violet…I do not want anything bad to happen to you."

At the thought of any kind of peril involving her, his heart squeezed. If anything happened to Violet…he could not stand it. It would tear him apart.

He bent forward and touched his lips to hers, lightly.

"I will make sure you are safe," he vowed.

They spent the next hour discussing plans for future séances and talking about yesterday's—when absolutely nothing had occurred. No feeling of weight, no hushed voice, nothing. Drew recalled his frustration and paced the room.

"Perhaps we will be more fortunate next time," Violet soothed. Her optimistic words reminded him of his aunt.

"Perhaps. All right, I better write the note to Donaldson," he said.

She promised to get some rest since this was her first day up and about since she had been struck. He walked her back to the house and upstairs to her room, then went to his study to write his letters.

Patricia stopped in his study to tell him that Henrietta and Harvey had decided to go back to New York on Monday, and he was a little relieved. He found Henrietta trying, and Harvey could be almost as annoying. They were scheduled to return for a visit in two weeks, and to perhaps join them in more séances at that time.

It would give Donaldson and his assistant ample opportunity to shadow Harvey and learn about his usual activities while he was in the city, however. So Drew was doubly pleased.

Being that it was Saturday, they had planned to have a festive dinner, then have a few neighbors over. After writing the letters and sending a footman to post them, Drew did the unusual: like Violet, he decided to rest. Stretching out on his bed, he closed his eyes and pictured her...

****

The gathering on Saturday evening at Covington house was fun. More intimate than Mary's ball, Violet found it a welcome change.

Violet was refreshed after her nap. She read a long, chatty letter from her sister telling her about neighborhood gossip, how she and her husband were faring, how the business was doing and that she had not heard from their brother since just before Violet left. But then, Joseph had never been much of a letter-writer.

Dinner was a delicious and pleasant meal. Afterward they gathered in the main drawing room and enjoyed the evening thoroughly. Betsey sang while RoseAnn, a young neighbor, played the pianoforte. Another neighbor, Gregory, a man of about Violet's age, performed some juggling tricks to many ohs and ahs. Patricia told a ghost story handed down by her grandmother about a ghost in a castle in Great Britain.

Even Henrietta rose to the occasion and told several amusing anecdotes about parties among the high society of New York City. Although, truth be told, Violet wondered if she might be exaggerating.

Harvey, too, participated, speaking about some of his adventures with friends in London. Time passed swiftly, and Violet found herself entertained.

Despite her nap, Violet found herself getting tired more easily than usual and remembered the doctor had warned her this might happen. So by ten o'clock, she said goodnight.

Drew insisted on walking her upstairs and gave her a chaste kiss before she slipped into her room.

She got ready for bed, and once under the covers, sighed. Drew had been so gallant, so caring...she dreamed of dancing with him again.

Sunday passed quietly, and Monday Harvey and Henrietta departed, loudly and later than originally planned. It was almost noon when they left, Henrietta dramatically in tears, Harvey more staid.

"We'll be back in a few weeks!" Henrietta gushed for the third time.

"We will be pleased to see you then," Patricia said somewhat formally.

It was quiet and peaceful after they left. Violet ate lunch with Patricia and Betsey, who was staying for another month, much to her delight. Drew had come back to see his cousins off and ate lunch, but then needed to return to the factory where they were having a problem with one of the machines. Patricia sat down to read, Betsey went to write a letter, and Violet excused herself to go read quietly in her room. When she grew sleepy, she napped.

She awoke in time for tea and hurried down to enjoy it in quiet with just Patricia and Betsey. They were fast becoming her favorite people, and she didn't want them to know she was secretly delighted Harvey and Henrietta had left.

But Betsey brought it up. "I must admit I am guilty of being quite happy that we can enjoy time without Harvey and Henrietta. I find them quite annoying, lately. They didn't used to be so—so negative and complaining, but they have become this way now."

"And it rather gets on my nerves."

Patricia balanced her teacup. "They were always rather selfish individuals, but I find them more so now than ever." She sighed. "A pity, really. I am glad we can enjoy ourselves without them. And their next visit will be brief, only a week or so."

"I must admit I find it more peaceful without them," Violet admitted. She didn't want to appear too negative but felt compelled to tell the truth. "But I am glad you are staying on," she told Betsey with a smile.

"Me too. And when I leave, I hope you will come visit me in New York, Violet."

"I would very much enjoy that," Violet said, "although I do not know when I will get a break from work."

"I will prevail on Drew to let you have a short vacation," Betsey said with a laugh.

Violet smiled in answer, reaching for a lemon cookie.

Drew did not return until late, looking rather weary. Dinner was a quiet affair, and then he disappeared to do some research. Violet, Betsey, and Patricia chatted in the green parlor for a while. Their next séance was scheduled for later in the week, and Violet was determined to go.

By nine o'clock Patricia announced she was going upstairs to bed, since she was tired. Betsey and Violet walked upstairs together by half past.

Before she got ready for bed, Violet walked to the solarium and stared at Drew's laboratory for a few minutes. She saw his shadow moving about among the bright lights, then nothing for a while. He must be researching again. She wondered if she would hear Charles' voice, but all around her the air was silent.

With a sigh she returned to her room and got into bed. She was feeling better, although more tired than usual. She just hoped she would soon be her normal self.

The week passed quietly, and Violet found herself happy for the peace after Drew's cousins left. Without their negativity, she could relax and recuperate fully.

The séance on Wednesday was only partially successful. Her neighbor Eddie came through, informing them that no one else was available or able to come through that night. Violet shared Drew's disappointment, but he was optimistic that they'd have more success next time, since Eddie assured them several spirits wanted to visit. Mrs. O'Grady was present, but she never went into a sleep, so they wondered later if that accounted for their mediocre results.

Still, someone had gotten through, even if it was only briefly. Drew remarked that although this séance hadn't achieved the results of some of their others, "It is still better than many of the ones we've had in the past."

Violet continued to read and research and began the job of cataloging Drew's books in his home study—the smallest of the collections. It took her until Saturday to finish, and then she asked his help in placing them in a logical order. "They will be easier to find now," she assured him.

She still had the library books and all those in his laboratory to catalog, but she was pleased that she had gotten this chunk of work completed.

By Saturday late in the morning, she was pleasantly tired but felt satisfied with the job she'd done. After lunch Drew invited her and Betsey to visit the factory.

They took two horses and the cart to the factory, with Betsey and Violet sitting behind Drew.

The factory was a large building, about two blocks from the main street, close to the first of the Twin Bridges. Violet observed many small houses around it, making it a quick walk for a good number of Drew's employees.

"Mrs. O'Grady lives there," Drew said, pointing out a cute, neat home that was slightly bigger than some others. Flowers decorated the front yard and porch. They drew up to the factory, and she could see it was an easy walk for Drew to come here. He helped them both out, and a young man ran up to lead the horses to a nearby stable.

Inside, she was impressed by the size of the building. The front was two stories high, and many men labored over shoes and boots at various work benches. A little dust filled the air and Violet smelled leather and polish.

Nearby two men were hammering on her right, and straight ahead a man was applying a heel. On the left a machine spun, doing something to a boot.

Drew led them around, introducing them to a few of the men. Each one seemed busy with his own tasks. Drew pointed out a pedestal he'd invented to help hold the boots so the worker could affix a heel; and another, a machine to glue the soles.

He then took them upstairs. A man and, surprisingly, a woman were working at two large tables, drawing designs for men's and women's boots and shoes.

"You have a woman designer," Betsey said in a hushed voice. "I am indeed impressed, cousin."

"I thought a woman might understand what another woman wants in her shoes and boots," Drew said. "So I hired Miss Abernathy here."

"Very good," Violet said approvingly.

The second floor balcony where they worked overlooked half of the first floor. At the rear of the second floor were several offices, including Drew's.

"The largest was my father's, and the one in the middle was the one Charles used," he said, showing them each in turn. The offices were spacious, with papers and shoe samples atop desks and credenzas. A few books lay about too.

"Mr. McDermott is my assistant, and now uses Charles' old office," he said. "He is downstairs right now; I'll introduce you later." He pointed out a small corner office. "That is where our bookkeeper, Elliott Dixon, prefers to work. He likes it because it's tucked away and quiet."

Drew's office was not as tidy as the others, which was no surprise to Violet, since she was familiar with the way he kept his laboratory and home offices. He liked to heap his work in front of him, as if he'd lose track of his projects otherwise. Here, too, he had several shoes and boots atop the credenza, and papers and envelopes lay haphazardly on his desk.

"I see your office here looks much like your office at home," Betsey teased.

Drew grinned at his cousin. "Yes, not particularly tidy. But I *do* know precisely where everything is."

"I have no doubt." She grinned up at him.

Listening to their words and camaraderie, Violet wondered if Drew would ever regard her with that same fond smile.

She wished desperately he would.

At that moment he looked up and met her eyes. Slowly, he smiled.

She felt a rush of warmth. He did look—caring.

****

It was on Tuesday afternoon that Drew received a post from the investigator. He announced over dinner that the following afternoon Mr. Donaldson would be by to give a complete report and invited Violet, Betsey, and Patricia to hear what the man had to say.

Mr. Donaldson came on the early afternoon train, and Drew brought him up from town. They gathered for tea in the blue parlor, and he told them what he had learned.

"First of all…Harvey," he began. "My associates in England wired that he has large gambling debts and is reported to have gone through the family money rapidly since his father died. He is trying one scheme after another to raise money. He has been spending a great deal of time with Lawrence Danforth, another Englishman who is visiting the states right now, who is also reputed to be on the verge of financial disaster."

"Not a good companion to have," Drew remarked.

"Indeed," Donaldson continued. He was a man in his late thirties, nice-looking and big boned, and seemed experienced in these types of investigations.

"They have spent a few evenings in the company of Louis LeBlanc, the other gentleman you asked me to investigate," he reported. "One of my employees overhead them in a pub, plotting to try to meet wealthy American heiresses. However, they were lamenting their luck. My employee did some nosing around, and it seems most of the wealthy heiresses they've tried to court know they are in financial trouble and don't want anything to do with any of them. Except for Miss Virginia Howell. Apparently, she has some money— although is not that wealthy—and is eager to snare a husband who has a British title, although her parents do not agree this is a good idea. Lawrence Danforth has been paying close attention to her as of late."

"Does a title mean so much to her?" Violet wondered.

"To some, yes, even to some Americans," Betsey said. "Although it is mostly the British women who are mad to acquire a husband with one."

"I myself heard them on another occasion, also in a pub just last night. They were talking about borrowing money from Louis' uncle to invest in a shipping business someone had heard about. They were hoping to make money hand over fist in a quick time period," Donaldson continued. "However, Louis said his uncle was reluctant to lend anyone money, and they were trying to figure how to persuade him. Harvey was boasting that perhaps with his familial connections he could persuade Louis' uncle."

"Hmph," Drew practically snorted.

"How are they managing to pay for their New York vacation?" Patricia asked.

Donaldson shrugged. "I believe they are living on credit. And of course, they have spent time visiting relatives such as yourself, living off others' generosity while visiting. They are set to visit some friend of Henrietta's this weekend in the Albany area."

Patricia made a tsking sound.

"And they spent a week at my home when they first arrived," Betsey said.

"Speaking of Henrietta…" Donaldson went on. "Apparently Harvey borrowed some money from her dowry at some point, and there isn't much left."

Patricia gasped. "How awful! In England especially, a woman needs a dowry to make a good match—unless her family is so noble or so esteemed or the one she is marrying into is so rich it doesn't matter."

"Well, the Covingtons may be esteemed," Betsey said, "but from what I have pieced together they are no more noble than dozens of others. Henrietta is fair looking but not a beauty; she doesn't have a lot of money or royal connections. Harvey's raiding the coffers is going to have an adverse effect on her."

"I almost feel sorry for her," Patricia said. "Except that, she told me she is making every effort to find a rich American husband—one who will be willing to return to England with her, since she prefers to live there. I do feel sorry for anyone who falls into that trap!"

"My conclusion is," Donaldson said, "that Harvey, Lawrence, Louis, and even Henrietta are in poor shape financially. Perhaps one of them was angry at your brother if he wouldn't lend them money—"

"That could be so," Drew acknowledged.

"You may be in danger, Drew!" Betsey said.

Violet's heart squeezed. Drew, in danger? The thought was horrifying.

But he was shaking his head. "That is doubtful. Besides, hurting me would not get them money. And Henrietta—why, the thought of her threatening me or anyone else is fairly ludicrous. She doesn't have the strength to yield a weapon, I'm sure, and most women do not like violence. I doubt she is the exception."

"Nevertheless, you should be on guard at all times," Donaldson cautioned.

"I will be. Now, as I mentioned on the way here, please stay and have dinner with us, and stay the night. I can get you on the train early in the morning to return to New York," Drew invited. "And I would like you to continue to investigate these people. There may be more to learn."

Donaldson agreed and sent a wire informing his

colleagues he would return the following day to the city. Then he and Drew went into Drew's study to put their heads together and work on some plans for Donaldson's investigations.

Dinner was a cheerful affair, as Donaldson told some stories of the city when he was a boy. He knew some people who Betsey did, as well, and everyone was happy he had visited.

Violet, though, wondered if Drew could be in danger and ignoring the possibility. She spoke to Betsey about it the next day.

"I am worried," she began as they walked back from town. They had bought some thread and a few things Patricia needed. "Charles was killed...what if Drew is in danger too?"

Betsey let a moment of silence pass. Then she said, "I worry too...perhaps someone wanted to get revenge on Charles...and now Drew, since he won't loan money to anyone."

Violet felt something clutch at her heart. "I hope Drew will be extra careful," she said.

"I keep telling him to—and so does Aunt Patricia." Betsey sighed. "But, you know, I have two older brothers...men do not listen."

"I have a brother too, and I know," Violet agreed.

Once they were back at the house, they separated to do their own reading. Later Violet went looking for Drew, to ask him for another book recommendation since she had finished the one she was reading. She had started working on the books in his laboratory library, but there were so many she was pacing herself and doing only a few shelves a day.

Patricia told her there had been a problem with a

machine, and he was staying late at the factory to work on it with several other employees.

"He may not even be home at dinner time," she said. "There was smoke involved."

"Oh dear. I hope no one was injured."

"I don't think so. I am going to send some food down to the factory for him and those staying late," Patricia said.

Without Drew, dinner consisted of more gossipy chatter, and although Violet missed him, she did enjoy talking about fashions and the latest gossip about the wealthy and privileged in the great city of New York.

It was much later, around nine o'clock, when hurried footsteps and a loud banging on the door interrupted them while they were all reading various books on séances together and sharing their thoughts.

"Mrs. Covington!" someone was yelling as he banged on the door.

The noise was loud enough to reach them in the parlor. Patricia sprang up, followed by Violet and Betsey.

"What is wrong?" Patricia gasped.

The three of them ran to the door, which Mr. Durham was opening.

A young man whom Violet recognized as a worker at the factory stumbled in.

"Mrs. Covington—ma'am—" he gasped.

"What is it?" She clutched at her throat.

"Young Sheldon Avery. He's been hurt."

Violet recognized the name of one of the young men working at the factory.

"Hurt—how?" Patricia was asking.

"Dunno. Mr. Covington sent for the doctor. They

found Sheldon outside, lying on the ground."

"Does he want us to come down to the factory?" Violet asked.

The young man shook his head. "No, he just wanted you to know what is happening."

"Thank you. Take a glass of water, Benjamin, before you go back," Patricia ordered.

The butler bustled away and returned shortly with a pitcher of water and a cup. The young man drank, then said he had to return, and left hurriedly.

"How strange," Betsey said as they resumed their seats. "That he was lying outside."

It was over an hour before Drew returned, looking weary, his brow furrowed.

"What happened?" Patricia asked as they all followed him into the library.

He reached for the decanter and poured himself a brandy. He drank it in one gulp, put the glass down, and poured another.

Violet had never seen him do this before and knew he was agitated.

"Sheldon must have been on his way home. He either slipped and fell against a log, or someone hit him from the side." Drew looked at them each in turn. "Marvin Middleton found him about an hour or so after he'd left."

"Is he all right?" Violet asked.

"He has a concussion, as you did. But I think his injury is worse based on what the doctor said."

"How awful," Betsey murmured. "Has he regained consciousness? What did he say?"

"He did, briefly, but he wasn't very coherent. Something about a shadow."

"Maybe he saw a shadow as I did!" Violet gasped.

"It is possible." He drank more slowly this time.

"Why would someone attack young Sheldon?" Patricia asked.

"That is a mystery," Drew declared.

A thought occurred to Violet, and she gasped.

"How is young Sheldon now?" Patricia asked, moving to put a hand on Drew's shoulder.

Drew grimaced. "As well as can be expected. The doctor feels his injury is worse than Violet's was, so he wants him to get plenty of rest and care. His father, Sheldon Senior, and his mother and his uncle, Daniel Avery, were all around him when I left. I promised I'd come back first thing tomorrow morning to check on him."

"Then perhaps you should turn in now and get some rest," Patricia urged.

Drew had turned his head to stare at Violet. "Violet, are you all right? You're white as a sheet."

Violet swallowed. A terrible thought had occurred to her, and she was hesitant to voice it—yet she couldn't keep still either.

"Sheldon Avery Junior is your height and has dark blond hair like you," she said. "Suppose in the dusk or darkness someone mistook him for you? Maybe you were the one they wanted to strike down—not him."

Drew gaped at her.

But even as she said the words, Betsey was nodding. Patricia looked horrified.

"No—" Drew said. "Why would anyone want to injure me?"

"Why would anyone want to hurt Sheldon Junior?" Betsey asked. "But the same person who struck Violet may have tried to injure you, Drew. Perhaps it's even the same person who killed Charles!"

Patricia sank to the sofa. "Oh, my Lord."

But Drew was shaking his head. "I cannot believe that—"

"Think about it. Violet makes a good point," Betsey declared. "What reason would anyone have to hurt young Sheldon? On the other hand, people know you and Violet are conducting séances, trying to contact Charles. Perhaps someone is determined that you won't succeed!"

Drew sat down rather abruptly beside Patricia. Now he had turned pale.

"Do you really think—"

"Yes," Betsey said.

"Yes," Violet echoed.

"I think it's very possible," Patricia concurred.

Drew looked visibly shaken. "If this is true, then we *all* could be in danger. All of us are participating in the séances." He sat back. "I shall have to hire several more footmen as guards for all of us, for our properties. And for my factory employees. I will tell everyone not to go about alone, to come to work and leave in pairs or groups. I do not want anyone else getting hurt because of me." He stood up abruptly. "I have a gun. Perhaps I should carry it with me at all times."

"You must protect yourself," Patricia urged, although Violet found herself worried. Would a gun really protect Drew if someone was stalking him with a club?

She voiced that thought.

"A gun is better than no protection," Drew stated.

She had to agree, although she was very worried.

The feeling gnawed at her stomach.

The others were worried too—she could see it in their faces.

"Well." Drew stood. "There is no sense in worrying. We will all take precautions, including me. I am going to get some rest now and suggest you all do the same."

They all nodded.

They trudged up the stairs together, Patricia and then Betsey separating to enter their rooms. Drew and Violet continued on down the corridor.

She paused to turn into the hallway toward her room.

"Please be careful," she whispered to Drew.

He stepped closer. "I will. You too, Violet."

She went to her room and readied herself for bed. But once she lay down, she found herself worrying about Drew's well-being, and it was quite a while before sleep claimed her.

****

The following morning Violet hurried downstairs for breakfast hoping to see Drew before he left. Patricia was already seated in the morning room and informed her Drew had left extra early with one of the footmen, to go visit Sheldon Junior.

"He said he would send word on his condition with Amos," she told Violet.

Violet poured coffee into her cup and placed it on the round table, then turned back to get a plate and food. Betsey entered the room and asked if there was any news. Patricia repeated what she had told Violet.

After breakfast, Violet wanted to work on further cataloging of the books in the laboratory. Mindful of her promise to Drew not to go anywhere alone, she asked Betsey if she'd be willing to help. Betsey accepted at once, making Violet wonder if Betsey, although enjoying her vacation here, may have been a bit bored or feeling restless.

Betsey plunged into helping, and with the two of them working, they got a considerable number of books catalogued that morning. In addition, they began straightening some of the shelves and putting the books in order by topic.

"This is wonderful," Betsey said, surveying their work. "I'd say almost half the books in this building are done."

"Thank you for your help," Violet said.

"It's nothing. I keep asking Patricia to give me something to do—I want to be useful while I'm here—but she doesn't usually have suggestions. This was fun, actually. And now I know a few more books I'd like to read about séances and spirits."

"Some of the books on astronomy and geology look interesting too," Violet said. They dusted themselves off, then went to wash up and have lunch.

Patricia relayed the news on young Sheldon. He was in pain, but the doctor felt he was doing better than expected.

"His family is quite distraught, especially his mother," she told them "I've met her many times…a nervous woman, always worrying." She shrugged. "Not that I can blame her for worrying about this incident—but she worries about everything."

She told them she wanted to visit the family and bring some soup and other items. Violet and Betsey volunteered to go with her. Drew had sent word he was staying at the factory this afternoon, so they set out in the carriage to visit the Avery family.

Mrs. Jean Avery met them at the door. She appeared flustered and invited them in, although unenthusiastically. Inside they met Sheldon Junior's uncle Daniel, his father Sheldon Senior, and his two sisters, Denise and Colleen.

Sheldon was propped up in bed, looking pale and weary. He thanked them for coming at once.

"We've brought you some soup," Patricia said, handing the basket to Jean Avery, "and an apple pie."

Jean sent her a look Violet couldn't decipher. Almost—suspicious.

"And some salves," Patricia added, taking off the scarf she had would around her head.

"Thank you." Jean's voice was stiff. "I'm sure that is not necessary."

Patricia sent her a glance, then focused on Sheldon. "I hear tell you've been stepping out with Farmer Parnell's daughter Elizabeth," she said in a teasing voice.

Sheldon flushed visibly.

"How nice," Betsey added.

"Yes, and she brought by an apple pie this morning," Colleen said, smiling at her brother. "Early, too. She must have baked it first thing, soon as she heard Sheldon was poorly."

"I'm not poorly," he protested.

"It's nice to have such a considerate girl baking for you," Patricia said. "Now, Mrs. White says this salve is good for headaches." She lifted it from the basket and placed in on a nearby table.

Behind her, Violet heard Mrs. Avery mutter

something about the devil's work.

She turned to stare at the woman. Her face was pinched with disapproval.

Violet swallowed. What was she saying? It didn't sound good.

They stayed only a few minutes, asking after Sheldon's head and his foot, which had some swelling. As they were leaving, Violet heard Mrs. Avery again.

"Heathen practices," she muttered. "It's no wonder there's trouble hereabouts."

This time Patricia turned to stare at the woman. So did Betsey, and Violet.

"Heather practices?" Patricia said, her voice taking on a chilly note.

Mrs. Avery raised her chin. "Yes'm. That's what I said. It's no wonder bad things are happening hereabouts. First this young lady"—she waved in Violet's direction—"now my poor Sheldon. I never heard of such terrible practices. Bringing back the dead, indeed. That's the devil's work!" Her eyes narrowed as she practically hissed out her statement.

Patricia flushed now.

"We are not practicing devil worship!" Betsey declared indignantly.

"Of course not," Violet said, championing the other two women.

"Only an ignorant person would think so," Patricia said rather cuttingly. "We seek to contact those who have passed on to gain knowledge."

"It's the devil's work!" The woman spat. "And now my poor son is being punished because he works for your nephew, him that is making this kind of trouble."

"Mother!" Sheldon shouted from the other room. He'd obviously heard his mother talk this way before—and didn't like it.

"I've told my boy and my husband they shouldn't be working there, for the likes of Mr. Covington," she continued.

"Now hold on there, Jean," Mr. Avery began. "He is one of the nicest people to work for—"

"He's practicing the devil's work!" she exclaimed, warmed up to her subject now. "I don't want that touching my family! Even our priest said last night it's unholy—"

"Perhaps your family should discuss it with my nephew," Patricia said. "I am very sorry your son was hurt, but our séances had nothing to do with the attack on your son."

"Jean—" Mr. Avery placed his hand on his wife and tugged her away.

She went with him, muttering.

"I'm sorry." Colleen had followed them from young Sheldon's room. She gave a hasty curtsy. "Please don't mind my ma." The girl looked anxious.

"It's all right." Patricia gave the girl a brief smile. "Your mother is—overwrought."

"Yes," the girl agreed.

They said goodbyes and left. The two footmen who had accompanied them were waiting by the carriage and helped them in. They started for the house.

Patricia sighed. "You just can't educate some people who are superstitious."

"That is true," Violet agreed.

As the horses clip-clopped, they heard someone shouting.

"Mzz Covington! Mzz Covington!"

They all turned to see Sheldon Avery Senior racing after the carriage.

"Stop!" Patricia shouted to the footman at the reins. He obliged. Mr. Avery caught up to them.

"Please," he panted. "Don't pay no mind to me wife. She's upset, is all, on account of the boy being hurt. She don't mean those things about Mr. Covington. He's good to us, he is, and we knows it. Why, he told me and Daniel to take the whole day off and attend to young Sheldon, and he's paying the doctor to treat him. We knows he's good to us."

"Thank you for telling me that," Patricia said gravely. "Drew cares very much about what happens to all the people who work for him."

"I know." Mr. Avery looked entreating. "Don't pay no mind to what my wife's sayin'."

"We will forget it," Patricia asserted.

Violet and Betsey murmured their agreement, and they took off again.

They stopped at the factory to check on Drew and the rest of the workers.

The factory was busy. Without the three Avery men, they were short-handed, and they'd just gotten a large order the day before, the foreman, Harold, told them. He was planning to hire another worker if he could find someone who seemed responsible. "I just sent word over to New Holland and Green Hills," he finished, naming neighboring towns. "There's no one else in town here looking for work, but perhaps over there, there may be some. And the Jackson family has rooms in their boarding house to put up a couple of men."

Drew greeted them and led them up to his office, where Patricia reported on the condition of young Sheldon. She mentioned Mrs. Avery's superstitions but didn't dwell on them.

Drew looked perturbed. "Ignorant people often think this way. I hope she does not turn others against us, or Mrs. O'Grady."

"I believe her husband will keep her in line," Patricia said.

"Well, I have made a decision," Drew said abruptly. "I need to do some investigating of my own regarding Charles' old cronies, and Harvey. I am going to New York City for several days."

"Oh! And I was just thinking that I need to go home for a few days, get more of my cold weather clothes, and check on my mother," Betsey said. "Please let me go with you! And Violet can come and spend a few days and visit New York. I believe we'd enjoy it immensely!"

Drew hesitated. "I don't know—"

"I would very much like that!" Violet declared, and she and Betsey turned to Drew. Betsey looked at him beseechingly.

"Please cousin? We would have such fun!"

"You can protect them more easily if they are in the city with you," Patricia pointed out, "then if you leave us alone here."

"I have plenty of footmen to look after you all," Drew said. "Still, I probably owe Violet some time off, and Betsey, I do understand you wanting to see your mother."

"Yes, and since you invited me to stay for another month, at least I can spend a couple of days with her,"

Betsey said. "And we would not get in your way, you could do whatever you have to. Plus, we have plenty of servants to look after us and keep us safe," she finished.

"I think it is a splendid idea," Patricia said. "I should like to see Matilda, and a few other friends in the city. If we stayed for five days, it should not be much trouble to Betsey's family, and we won't be gone from here for too long. Perhaps we can even try a séance while there!" she added.

Drew smiled. "All right, you have convinced me."

Betsey leaped up and ran to give Drew a kiss on the cheek and an enthusiastic hug. "Thank you, Drew!" She turned to Violet. "We shall have a splendid time!"

Violet felt her excitement growing. New York! She had always wanted to see the city again. She had been there once, as a young girl of four or five, and all she could remember were tall buildings, heat, and noise from many people and horses in close proximity on the streets.

Drew said he would send a wire to Betsey's family, and they agreed to leave on the next Wednesday. He would procure the train tickets. The women left, chattering about their trip.

Once back at the house, Patricia called several servants to the parlor and gave instructions for their trip. Since it was Thursday, they had plenty of time to pack, but she wanted to let the staff know when they were leaving.

Betsey went to pen a letter to her family, and Violet decided to write her sister.

"And make a list of some things you want to do in the city!" Betsey suggested as they went upstairs together.

As she walked to her room, Violet daydreamed of doing some activities with Drew. Perhaps an elegant meal out, or walking down an avenue together if the weather was fine.

She was looking forward to this trip a lot.

****

Violet and Betsey were in high spirits when they left Twin Bridges on Wednesday. The week had been quiet, and Drew has been so busy at work, both catching up and preparing to be away, that he'd declared there would be no séances until they returned, unless they decided to try one in New York. Violet had noted his disappointment as he said that.

It was late afternoon when they pulled into the train station in New York. The number of travelers, noise from the trains and the street, people jostling her left and right was a bit overwhelming at first. But Violet quickly became accustomed to it. By the time Betsey's family coach had met them until they disembarked, the noise had become more of a background roar and Violet felt more at ease.

Drew was planning to spend the day tomorrow with Donaldson and some of his investigators, and was going to "nose around" a few of the pubs Charles used to frequent. Betsey had declared that this left Thursday for them to shop at several dressmakers, and a book store which Drew highly recommended.

Violet had enough money from her generous salary saved to buy a few books and perhaps one dress, so she was looking forward to the excursion. Friday night, Betsey's extended family would be gathering for dinner, and she looked forward to meeting them.

Betsey's mother was a soft-spoken woman who

welcomed them warmly. Their home, in a fashionable part of the city, was almost as large as Drew's and decorated sumptuously. Betsey's maid helped Violet unpack after she helped Betsey.

Dinner in the city was later than in the country, and although Betsey said it wouldn't be a fancy meal, there was nevertheless plenty of food. They spoke about their séances and Mary and her family.

"Your brothers and their wives will be here on Friday," Mrs. Collins said to Betsey. "And I was thinking of inviting Harvey and Henrietta too. I have not seen them since they returned to New York from Twin Bridges. And Louis Le Blanc will be here."

"When should we try a séance?" Drew asked.

"Saturday, we have all been invited to a party," Matilda said. "Will Sunday be all right?"

"That is fine. I think I would prefer to keep it to just the five of us," he said, glancing around the table. "Or perhaps your sons could join us too."

"Certainly. You can ask them on Friday," she said.

Traveling was tiring, so they all went to bed early. The noise from the busy streets crept through the window, and at first Violet found it harder to relax than usual. Eventually, she did fall asleep and woke refreshed at her usual time.

They hurried through breakfast, eager to get to shopping. Betsey's mother and Aunt Patricia accompanied the girls along with two footmen. They visited two dress shops and a milliner.

Violet was shocked to see how much more the prices of dresses were in New York. Although she found a soft sea green dress she loved, the price was above what she could spend.

Patricia, however, insisted she pay for part of it as a gift. "You are my friend," she said, "and not just an employee of Drew's...you are almost family, Violet."

Betsey agreed when Violet protested. "Please, Violet, let Patricia and I make up the difference in what you can spend," she urged.

In the end, they wore Violet down, and she agreed to let them, although she felt guilty.

Betsey found a bright blue dress she liked, too, and at the second store, Patricia selected a yellow and red-flowered dress for herself. Once at the milliners, they looked over dozens of hats, but only Betsey purchased one.

They sent their packages home with one of the footmen while they had lunch at a fashionable restaurant. Violet was surprised to find that for restaurant fare, the food was delicious, and they had fun talking about fashions while they ate.

Betsey's mother, who tired easily, had the coachmen take her and Patricia home after they dropped Betsey and Violet at the first bookstore.

She had looked forward to the book store excursion as much as she had to the dress shopping, and she was not disappointed. She and Betsey wandered about the store, studying various books on the occult, other topics, and some of the new novels on display.

Violet found an intriguing book about séances in upper New York State, while Betsey selected one about séances in England. Then they looked over popular novels, each choosing a romantic book to read.

Feeling even more excited about this purchase than the dresses, Violet and Betsey returned to Betsey's home. Both Patricia and Matilda were still resting when they arrived. Betsey and Violet sat in a gold and cream colored parlor and read.

Dinner was fun, but Drew did not appear.

"Perhaps he is getting some good information," Patricia said.

They sat together in the evening, talking, hoping Drew would return soon. By ten o'clock Matilda announced she was worn out, and Patricia also followed her upstairs to bed.

Betsey and Violet tried to stay up late. But by eleven, they were both yawning.

"I guess we'll have to hear about Drew's adventures tomorrow," Violet said.

"Yes...I did so hope we would hear something interesting this evening," Betsey said with a sigh. "Oh well, I guess we'll hear all about it in the morning."

They went upstairs. Violet was staying in a lilac colored guestroom which was a good size but had a cozy feel. Before she got into bed, she studied the beautiful gown the others had helped her buy and decided to embroider a handkerchief for each of them as a way to thank them.

She lay in bed, wondering what Drew was doing this very moment. Was he creeping around corners in a dark and deserted alley, listening to men of questionable reputations? Was he drinking at a pub and getting information from someone who had known Charles? Or perhaps he was sharing a drink with a woman of loose morals who was giving him information about Harvey or some other characters...

****

Drew sat in the booth of the rather seedy bar with Phillip Donaldson opposite.

They were both in disguise. Donaldson had managed something to make his hair gray, and Drew wore a dark wig and rather shabby clothes. He had a battered hat pulled low over his forehead.

They each held beers and were talking about gambling, in case anyone overheard them.

Mostly they were listening. In the next booth sat Harvey and Louis.

They hadn't seemed to pay any heed to Drew and Donaldson when they took the booth behind them and ordered their drinks.

Harvey and his friend were speaking French. Drew's French was passable but not great, so he missed some of the conversation. Donaldson spoke very little French but did understand some; he hoped that between the two of them they would glean some valuable information.

Apparently, Louis was pursuing Henrietta romantically.

"You have not a penny to your name," Harvey told him in French. "Why would I want you to marry my sister? And you are my friend…why would you want to marry a woman who spends money so carelessly and feels she should have the latest fashions?"

"Your sister is a beauty," Louis replied. "And I find her intriguing."

Harvey snorted. "Intriguing? Or do you just want her because she does not want you?"

"That is not true! She has said she cares about me. She talks of one day marrying me."

"You know she has almost no dowry."

Louis sighed dramatically. "More's the pity."

There was a moment of silence, then Harvey's

voice dropped. "Now if this scheme with Burlingame works out, things could change."

Louis responded in a low voice, and Drew could not hear what he said.

"So what horse are you favoring in the next race?" Donaldson asked loudly.

"I'm not sure...mayhap Leon's Lightning," Drew said, recalling the name of a horse he'd heard talk of.

They fell silent again, straining to listen to whispers form the next booth. Louis was saying something about getting people to invest in a shipping business. "But on top of getting many investors to put up cash, they'll actually be shipping some stolen jewels," he said to Harvey.

"I'm not sure about this," Harvey said. "Stolen jewels...I don't know if I should get involved."

"Come now, man, it's perfectly safe. They're shipping them to England. No one will ever find out."

"It may be easier for me to try to court Cassandra Wagner. She certainly has enough money and is plain enough that she is flattered when I call on her."

"Yes, but her father is an ogre, even if you were to marry the chit, he'd probably control every penny," Louis said. "Now, if we go along with Burlingame's idea regarding this shopping business, and we can persuade others to invest..." his voice dropped again.

Drew had heard enough. Harvey and Louis were cooking up a scheme to part people from their money, and possibly for Harvey to marry an heiress.

Had Charles been aware of this, or another such scheme? Had he refused to take part in it, perhaps even threatened to warn others and was killed because of his intentions?

As Drew mulled over these possibilities, the door at the front of the pub opened, letting in chilly air that felt refreshing against the stale, smoky air of the pub.

A man walked past his booth and greeted Louis and Harvey in English. He slid in on Louis' side.

"The job is done," he said in a hoarse voice. "Parkin won't bother no one no more."

"Dead? Shhh…" warned Harvey.

Louis switched to French. "That is good. He was getting too greedy."

Their voices dropped, and it sounded like the newcomer said "threw him in the river" but Drew couldn't be sure, between the low voices and the French language. Harvey seemed disturbed to learn of Parkin's death. Louis seemed unsurprised.

The three men ordered another round of beers and started talking about good French brandy.

Drew had heard enough.

Donaldson raised his eyebrows.

Drew finished off his beer and tilted his head. "I better get back home," he said. Louder, he declared, in an Irish accent, "the missus gives me hell when I'm out too late."

"Sure enough," Donaldson responded, "I better be on me way too."

They left. Walking back to a more popular area, he gave Donaldson the info he'd gleaned from the men.

"I'll ask around about any bodies being found in the river," Donaldson said. "I still have friends on the police force."

They parted ways several blocks later, Donaldson to walk home and Drew hailing a hansom cab to take him back to his cousin's house.

It was a few minutes after one when the night footmen let him in. The house was dark and quiet, with only the ticking of the large grandfather clock to punctuate the night.

He quickly got ready for bed, wondering what to do about this new information. Once he slid beneath the covers, his mind whirled with the information he'd gleaned, and he had trouble going to sleep for a while. Finally, exhausted, he slept.

****

Violet was startled but not totally shocked to hear about the meeting between Harvey and Louis.

"They are up to something nefarious," Drew concluded. "Donaldson has sent word no one has heard of a fellow named Parkin recently...and no bodies have shown up today, but he's keeping his ear to the ground."

"Well." Matilda's hands shook slightly. "Harvey and Louis are certainly disreputable people. I wish that we had not invited Harvey and Henrietta over tonight."

"But perhaps, Mama, they will slip up, and we will learn something," Betsey said.

Violet nodded. "Let us all be on our guard and listening carefully."

"The séance on Sunday should prove interesting," Drew concluded. "Violet, perhaps after lunch we can go over the details and set things up. Matilda would like us to use the summer parlor at the back of the house, which is the quietest room."

"It will be cold there," Betsey warned. "And Mama, you will have to act the perfect hostess."

"Yes, do not let on that we have any suspicions at all, any of you," Drew cautioned them.

They agreed to do their best to act natural, but Violet was a little worried about Betsey's mother. Later, when Betsey and Violet were alone, she expressed her own fears to Violet.

"I hope my mother can act normal," she said as they sat together in Betsey's large blue and white room. "If not, if anything makes Harvey and Henrietta suspicious—I just don't know what we'll do."

"Perhaps Patricia can keep her busy with conversation," Violet suggested.

"Yes, and our neighbor Claudia—the Stilton's daughter—will be here. She is quite the flirt. She should keep Harvey and Louis occupied. Harvey met her last year and was taken by her…but of course, she is an heiress and has many men pursuing her."

"Who else shall be present at the party?"

"Mrs. And Mrs. Stilton, and their son, Ambrose. He is a few years younger than Claudia. They have another son, too, but he is but a lad and won't be present. And our neighbor Mr. Eckert. He is an older gentleman, quite educated, and lives with his sister Maureen. Neither ever married. She is in Canada visiting friends before winter sets in, but he will be here."

"Let us hope all these people will distract your mother," Violet said. "I will try my best to keep her busy."

She, Betsey, and Patricia went downstairs early for dinner and offered to help Matilda with anything she needed. Everything appeared well in hand, though, so they kept the conversation cheerful and breezy, hoping to keep her mind away from the séance, Harvey, and Henrietta.

Joseph Eckert arrived first and was describing his trip this summer to Italy when the Stiltons arrived. Trips to Europe became the topic of discussion, with Claudia attempting to flirt not-so-subtly with Drew.

Betsey's brothers and their wives soon appeared. Then Louis arrived and joined in the discussion with tales of his recent trips to England and France. Harvey and Henrietta finally appeared, and they sat down to supper.

Violet was relieved to see that Matilda appeared her usual self—only slightly nervous, checking to see that her guests had all the food and drink they desired. She noted that Mr. Eckert had a hearty appetite, as did Harvey.

Louis drank quite a bit of wine, but it seemed to have no effect on him. He must be used to it, she concluded.

After dinner, Betsey's brothers and their wives left, saying they had early plans for the next day. The other men retired to drink port and smoke cigars in the library, a large room filled to the brim with books. Betsey had told Violet that her father had been an even more avid reader than she was, and many of the books had been read—they were not merely used for display as some people did. The women sat in the red and gold parlor, with a fire burning to ward off the chill of the late October evening.

Twenty minutes later Drew appeared.

"Everyone has requested that we not wait for Sunday, but that we do a séance this evening," he said.

Violet studied him. He did not appear opposed to the idea.

"This evening?" Matilda gasped.

"I'm sure it will be fine, Mama," Betsey said, placing a hand on her mother's arm.

Henrietta looked pale, but she nodded.

Drew invited them to the summer parlor. The room was dark and cool, with no fireplace, and he instructed Violet to light a few candles.

They sat around an oval table, which had been pulled to the center of the room. Drew was at the head, with Harvey, then Henrietta, then Louis to his left. On his right were Violet, Patricia, Betsey, and Matilda, then Mr. Eckert, Ambrose, Claudia, and Mr. then Mrs. Stilton, and Mrs. Stilton joined hands with Louis.

"Now we will be quiet, and wait," Drew directed as their hands joined.

The faint ticking of a clock in the hall was the only sound except for their breathing. Without Mrs. O'Grady, Violet wondered how much success they would have.

A sudden breeze stirred the air. The window was closed, yet the breeze was definitely there. Violet listened and suddenly felt that strange heaviness she often felt as a spirit occupied space nearby.

"Someone is here," she whispered.

She saw Henrietta flinch. Claudia made a small noise.

They remained quiet, and then they heard a voice say, "I am here." Red Feather's voice.

It seemed to be coming from Mr. Stilton, who had slumped into his chair and was breathing deeply.

"Red Feather?" Drew asked.

"Yes. There is one who wishes to come through." There was another moment of silence, and then a female voice came forth.

"*Mon cher*," the voice whispered.

Patricia gripped Violet's hand harder.

"Maman?" Louis asked, sitting upright, his face white in the dim light.

"Yes, my dearest. It is I," was the reply.

"Madame LeBlanc?" Drew asked quietly.

"*Oui*." The Frenchwoman's voice was low and breathy.

"Maman, are you all right? I have missed you—how are you? It is three years, but it seems like only yesterday—"

"I am not here to talk about me, but about you," she answered. "*Mon cher*, you must be careful. I do not like—" There was a pause. And then she switched to French.

Fortunately, Violet's French, from school, was fairly good. She understood what the woman was saying. "I am worried about you, my dear. I see you are surrounding yourself with some people I do not like. You must be careful, you must avoid them!"

Henrietta sucked in a loud breath, and someone—she thought it was Claudia—gasped.

Violet suspected that most of the people here spoke passable French, which was taught in the best schools, and could understand the gist of what the woman was saying to her son.

"There is nothing to worry about, maman," Louis answered swiftly, also in French.

"Be careful," was the whispered response. "Do not trust easily, *mon cher*."

"I will be careful," was his whispered vow in response.

The air lightened, and a cold breeze swept through

the room. Violet knew the spirit had departed.

Betsey let out a long breath. She must have felt it too.

Drew glanced around. No one stirred, no further air moved.

They waited, but the woman did not return, although Louis asked hopefully, "Maman? Are you still here?"

There was only silence.

Finally, after about ten minutes, Drew asked if Red Feather was still present. There was no response.

"I believe we are done for the night," he declared.

Henrietta let out a shaky breath. "How frightful!"

Betsey shot her a look. "Not at all. I believe Louis was glad to hear from his mother."

"You must be careful," Mr. Eckert advised Louis.

Louis appeared quite pale. "I will be."

"Samuel?" Mrs. Stilton pushed her husband warily. "Are you still asleep?"

He came to with a start. "Huh?"

"You fell asleep," she said accusingly.

"Mrs. Stilton, I believe your husband was the medium—the vehicle—for Red Feather to reach us," Drew said.

"What?" Mr. Stilton asked.

"I believe Red Feather—an Indian guide—reached us through you," Drew repeated.

Mr. Stilton looked taken aback, Mrs. Stilton disturbed, and both their children fascinated.

"You were, Papa," Claudia said.

"I would not have believed it if I didn't hear it with my own ears," Ambrose affirmed.

"Really?" Mr. Stilton looked around the table.

The others nodded.

"The spirit of my Maman came through," Louis told him.

"Why do you think she told you to be careful?" Patricia asked.

He shrugged. "Who knows? New York City—any city—can be a dangerous place."

"Perhaps you should not play cards so often," Henrietta said, rather tartly.

Louis sent her a dark glance. "I am sure a little card-playing is not harmful."

Unless, Violet thought, he played for high stakes. But she did not voice the thought.

People began to get up and leave the room. They gathered in the red and gold salon and Patricia, Drew, and Matilda poured drinks for anyone who wanted one. Violet found the small brandy she asked for warming and sipped it slowly as she sat near the fireplace.

Louis tossed back his brandy. He looked pale and shaken, she observed.

Within a few minutes the Stiltons and Mr. Eckert departed. The others only lingered about ten minutes more, discussing the séance. As a footman brought in their wraps, Violet was standing near the stairs in the hallway, and Henrietta and Louis were close by. Louis helped Henrietta with her navy blue cloak.

She put a hand on his arm. "Do not worry about what you think your mother said. We do not even know if it was truly your maman who spoke."

He murmured in French, in a low voice, "I am concerned. I must reconsider all my options."

Henrietta sent him a glowering look.

Was he speaking, Violet wondered, of courting

her? Or…something more sinister?

Henrietta pulled on black gloves. "We will see you all at our party tomorrow, yes?" she asked, glancing about.

"Of course," Matilda answered.

The others murmured their assent.

"I look forward to it," Violet said.

Henrietta shot her a look she couldn't decipher.

"We will see you tomorrow," Patricia said.

"It will be fun," Betsey added.

Once they left, Matilda stifled a yawn. "This has been most fascinating, but I am fatigued. Goodnight everyone."

Betsey accompanied her mother upstairs, saying she was getting tired too.

Patricia lingered with Drew and Violet for another few minutes.

"I do believe that was a successful séance," she said. "It certainly seemed that Louis' mother came through."

"Yes, he undoubtedly recognized her voice," Drew agreed. "I wonder if she was warning him about Henrietta and Harvey among his shady associates."

"It is very possible," Violet said.

Once she went to her room, she sat and made notes, which took her nearly an hour. Tucking the papers in a drawer, she finally went to sleep.

And dreamed, not of séances, but of dancing with Drew.

****

The house that Harvey and Henrietta were renting in New York City was on a fashionable street, but the inside was dark and gloomy. Heavy, dark wood furniture, and dark-colored crimson draperies brought little life to the home. Large couches, clothed in brown velvet, provided almost no color and the oil lamps were black and gold, and shed little light.

Henrietta greeted them all and proceeded to latch on to Drew and steer him around, introducing him to her friends. She paid scant attention to Violet, Betsey, Patricia, and Matilda.

Besides Louis, there were two other men and two women present. Sir Francis Langford, also from England, was visiting New York. Frank, as he asked to be called, had arrived only a week ago but apparently knew Harvey well from London. Jonathan Rimes was from Philadelphia but had friends in New York and apparently visited here often.

Jonathan's cousin, Celeste Rimes, lived in New York and knew Harvey and Henrietta from previous visits.

Cassandra Wagner was also present. Violet remembered Drew mentioning that Harvey was pursuing the woman, who was an heiress.

The two men and women appeared to know each other well, and also knew Harvey and Henrietta.

The dinner in a drafty dining room was, fortunately, well cooked and included roast chicken, fish and vegetables in a cream sauce, and Napoleon pastries.

Conversation during the meal was light-hearted. Violet was seated next to Jonathan and found him to be amusing. Betsey, on his other side, had Louis and then Cassandra on her right. But she seemed to prefer the conversation with Jonathan.

After dinner, the women returned to the dark

parlor, and the men to the library to smoke and drink port.

Henrietta was a decent hostess, moving from one person to another, making casual conversation about shopping and clothes. She asked Violet what shops she had been to in New York and asked Betsey about her preferred milliner.

Violet excused herself to find a water closet. She followed Henrietta's directions, but the narrow hallways twisted and turned, and she got lost. A maid found her in a back corridor and led her to the nearest water closet, with directions to return to the parlor.

When she was done, Violet stepped out into the silent hall. It was dark back here, with only one very small oil lamp on a table flickering to light the way. She started forward, then paused, hearing whispered words from behind a nearby door.

"I am through. Finished." She was positive it was Louis' voice.

There was a murmur, but Violet could not tell if it was a woman or a man who spoke.

Shadows flickered wildly on the wall as she passed by the lamp.

"I tell you; I am done! Finis!" Louis exclaimed sharply.

The other voice spoke again, too low to hear the words, or to identify the speaker.

Violet sighed. Much as she would like to eavesdrop and find out more, she knew she should return to the others.

Besides, now there was silence.

She stopped but heard nothing. Then the whispered voice spoke again. The two people seemed to be disagreeing.

She went on down the corridor, turning to the right, and proceeding down the next hall to the front of the building.

She found the parlor easily and realized she must have passed the nearest water closet originally and found a different one when she saw Patricia coming out of a narrow door.

Matilda, Betsey, and Celeste were seated on chairs near the fireplace. As Patricia joined Violet, they stepped into the room.

She noted that Henrietta and Cassandra were missing, and the men had still not returned from drinking.

Shortly afterward Cassandra returned, looking flustered, her cheeks pink. Then Henrietta entered the room, her expression her usual haughty one, her hair smoothed as if she had recently combed it.

Studying both women, Violet wondered if one of them had been with Louis.

It was another five minutes before Jonathan and Drew entered the parlor. Louis was still missing, and apparently Harvey and Frank were still smoking or drinking—or somewhere else

Fifteen minutes later those two strolled in, joking about a billiards game.

Violet spoke to Matilda for a while, then to Celeste, who seemed genuinely friendly. She was most interested in hearing about life in Twin Bridges.

"Some of these sophisticated city parties are stuffy, boring affairs," she whispered conspiratorially.

Violet grinned.

"Has anyone seen Louis?" Betsey asked suddenly.

They glanced about the room.

"He was with us, drinking port," Drew said. "He excused himself and said he would be back shortly."

"He was—attending to personal business," Jonathan said. "I assume."

Meaning the water closet, Violet guessed.

"I shall ask a servant to check on him, and I'll look around the house," Henrietta said.

"He can't have got lost, can he?" Matilda asked.

"It's a big house," Harvey said, shaking his head, "but he's been here dozens of times."

Violet sat perched on her chair as Henrietta bustled out, and Harvey, too, left the room. She suddenly had an uneasy feeling, recalling the conversation she'd partly overheard.

"I heard him in a room near the water closet I used in the back of the house," she whispered to Betsey. "It sounded like he was arguing with someone."

Betsey stared at her. "Really," she breathed quietly. "I wonder who?"

Violet did too. A strange, uneasy sensation curled within her.

"Perhaps we should all be searching," Drew suggested.

Celeste got up. "We can cover the house more quickly that way."

Since Harvey and Henrietta had left the room, Drew split them into parties of two to search. Betsey and Violet were paired together, and he directed them to check the second floor. Patricia and Matilda would also be on the second floor, checking the back of the narrow house. Celeste and Jonathan, Frank and Cassandra would be checking the third story, while

Drew joined the others on the first floor.

"I believe it is more likely he'll be on the first floor, since he is a guest," Drew said. "And I will check outside, in case he went out for fresh air."

Violet had placed one foot on the first stair when a shriek pierced the quiet house.

Together they raced en masse to where the sound had come from—the corridor near where Violet had heard the argument.

Henrietta stood in the doorway of the room close to the water closet. Her expression was shocked.

"Oh-oh—" she moaned.

"What is it?" Patricia asked.

Henrietta waved a hand wordlessly.

Harvey appeared from the other end of the corridor. Henrietta stepped aside, and Harvey and Drew shouldered into the room, followed by Jonathan and Frank.

"My Lord," Frank breathed.

"What is it?" Matilda asked, wringing her hands.

"Lou-Louis," Henrietta rasped. She pointed with a shaking arm.

Violet peered around Henrietta. Drew and Harvey were bending over a man who lay on the floor.

Drew looked up. "He's gone."

Patricia gasped loudly, as did Cassandra. Slowly they filed in to surround Louis. Drew and Harvey both stood up.

"Gone? *Dead?*" Cassandra squeaked as they moved.

"I'm afraid so." Drew straightened. "We should send someone for the police."

"The police?" Henrietta gasped. She teetered, and

looked about to faint.

"There is a wound on the back of his head," Harvey told them, "as if he's been struck by something."

The others peered at Louis' head. Dried blood capped his brown hair.

"Oh!" Matilda cried out, and swooned.

Jonathan was behind her and caught her before she fell to the floor. He and Harvey carried her to a nearby couch.

"Yes." Drew's voice was grim. "Harvey, can you send a footman for the police?"

****

Two hours later, the police had come and gone. Violet, Betsey, Drew and Patricia and Matilda—now recovered from the shock that had made her faint—were in a carriage, heading back to Matilda's home.

The police had examined Louis and taken away his body. An inspector had pointed out a candleholder, made of silver, sitting on a nearby table. It was heavy and when he turned it around, dried blood stuck to the underside.

"This is the weapon the killer used," he pronounced.

They had questioned everyone, including servants. No one had seen or heard anything more than Violet, who reported the argument she heard.

"Perhaps the killer was the one he argued with," the inspector said. "But it is also possible it was someone else."

Everyone, at some point, had been out of the parlor while Louis was too. Either checking on him, using a water closet, or in Frank's case, finishing his brandy and cigar after the other men left. Only Celeste and Matilda had remained in the main parlor the entire time.

"So, Celeste seems to be the only persons with an alibi for the entire time Louis was absent from the room," Drew mused now as they sat in the carriage, the clip-clop of the horses a soothing background to Violet's tumultuous thoughts.

"Yes, my mother and Patricia were there and could vouch for her presence when each left the room and returned," Betsey said. "Whereas Violet, I, Cassandra, and Henrietta were in and out of the room—along with all of you men."

"That is correct," Drew said. "So any one of us, in the eyes of the police, could be guilty. Even Violet could have reported falsely on the conversation she heard. "Not"—he added, when Violet started to protest—"that you would, Violet. But the police might think it is possible."

"Was it a man or woman you heard?" Betsey pressed. "Could you tell at all?"

Violet shook her head. "Honestly, I could not tell. The voice was low, and I could make out few words."

"It might have been Louis' killer!" Matilda exclaimed. She clutched her cape. "Oh, my stars. I declare this is so frightening."

"Shh, Mama," Betsey soothed her distraught mother.

"It's all right, Matilda," Patricia said at the same time. "They will find his killer. I am sure."

"We must learn who had a motive to kill Louis, as well as opportunity," Drew declared. "For example, Cassandra is a pampered heiress. She has money to spare and probably would not resort to violence. What motive could she possibly have?"

"Revenge? Perhaps Louis did something to her?" Violet hazarded a guess. "Harvey, on the other hand, needs money…but how could killing Louis benefit him?"

"Who knows?" Drew said. "But I do believe the police will investigate thoroughly, since Louis came from a well-known family in France. And…I am going to see Donaldson after I drop you ladies at the house, and discuss this with him. I want him to see what else he can find out."

"It's getting late, Drew," Patricia said. "Can it not wait until tomorrow?"

"No." He shook his head.

"I don't trust Harvey," Betsey said suddenly. "Perhaps he thought Louis would lend him money, and when he didn't, Harvey got mad."

"Louis did not have much money," Drew said.

The carriage slowed. "We're here," Matilda said faintly. She looked pale and upset, and Violet thought the night's events had been hard on the older woman.

Drew and a footman helped the women to alight, and then he bowed and left them to go see Mr. Donaldson.

Inside, they shed their cloaks, and Matilda went immediately upstairs to bed, with Patricia holding her elbow as she ascended the stairs.

"My mother is worn out," Betsey whispered to Violet. "And upset. Violet, would you care for a sherry? I could use a drink after tonight's events."

"Yes, thank you," Violet said, thinking the liquid would warm her. She'd been cold, quite cold, since Louis' still body had been discovered.

Betsey moved into a small blue parlor and took a decanter from the sideboard. She poured the sherry into small glasses, handing one to Violet.

Violet let the smooth sweet liquid slide down her throat slowly, feeling the warmth, and found herself relaxing. She sat down beside Betsey.

"This is awful," Betsey said. "I didn't care much for Louis, but to see him lying there, dead...!"

Violet agreed. "It is terrible," she said, "and he was young."

They sat talking for a few minutes, wondering who could have murdered Louis, and why. They conjectured about each person in the party—rejecting any thought of Patricia, Matilda, Drew, or themselves. Violet knew no one of their group could be responsible. The others—they really didn't know them well, except for Harvey and Henrietta, but what would they gain by Louis' death? And could Cassandra or Celeste or Jonathan or Frank possibly be guilty?

"What if," Violet asked, "someone sneaked into the house and killed him, then took off?"

"Harvey did suggest that to the inspector, remember?" Betsey asked. "And the inspector thought it unlikely."

"That's right." Violet recalled that now. "The inspector said it's usually the case of someone who knows the victim, unless it was a robbery or something."

"And Henrietta said nothing was taken from the room," Betsey added.

Betsey gave a wide yawn. "This—commotion—has tired me out. I need to get some sleep."

Violet accompanied her upstairs in companionable

silence. Once they separated and she got ready for bed, she found herself unable to relax, and tossed and turned for at least an hour.

Who had killed Louis? And was that person running around, lurking nearby, ready to hurt someone again?

****

The following day they were up early since the police wanted to question them again. Most of the day was spent talking, their voices low and concerned, or reading. Sunday they were again up early to attend church services along with Harvey and Henrietta. Violet found herself praying for peace for Louis. She hadn't particularly cared for him, but the way his life ended, at such a young age, was sad.

Of course, if he had had anything to do with Charles' death then perhaps he deserved his fate.

After a luncheon at Betsey's house, which included Harvey and Henrietta, the brother and sister left, and the rest of them went to pack. Betsey would be returning with Violet and Drew and Patricia to New Jersey the following morning, so she spent some time alone with her mother. Since Louis' death, they'd decided to postpone another séance.

That evening Drew told them about his meetings with Donaldson on Friday and again on Saturday. Donaldson had been shocked to learn that Louis was killed. He was not able to find out anything else, except that a body had washed up on the banks of the Hudson River sometime on Friday, and he suspected it might be the man, Parkin.

They all retired early and were up early on Monday to start their trip back.

The train was fairly crowded, so they kept their conversation to non-personal topics. Once they arrived in Twin Bridges in the early afternoon, after having eaten lunch on the train, Drew went directly to the factory. A wagon with two footmen met them and transported the rest of them back to Covington House.

Betsey began chattering excitedly about the next séance, which was scheduled for a week from Tuesday when the moon would once again be full. Drew had asked Violet to send a note to Mrs. O'Grady reminding her, and she did so as soon as she had returned to her room and unpacked.

At dinner, Drew told them he had received a telegram that afternoon from Donaldson, saying the man who had been found dead by the river had been positively identified as Parkin.

"Donaldson also checked around further about Louis," he said. "He owed money to several people…so anyone might have been angry with him."

"But if he's dead he can't pay them back," Violet pointed out.

"True…but maybe it was a crime of revenge," Drew said.

Violet felt this wasn't correct and voiced her opinion. "What if, perhaps, he knew who killed Charles—and someone was afraid he would confess it?" she suggested. "Remember the last séance? He seemed to be genuinely scared and wanted to change."

"That's plausible," Betsey concurred.

"It is," Drew agreed, and Patricia nodded.

The week sped by. Drew spent most hours at the factory, making up for the days they were in New York City. Betsey helped Violet tackle the house's library, and by Friday at dinner time, with her help, Violet had catalogued most of the books and put the ones Drew was not using currently in a semblance of order. She had only to finish his laboratory office.

"I think we can finish that on Monday and Tuesday," she said, wiping her brow with a handkerchief. She felt dusty and in need of a bath.

Betsey surveyed their work. "This was quite a job, but it looks much better, and now Drew will know what books he has. He probably has no idea he has duplicates and triplicates of several."

"And four copies of Elmer's *Séances of Edinburgh!*" Violet agreed, laughing.

She smiled at Betsey. "Thank you so much for your help. It would have taken me more than twice the time to complete this on my own."

Betsey smiled back. "I enjoyed it, really. Besides giving me something to do, I found it interesting to look at the books. I plan to read the Edinburgh one this weekend."

"We only have the one additional room to complete," Violet said. "That will not be too difficult."

"Yes, but those books are partially in order already. Drew seems to have them separated, roughly, by topic. And you started on them already so it should go quicker. I will help you while I am still here," Betsey promised.

The two returned upstairs to wash before dinner. They were happy to tell Drew about their progress.

He was pleased, and at dinner they discussed the séance that would occur on Tuesday.

Mrs. O'Grady would attend, along with Henrietta and Harvey, who would arrive on Monday.

"Is young Sheldon's mother still talking about the devil?" Patricia asked.

"Yes. Fortunately, most of the other people in town are paying her little heed; or if they do, they are wise enough not to talk about it in my presence," he told them. "Mrs. O'Grady has gotten some criticism, I am sure; but she is staunch in her beliefs that contacting the dead helps the living."

"Fortunately," echoed Betsey.

The following day, Saturday, Drew wanted to return to the factory and finish catching up on work there. Betsey and Violet walked with him, intending to bring some freshly baked bread to the Avery family.

They were greeted in a subdued manner. Mrs. Avery did not appear, but Sheldon and his sisters were friendly, although rather restrained. Sheldon appeared much improved.

"I bet," Betsey said after they left and strolled toward the factory to peek in on Drew, "that Mrs. Avery made them promise not to be too enthusiastic with us or too welcoming."

"I believe you're right," Violet agreed.

They reached the factory in a few minutes. Only one designer was there on this Saturday morning. She was busy sketching and showed the boots she was drawing to them.

"They're beautiful!" Violet said, noticing the flower peeking out at the top of the boot. "I would love a pair!"

"Me too," Betsey said. "Is Drew around?"

"In his office, with Arnold, the bookkeeper," she told them.

They knocked, and he bade them enter.

The room had a distinctly chemical smell. On a small table Drew was leaning over examining something. The bookkeeper was standing at Drew's desk, frowning at some papers.

"I will reconcile these statements," the bookkeeper said, "before I leave this afternoon." He brushed past them, still frowning as he stared at the papers in his hand.

"Hello," Drew said absently. He was applying something to a shoe heel with a thin brush.

"I hope we're not interrupting," Violet began.

"No, no...I am just trying out a new adhesive for heels." He straightened.

Betsey had picked up a glass bottle from the table and was staring at it.

"Be careful," he warned. "I have some dangerous items here. That's a chemical which can be used in explosives."

Betsey put the bottle down gently. "Oh. Well, Cousin Drew, you are a scientist and inquisitive by nature, whether it is in inventing a better shoe or conducting a better séance."

He grinned at that. "Thank you."

Violet glanced around the room. He had several bottles of mysterious-looking substances on the table, plus a few tools. She studied several of them. A few of them had dangerous-sounding names.

"I have tried to make my own glues and adhesives," he told them. "I just applied this new mix...we will see if it works. I will leave it, then check on Monday."

"Harvey and Henrietta sent a telegram a little while ago," Betsey said. "They will arrive on the train

Monday afternoon."

"That is good. We will spend Monday evening and Tuesday afternoon readying for the séance. The full moon—and being so close to All Hallow's Eve—bodes well for our success." He gave them a wide smile.

Violet's heart skipped, and she smiled back. Just a smile from him had her feeling wonderful.

Dinner that evening was cheerful. This was the first Saturday night in weeks when they hadn't been at a party or gathering or entertaining. Violet enjoyed the quiet and relaxing evening at home—she found herself often thinking of Covington House as home. They sat in the parlor, speaking of the séance, and Betsey did sing a few songs and Violet, Drew, and Patricia joined in.

Although Violet wished heartily for time alone with Drew, he seemed absorbed in his various pursuits and had been busy the entire week. They had no time alone; and she didn't want to deliberately try to get him by himself, afraid he would think of her as a scheming female like Henrietta.

Sunday passed quietly, but Monday was busy. The staff had readied the usual rooms for Harvey and Henrietta. The train was on time, and they soon arrived at Covington House. Drew stayed at the factory until late afternoon, sending his regrets for not being there earlier; but his glue experiments were keeping him busy. When he arrived home, he went for a walk with Harvey almost until dinner time.

"We will do some work in the laboratory after dinner, if that is all right," he told Violet as they walked into the dining room. "We will start preparations for tomorrow's séance."

"Of course," she agreed.

Dinner was again cheerful, although Henrietta appeared very subdued. Harvey whispered to Violet just before they sat down that she was quite saddened by Louis' death and had been morose since that day.

After dinner, Drew and Violet retreated to the laboratory.

Earlier in the day, she had dusted in the laboratory with one of the maids. Now Drew and Violet checked to see the table in the séance room was centered, the cloth on it clean, and that the trumpet and candles were set in the usual places. Drew added the meteorite to the table and a large clear and milky-white crystal he had been planning to add.

He returned to his office to do some reading, and Violet wandered in the main room, looking at the improved shelves with their more organized books, and the tables which held a few additional crystals, a couple of books Drew wanted left out, and a large envelope with her notebooks.

She touched the envelope. This was weeks of accumulated work, and she wondered if she should copy the notes.

She moved back to the séance room. It was quiet and ready…almost…waiting.

She said a quick, silent prayer. *Please Charles, appear to us…please…this time come through…*

Taking a deep breath, she returned to the main room.

Drew stood up in his office. "I'll walk you back to the house if you want to go back."

"Yes," she said, "although you really don't have to keep walking me back and forth."

He shook his head. "There may still be dangerous

characters out there." He showed her his inner pocket. A gun rested there. "I bring this with me everywhere now, just in case there's trouble."

"I'm glad," she said. "You must protect yourself from danger."

His eyes met hers. Warmth suffused her.

"I will be fine." His tone was reassuring. "Come, let us return to the house."

He walked back with her, and Violet was glad of his company.

"I think," she said, "that our séances are more successful when Mrs. O'Grady is present."

"Do you think so?" She thought she saw amusement in his eyes. "I was just thinking, it seems my séances are much more successful since you have been present, Violet." He reached for her hand and clasped it in his larger one.

Warmth swept up her arm.

"Since you have joined us in our quest, Aunt Patricia and I have noticed that we have been much more successful in contacting the dead—with or without Mrs. O'Grady."

"Really?"

"Yes," he affirmed.

She smiled at him, and he tightened his grip on her hand as they drew closer to the house. Once they reached the door, he leaned forward and brushed a kiss across her lips. "Yes," he whispered.

Tingling shot through her. They proceeded inside, and then he went to his study, and she upstairs, to her room. Once she was in bed, she found herself dreaming of being held by Drew...

****

The following day passed quietly. Violet kept herself busy with reading, both a book on ghostly visitations and the novel she had bought. She saw Betsey but except for meals, no one else.

By seven thirty Mrs. O'Grady had arrived at the laboratory, escorted by her younger son, who left immediately. Violet had accompanied Drew earlier and they had checked again to see all was ready. Betsey, Patricia, Harvey, and Henrietta came right on the heels of Mrs. O'Grady.

They took seats around the table. The night was dark, with many clouds, and the full moon showed between them only intermittently. Wind blew briskly, and the scent of damp air heralded rain.

Drew sat at the head of the table, as usual. To his right sat Violet, and to his left, Mrs. O'Grady. Beside Violet sat Aunt Patricia, and to her right Betsey, then Henrietta, then Harvey, Mrs. O'Grady, and then Drew completed the circle.

The window was open slightly, and as Violet lit two of the three candles, one gusted suddenly, sending shadows flickering about.

Drew lit the third candle, and they all sat down.

"We are here to reach those who have crossed over," he said solemnly.

They sat silently. Gradually Violet realized Mrs. O'Grady's breathing had slowed. Patricia seemed to grip her hand more tightly.

"Greetings, friends." The voice of Red Feather broke through the quiet suddenly.

"Greetings. Red Feather, is it you?" Drew asked.

"Yes, friends."

There was a minute of silence.

Violet felt the now familiar heaviness in the air, between her and Drew. But it seemed heavier, stronger, and more dense than usual.

"Who is trying to come through tonight?" Drew asked in a conversational tone.

"I think...there is more than one person trying to come through," Violet whispered.

Wind blew suddenly, and Violet saw Henrietta shift in her seat as if cold.

"My friends, it is I." The slight French accent had Henrietta and Harvey dropping their mouths open. "I am not alone."

"Louis? Is it you?" Drew asked, an eager note in his voice. "Is Charles with you?"

There was another minute of silence.

"I am here." It was a different voice...Charles'? This time it was quite clear.

One of the candle flames flickered and sent up a wisp of smoke.

Drew's expression changed from serious to happy. "Charles!" His whisper was lilting.

"Yes." The voice was thick, almost sluggish, as if the person struggled to use it.

"Charles, we have tried so long to contact you...I miss you," Drew said eagerly. His hand gripped Violet's tightly. "Tell me, please...do you know who murdered you?"

"The person who...who...killed...Louis."

Patricia gave a soft gasp, her hand tightening in Violet's.

Violet felt a shiver move through her.

"So you were both killed by the same person?" Drew pressed.

"Yes."

"Yes."

The two voices—Charles's and Louis'—spoke at almost the same moment.

Nearby, Violet heard Harvey suck in a breath.

"And can you identify that person?" Drew asked, his voice raspy.

There was another moment of silence. Then a breeze blew strongly through the room, stirring the curtains, and the flames on the candles danced wildly. Violet shivered, and noticed that everyone around the table was doing the same. The cold in the room was palpable.

"Murderer…" Louis' voice hissed through the air.

"The killer was hired!" Charles' exclamation split the air, his voice stronger this time.

Patricia gasped loudly.

"Who hired the killer?" Drew pressed on.

"The trumpet!" Harvey exclaimed.

The trumpet was moving slowly upward. It hovered for several seconds before it sailed through the air, narrowly missing Harvey's head.

Henrietta shrieked as it swept by her before crashing into the wall and falling to the floor with a discordant note.

Harvey? Could it be Harvey? Violet wondered. Had Harvey hired the killer?

But Drew was not done with his questions. "Can you identify the one behind this? The one who hired someone to kill you, Charles? And Louis?"

"Parkin's brother…was the hired killer." Charles now sounded like he was gasping for breath, as if every word was difficult.

And then, in the dark, Violet saw it.

The vague outline of a body...a head...a face.

Charles' face!

This time it was both Betsey and Henrietta who gasped.

"Charles! Brother!" Drew exclaimed. He started to rise from his seat.

She could see it now, the narrow nose and full lips, the mustache, the eyes so similar to Drew's...and a smile. A sad smile on Charles' face. His form, which was partly transparent, wavered, as if folded.

"Brother..." he echoed. "My...brother. Drew."

Violet's whole body tightened with excitement.

"Parkin's brother killed you?" Drew asked. "I understand Ernest Parkin is now dead."

"Killed by...his brother...Allen Parkin...killed me..." The words were coming out in fits and starts, as if Charles was having trouble getting them out. His mouth was moving, but the words were disjointed.

And well he might be having trouble. For in materializing, Violet surmised he was using his strength to project his image, the image Drew had so wanted to see...but his voice was having problems.

Even in the dark, Violet could see Henrietta's face had gone white. Was she afraid her brother was implicated in these two deaths? She looked like she might faint any moment.

The image of Charles seemed to flicker, then came back stronger. She could almost sense him trying to maintain his appearance.

"Charles? Can you tell us anything more? Who hired Allen Parkin?" Drew rushed on, as if afraid the connection would end.

"Here…here…" Charles' voice was fading. His image flickered again, more rapidly.

"Louis? Can you help?" Drew asked sharply.

But Louis had gone silent, perhaps unable to control his own ability to speak.

"Drew…brother…bring justice…" Charles gasped.

And the image faded away, until all that was left was a thickening column, almost smoke-like, where his image had floated near Drew.

Violet sensed the disappointment emanating from Drew. His hand, which had gripped hers so hard, slackened in its strength.

"Charles? Louis?" he probed.

"I am here, my dear." The woman's voice, clear and low, was startling in the darkness.

A sudden fear gripped Violet. She knew that voice, had heard it before. What if she was here to chastise Violet?

"Mother?" Drew asked.

"Claire?" Patricia questioned softly at the same time.

Violet shivered.

"They have been here in this realm such a short time. It is most difficult for them to get through, to communicate to you, my dear." The woman's voice was sad, resigned. "But I can."

Her voice was stronger than it had been the two previous times their group had heard it.

"What can you tell us, Mother?" Drew began.

A crackling sounded nearby, and a spark flew across the room, as if electrical energy had spit out of nowhere.

"You." The voice had dropped to a low hiss. "I

tried to warn Charles. I asked for your help!"

Violet shivered, and her insides seemed to be slowly freezing.

"You," the voice repeated. Slowly, another being began to materialize. A hand, an arm...and a finger. Pointing at her, at Violet! "You did not do anything!"

Bestey's mouth fell open, and Henrietta cried out.

"I—I didn't think—you were real," Violet whispered. She began to shake as the cold crept into her bones. "I had been to so many false séances...had you tried to get through to Drew yourself?"

"You were the only one I could reach." Her voice was a moan. "Even now—it is difficult—to get through—"

Slowly, the hand and finger disappeared.

Drew was staring at the space where it had been. "Mother?" he questioned. Then he turned his head, focusing on Violet.

A pop sounded, and Violet knew that she, like Charles and Louis, was gone for now.

Silence reigned.

"Claire?" Patricia whispered.

There was a small moan. Violet turned to see Henrietta, looking rather sick.

She felt as sick as Henrietta looked.

What was Drew going to say? She should have told him, told him about the contact with his mother, before he had to learn it this way.

He was looking quite flabbergasted, as if he wasn't sure what was going on. An unusual state for him.

The heavy feeling in the air lifted. A swirl of a breeze seemed to carry away the very air—and the spirits. Violet felt the atmosphere lighten.

"Mother?" he whispered. Then, "Charles? Louis?"

After a minute he added, "Red Feather?"

But there was no answer to any of his inquiries.

They sat in silence for a few minutes. Patricia sighed loudly.

"I believe they have left," Drew said, reluctantly. "No one appears to be remaining."

"Louis?" Harvey asked suddenly. "Charles?"

Only continued silence met their ears.

A few minutes later, Drew sighed heavily, and his hand grew limp in hers. "They have gone." But he didn't sound disappointed. Rather, he sounded cheerful.

As well he should be. They had experienced great success—they had contacted four spirits!

As if Betsey could read Violet's thoughts, she spoke. "We contacted four people," she said, her voice filled with awe. "Four of them!"

"Yes," Drew said, his voice calm but with an underlying note of excitement. Even his face looked excited—flushed, his lips tipping up in a half smile, his eyes wide. "We did!"

"We must immediately make our notes," Violet said guardedly.

"Of course. I will wish most of you goodnight—and thank you for being here." He nodded, sending a brief smile around the table.

Violet went to get her papers and Drew's, which he had left on his desk. Betsey also went to gather up pen and paper. Harvey and Henrietta stood, murmured goodbyes, and left with Patricia, who also said a hasty goodbye to the others. Henrietta looked shaken, and Harvey more serious than usual. Mrs. O'Grady said her son was returning for her and waited at the window until she spotted him.

For at least a half hour, Violet, Drew, and Betsey scribbled on paper, writing their impressions of what they had observed.

Betsey finished first. "I am done. I will return to the house."

"Not alone," Drew commanded. "Wait a few minutes, and we shall all return together."

Violet felt relief sweep through her. Apparently, Drew was not going to ask her about his mother's accusation. In fact, she was surprised that no one had. The appearance of Charles must have been foremost in everyone's minds.

She finished her notes at the same time Drew did and held on to them as he put out the lamps and made sure the laboratory was locked up.

They returned to the quiet house. The wind that blew was stiff, and clouds chased each other across the sky, sometimes obliterating the moon. Other times the white orb shone brightly.

"I am tired. Goodnight," Betsey said, and Violet wondered if she was trying to maneuver her to have time alone with Drew.

"Violet, may I see you in the study?" he asked her formally as Betsey went toward the stairs.

A feeling of dread was like a stone in her stomach. "Certainly," she said, forcing herself to sound calm. He indicated she should precede him, and they walked down the hall to his study. Once inside, he shut the door.

Violet perched on one of the chairs by his desk, and he took a seat behind the desk.

He stared at her for a moment, his gaze almost

benevolent.

"What," he began slowly, "did my mother mean about asking for your help...and you doing nothing?" He sounded confused.

Violet took a deep breath. She'd been afraid of this.

Chapter Eleven

Violet made a conscious effort to relax her body.

"About a year ago—a little more than a year, actually—" she began, "I attended a séance at a neighbor's. This particular neighbor had had one once before and trumpets went flying, voices came to us and—to make a long story short, several of us were convinced it was faked." She took a breath. "Supposedly my mother came through, but her voice didn't sound like her, and she could not give specific answers when questioned by me. So, I felt the séance was fraudulent.

"However, a few months later, they asked me to attend another one. Curious, I did. It was the same medium, so I was immediately suspicious."

"You thought another fake séance was about to happen," he said slowly, leaning back in his chair.

"Yes, precisely. So when a woman's voice came to us—one I didn't recognize—and she seemed to be addressing me, I was surprised. And suspicious. She said her younger son was in danger, although she wasn't sure from who, and I should try to warn him. Charles Covington." She took a deep breath, her insides tightening, her whole self growing cold. "I asked for more details, and she only provided the information that he was in danger, and he came from Hunterdon County."

"She said his name?" Drew went pale.

"Yes. I questioned but received no further answers. Afterward I pondered the problem. She hadn't told me exactly where he lived, only said that comment about Hunterdon County. I made a few inquiries and found out there was a Covington Family in Twin Bridges. But," she said, taking another breath, "the information was so vague I was sure the medium was making it up, trying to get me, and the others there, to believe something. I was afraid I was being taken advantage of. I considered writing, and thought that the family would think I was either looking for money or a lunatic. I had found out that the Covington family was wealthy and didn't want you to think I was looking for a hand out of some kind."

She paused, clutching her hands together. "I had no idea at the time you were interested in the—occult. I was simply afraid I would be thought a lunatic, as I said—or a greedy person looking for money or something. So…I said nothing. I did discuss it with my sister, who thought it was highly suspicious and the medium was just trying to start trouble. So…I'm afraid…I did…nothing, at first." Her voice dwindled. "After a few weeks of debating with myself over the issue, I decided to write him a letter."

"You wrote to Charles?" Drew's eyebrows shot up.

"I didn't know what else to do. I still was unsure of the legitimacy of the séance."

"Did you keep a copy of the letter?"

She nodded. "I did. And—the original was returned to me—I think perhaps it was delivered after his death, so someone returned it. I felt so bad when I learned he was dead. And that I had been—unable—" she choked out—"to stop it."

Drew looked, frankly, shocked. "I find it difficult to believe that my mother contacted you…she didn't know you…why would she do that?"

She swallowed. "I don't know. But when I read of your brother's death in the papers I felt terrible." She tightened her fingers together in her lap.

He stared at her. "Why did you not tell me all this?" He looked perplexed, shocked.

"I—I felt—badly. I kept thinking there might be an opportunity—but I also felt—ashamed. You do not know how many nights I was sleepless, wondering if I could have prevented—"

"You should have said something, told me, when I hired you." His voice was much harsher than she'd ever heard it. "You should have been honest."

"But what could I say?" she asked, spreading her hands open. "That I got a warning—from someone I didn't know, about someone I didn't know—and thought it just part of a fake séance? That is the honest truth!"

"But now you know it *was* true. That my mother—or someone—came through to warn Charles. You should have told me what happened." He stood abruptly and began to pace around his study. He looked large and agitated, and the room seemed to shrink, the walls closing in as he strode about. "You should have told me!"

"But there was nothing you could do!" she protested. "Charles was already gone, and you would have felt badly, too, as I did. I did not want you thinking something could have been done when it was too late."

"But maybe something could have been done!" His voice blazed. "Maybe we could have prevented his death!"

"Not if someone was bent on destroying him," she said, but her voice sounded unconvincing to her own ears. "I had no indication of who, or where or when—or even if it was the medium's imagination—so what could I have done?"

"Warned us. Warned him. He could have been more careful—"

"Do you think he would have listened?" she asked pointedly.

He stopped pacing for a moment to stare at her.

"I don't know," he said, shaking his head. "I don't know."

"Please, Drew, I tried—"

He cut off her words. "Even if you didn't believe what happened, you still should have discussed this with me from the beginning. My God, I trusted you, Violet. Trusted you as I have never trusted another woman—"

"I know," she whispered. Her stomach twisted. "But I did not want to wound you further. You were hurting too much...and then, as I got to know you better, the opportunity never seemed to come up..."

"You should have made an opportunity." His voice was cold now. He ran a hand through his hair. "I—I don't know what to think, what to do. After our success tonight—I am so—" He broke off and stared at her. "I have to think about all this." He sounded so sad and bewildered, that her heart wanted to break for his pain. "I trusted you, and you—and you..." His voice faded.

She knew it was not like him to be at such a loss

for words.

"I am sorry," she said. "I have lived with the anguish of wondering if there was something I could have done...even after I sent the note...and then wondering when and how I should tell you..." Her own voice faded.

Abruptly she stood up. "I will go now," she said softly. "I am so very sorry, Drew."

He nodded, as if lost in thought, as if he felt hopeless.

She almost ran from the room and up the stairs, choking back tears until she reached her room.

If only she'd told him...if only she had been able to warn Charles...!

But it was too late for that. She reached her room, locked the door, and threw herself on the bed, crying quietly into her pillow.

Had Drew lost all respect—and perhaps loving feelings—for her?

She'd never felt so desolate, so alone, so without hope.

****

Drew sat in the cold room. In an effort to conserve wood—whether they could afford it or not—he had the servants refrain from lighting fires if a room might not be used at night, or used only briefly, like his study.

He stared at the dark fireplace. Violet had known something might happen to Charles. Well—she was afraid something would happen, although not certain.

He could understand her perhaps not being convinced the séance was real. He'd been to enough fraudulent ones to realize they were a dime a dozen. But to not tell him—to refrain from explaining what had happened—

He had thought she was trustworthy. Completely. And now he had learned she was not.

He sat, staring, barely able to move, to think. The fact that they had finally heard and seen Charles seemed secondary compared to Violet's—what? Lack of honesty?

Why? Why had Violet not told him about her experience? Her warning for Charles that came too late?

Something inside him seemed to curl into a tight ball, and he sat, numb and miserable, wondering what on earth he should do.

****

The following afternoon Betsey, Violet, and Drew gathered in the library and reviewed their notes. Drew was cool and collected, and Violet, her mouth dry, found herself talking as stiffly as he did. Betsey kept glancing at them both.

Violet's notes were the most detailed, although Drew's and Betsey's were quite good. They spoke a little about the things each had especially noticed, and then Drew excused himself to go to his laboratory and study the notes all had taken.

As soon as he left, Betsey turned to Violet. "What is the matter, Violet? I could hardly stand the tension between you and Drew."

Violet sighed and wrapped her shawl around her more tightly. There was a small fire burning in the fireplace, but the library was a large room and the damp, chilly day seemed to permeate even this cheerful room, which she normally loved.

She sat beside Betsey and decided to confess all.

She started with the séance she had thought was faked, the warning for Charles from Claire, her note that arrived too late, and then her failure to tell Drew about it.

As she spoke, she began to cry. By the end of her speech, she was sitting next to Betsey and crying into her shoulder.

"He is so angry and upset... I don't think he'll ever feel the same about me," she confessed to her friend.

"Nonsense!" Betsey said staunchly. "I've seen the way Drew looks at you—he's in love! And I'm so happy about it. I feel we are friends. I hope we shall be cousins, in truth, some day."

Violet shook her head. "I don't think that is going to happen, now, although I have dreamed of it."

"Drew will act sensibly after the shock wears off," Betsey predicted. "Just give him time. If you'd like, I will be happy to speak to him."

"Would you?" Violet asked, knowing she sounded too eager and grasping. But anything, anything that would help Drew to be more understanding sounded good.

"Of course. You know, Violet, had I attended a séance and heard your mother speak, for instance, warning about you, I would not have done anything either. How would I have known it was really your mother? And I would have had no idea who you were. I would have acted in the same way you did."

Violet sniffed. "You would?"

"Yes, and I will certainly tell Drew so." She hugged Violet.

Violet wiped her tears. They spoke for a little longer, and then she went up to her room to bathe her face in cold water and refresh herself, promising to go for a walk with Betsey in a few minutes.

As she walked down the hall to her room, Henrietta's door opened, and she came out. She was the last person Violet wanted to see, knowing her face was probably puffy and she didn't look good

Henrietta sent her a sharp glance. "Hello," she said cooly. She did not ask if Violet was all right—she probably would never care—and for that Violet was grateful. She did not want to talk about how she felt to this woman.

"Hello," she replied, and continued walking to her own room. She could feel Henrietta staring at her as she did.

The rest of the day passed quietly. Drew did not appear at dinner, and Patricia informed them he was eating while researching in his laboratory, which he did on occasion.

Violet suspected he did not want to be in the others' company—especially hers. She felt badly and as soon as the meal ended went up to her room.

Betsey found her there and talked sympathetically to her for a while. But she went to sleep early, and Violet attempted to sleep herself, but it was a long time until she could.

The remainder of the week passed quietly. Drew spent a lot of time in his laboratory and did not seem to want to discuss their exciting séance when so many entities had been present. Violet felt bad that he was avoiding the rest of the family because, she assumed, of her.

Betsey did not agree. "He's wrapped up in séances and catching up with work, I believe," she told Violet.

"And perhaps he feels awkward about discussing things with you as much as he used to. I have tried to talk to him, but he keeps telling me he is busy." She gave Violet an apologetic smile.

"He's angry and disappointed," Violet said. Every time she thought about Drew, she felt like a rock had settled in her stomach.

Henrietta and Harvey were set to leave on the following Monday. On Saturday they went into town to do some shopping after lunch, and since Drew had decided to work at the factory—he'd sent word to his aunt—Violet found herself wandering listlessly in the afternoon. She'd spent the morning finishing work on the library catalog again with Betsey, and it had felt good to accomplish something, but Betsey wanted to read this afternoon and Violet was too restless and disturbed to read for long.

The weather had turned colder with a strong wind, and dark clouds seemed to press down on the house. Violet found herself pacing, a feeling of dread growing inside her. She could not get rid of it. Something, she was sure, was going to happen, and it wasn't just because of the ominous clouds outside.

She thought of Drew, in the factory, and wondered how he was feeling now.

She couldn't stay in her room. She left, pacing the hall, and then went into the conservatory.

She found herself staring out the big windows at the laboratory, just as she had the night she had sensed Charles' spirit. The dark afternoon seemed to press in on her.

Perhaps Charles could help her again—help them all. She had never tried to specifically reach out to him, and it was day, not their usual night time setting, but she found herself speaking as if he were nearby.

"Charles, please help me," she requested, and heard the desperate note in her voice. "We are trying so hard to reach you—and I am trying so hard to help Drew. I am sorry I didn't try to warn you earlier. So, so very sorry. I wish so much I had done more—but please, help us now. Drew needs your help. I feel— something, some danger, and we need your help to discover who harmed you."

After that impassioned plea, she stood still, waiting.

The wind keened loudly. She could feel the storm approaching. There was a heaviness in the air—

A heaviness.

She strained, her whole being listening, her nerves aware, waiting for a further sign.

"Charles?" she whispered.

Lightning flashed suddenly. And in that instant, she saw an outline—a shape. A person.

"Charles?" she asked. Holding her breath.

"I am here." The voice seemed to whisper on the wind. "Tell Drew—you should not—be sorry. Louis tried to warn me—I didn't listen." He sounded as if he was having difficulty getting the words out. "Top drawer of my—night stand—Drew must look."

"The top drawer of your nightstand. I will tell Drew to look," she repeated.

"Yes-ss." There was a pause. His outline flickered, then came back again, strong. "Hurry. Drew—in trouble. Must go—help him."

"Drew is in trouble?" she gasped. "Now? I should help him?"

"Help him," Charles said again. "Yes...now..." he flickered again as his voice faded. "Quick—ly."

"I will go!" She darted for the door, then paused to look back. The heaviness remained in the room, but she could no longer see Drew's brother. "Thank you," she said, then ran out of the room.

She had to help Drew. She would not fail to warn anyone again!

She had to—reason reared its head as she hurried down the corridor.

She might need more help. The police? But she didn't have time to get them.

Betsey. She was nearby, reading.

Violet ran to her room and rapped loudly on the door.

"Yes?" Betsey's voice called. "Come in."

She opened the door and almost leaped inside. "Betsey—I tried to contact Charles—and his spirit said—Drew is in trouble," she cried, the words tumbling out.

Betsey didn't stop to interrogate her or act like she didn't believe. Instead she sprang up from her chair. "Yes? What can we do?"

"I'm going to the factory to find Drew and warn him—or if there's trouble right now, see what I can do," Violet said. "Can you go to the police and bring them?"

"Of course." Betsey grabbed her cape. "I will go straight away."

Violet did not stop for her cape, but Betsey thrust a shawl at her which she gratefully took. Then she led Betsey down the hall, down the stairs, and out the door.

They hurried, half running and half walking, into

town. As they neared it, Betsey called over the noise of the wind that she would go to the police. She sprinted down the hill, and Violet made the right at the street leading to the factory.

On a Saturday, the factory was quiet. When she opened the unlocked door—thank goodness it was unlocked—the air was still and no one was about downstairs.

She hurried, almost out of breath from her journey, to the stairs. "Drew?" she called up, and started up the stairs. "Drew? Are you all right?"

"Violet? Violet!" Drew answered. "Don't come up here! Get away—"

It was too late. When she reached the top of the stairs, something swung out at her. She caught sight of brown material when a bag swept over her head, and she found her arms grabbed and pinned by her sides.

"That's enough of that." She recognized Henrietta's smug voice. "This is amusing—little Miss Perfect, riding to the rescue of the handsome hero. Put her in with him, Reggie," she commanded, and Violet felt herself dragged. She struggled, barely able to breathe. She heard a door open, and then she was shoved.

She put out her hands to brace herself and felt a hard floor as she stumbled onto her knees.

Chapter Twelve

For a moment, the breath was knocked out of her. Then she became conscious of her hands against wood, of the stuffy burlap bag around her head.

A second later it was lifted off. "Violet?"

Drew knelt before her, and she realized she had been thrown into his office at the factory.

"Drew!" she gasped.

"Are you all right?" His expression was anxious. He reached out and gripped her arms, pulling her into his lap as he slid to a sitting position on the floor.

She nodded, trying to catch her breath, hardly able to speak. "Drew! Are you—are you all right?"

"I'm fine." He frowned. "I've been trying to"—he lowered his voice to a whisper—"figure if I have the right chemicals in my office to blow the door open and escape."

"Was that—Henrietta?" she asked shakily.

"Yes. She and that henchman of hers trapped me in here." He frowned. "I told her in no uncertain terms last night I *wasn't* going to marry her, when she practically proposed to me. Apparently, she has now decided if I die—like Charles—she might have a chance to inherit, with Harvey, my family's money anyway, since they are distant cousins."

"Charles? Henrietta killed him?" She stared up at Drew and clutched his coat. "No wonder that trumpet almost hit her. Charles must have been trying to tell us—"

"Yes, yes. With that man Reggie's help, I'm thinking." Drew hugged her suddenly. "Oh God, Violet, when I heard you downstairs I tried to warn you. The last thing I want is for you to be in danger—"

"I sent Betsey to get the police," Violet told him. "They should be here soon."

His eyebrows shot up. "How did you know I was in danger?"

"Charles. I tried to contact him on my own. I—reached him, Drew, and he told me about a letter—never mind, I will tell you that part later. The important thing is, he told me you were in danger. And I got Betsey. Help is on the way."

"Thank God." He stood, pulling her to her feet with him. "But we can't wait. We don't know what they're planning, but I'm sure it's our demises."

All she wanted was to move into his arms, but she knew he was correct—they needed action right now. "What should we do?"

"I won't have to blow open the door and try to rush out and not get shot, if the police are arriving soon." He tilted his head, considering. "I have it. I'll create that glue and wave it under the door. Once they begin to breathe it, they will be light-headed, possibly delirious. That should incapacitate them somewhat and help us to get away."

He moved to the table in the room.

"How can I help?"

"Hand me that mortar and pestle." He pointed to a dark-colored bowl and some kind of tool that looked similar to a spoon.

He grabbed for a bottle, then another. "I'll make a potent mixture," he whispered. "And—can you grab that tube over there?—we'll pipe it under the door and try to get them to breathe it."

He was grinding some kind of powder, then pouring liquid over it, and mixing rapidly with another tool. Violet watched, fascinated by his quick thinking and knowledge.

She held the rubber tube in her hand. As she watched, a smoky fume began to emerge from the bowl of ingredients he was mixing.

"Quickly," he hissed, and holding the bowl, strode toward the door.

She swallowed and followed him, walking rapidly and quietly. He took the hose from her when she reached the door and placed part of it under the door so it just reached the main room.

Bending the tube, he slowly poured the mixture into it. When he finished, he set the bowl down and looked up at her. "There." He smiled briefly. "Let's back up. Cover your mouth and nose so we don't breathe in much. Hopefully, they will breathe this in and be incapacitated by the time the police show up. And the fumes won't come back under the door to reach us." He covered the lower part of his face with his hand

She covered her mouth and nose too, backing up with him.

She strained to listen. After two or three minutes, she heard a masculine cough, and then Henrietta asked "What's that smell?"

Sudden footsteps pounded up the stairs. "Henrietta, you haven't—what the blazes?" It was Harvey's voice.

"Yes, I have Drew locked in there, along with that meddlesome Violet. After it gets dark, we will kill them both. No more waiting for him to marry me and make me wealthy. We're going to be left his fortune, Harvey. We are close cousins after all. I will finally be rich and get what I deserve!"

"I hope she does get what she deserves," Drew muttered grimly.

Harvey called out. "No, Henrietta, you can't!" He began coughing.

"What—what—" Henrietta sounded woozy.

Drew whipped a handkerchief from his pocket. "Use this." He handed it to Violet. "Once we get out there, we don't want to breathe in—"

The coughing from the other room had grown in intensity.

There was a sudden, loud commotion from downstairs.

"Police!" someone yelled.

Henrietta shrieked, then coughed fitfully.

Drew yelled "Cover your mouths!" to the policemen who were thundering up the stairs. Violet could hear many footfalls, voices and someone yelling "Mr. Covington!"

She stood by the door with Drew, awaiting someone to unlock it.

The door pulled open, and smoke wafted in.

They practically tumbled out the door.

"Drew! Violet!" Betsey shrieked, pounding up the stairs behind several men, calling and coughing at the same time. She embraced them both, laughing and crying. "Thank God you're all right!"

There were at least four policemen there. Two were

restraining Reggie, one stood by Harvey, who was coughing hard, and one stood over Henrietta, who had crawled into a corner and was weeping hysterically. "My brother—Harvey—he made me do this!"

"I did not!" Harvey shouted, then collapsed on the floor too, coughing fitfully.

"Ma'am." The policeman pulled Henrietta up, but she was woozy and could barely stand, as if she'd had too much to drink.

Violet hugged Betsey back, then glanced up at Drew.

"Thank goodness you are unharmed," she said to him in a low voice.

"Thank goodness you got here and thought to send for help," he responded. He lifted a hand to her face and stroked her cheek with two fingers, which shook. "You are certain you are unharmed?"

"Yes." She nodded, choked up. Drew cared. He might be angry, but he cared. She could see it in his eyes, hear it in his voice.

"Come, let's get away from here," Betsey said, tugging them both. "What is that awful smoke?"

"A potent mixture—very potent—of my new adhesive," Drew replied, coughing slightly. "The effects won't last long—but those who were out here will be a bit incapacitated for a while."

"Very clever, Mr. Covington," the policeman who seemed to be the leader remarked. "You men—bring him to the jail cells," he said, indicating Reggie. "And Miles—bring her along. The rest of you, come with me downstairs." He cast a glance at Harvey.

"He was not involved, as far as I know," Drew said. "It was Henrietta and her friend Reggie who locked me—and Violet—in the room, and said they were going to kill us."

Drew opened windows, and then they went downstairs, where he opened more. The three other policemen practically dragged both Reggie and Henrietta, coughing and wobbling, out the door.

"My brother—made me—do this—" Henrietta was saying as they left.

Harvey, still coughing as well, plopped down in a chair near Drew. "I didn't—"

"Now," said the head investigator, who told them his name was Carson Bentley, "Mr. Covington, go first, and tell me exactly what happened."

Violet and Betsey took seats at one of the work tables.

Drew launched into his story. He'd been working at the factory when Henrietta approached, saying she felt unwell, and could he come help her? She'd been sitting on the floor, claiming she was dizzy. When he'd reached down to help her, Reggie jumped from behind the door to the bookkeeper's office and struck him on the head. When he regained consciousness, he was locked in his office and could not get out the windows since the second floor was too high to jump.

"As I was trying to find ingredients to blow the door open, I heard Violet calling for me," he told them. "I yelled at her to stay away, but she didn't listen." His expression as he looked at her was serious. "I was afraid they would harm her."

"Why would they hurt you or her?" Carson Bentley asked.

Drew sighed. "Henrietta wanted to marry me," he said, "for my money. She practically proposed to me last night. At first, it was Charles she wanted—she thought he was exciting, I gather, and she was very attracted to him. When Charles realized she wanted his money, he told her he'd never marry her. I heard her discussing it with this Reggie guy. Apparently, she got so mad she had him kill Charles because he was going to tell me what she was planning. She and Harvey had run out of money, and she was getting desperate. She had Reggie corner him after he'd been out drinking with Louis LeBlanc and some other friends, and Reggie killed him and made it look like a robbery. Charles never had that chance to warn me. Then she plotted to marry me. When I"—he turned to Violet—"was drawn to you, she got desperate and tried to kill you. She didn't succeed and decided it might be easier to kill me than to try to marry me—after I told her I wasn't about to marry her. Henrietta figured she was next in line to inherit from my parents, especially if something happened to my sister Mary next."

"How awful," Betsey said. "She is mad if she thinks she could get away with Charles', yours, and Mary's deaths."

"Mad—or desperate?" Drew asked, looking at Harvey.

"It's true, we had no money," Harvey said, his voice raspy. "She was not content to live quietly in the country. She wanted a rich husband, or to be independently wealthy—to have gowns, and jewels, and be able to go where she pleased."

"She'll go nowhere now," Bentley practically growled. "What happened after you got here?" he asked Violet.

She described how she had found Drew, and how

after being locked in together he had concocted the mixture to make the villains woozy and coughing.

"It was brilliant," she finished.

"It certainly was!" Betsey exclaimed.

There was a commotion just then, as Patricia arrived with two footmen, anxious to find out where everyone was and why no one was in the house.

They gave her a brief explanation, and then Mr. Bentley stated how Betsey had come running to get help, and he and three others had come to their aid.

Harvey explained that his sister had become increasingly volatile, spouting more venom against Drew and Violet, and he had begun to wonder if by some chance she had done away with Louis. "He had no money, and she was stringing him along because he indicated he might be coming into some," he told them. "I am afraid he may have guessed she had something to do with Charles' death. He wanted Charles roughed up, but not dead. Remember, after the séance in New York he seemed to feel guilty?"

"Yes," Drew said. "She must have been afraid he was going to say something, and when she had the opportunity, struck him with the candlestick."

Harvey nodded, looking quite miserable. In that moment, Violet felt sorry for him. She had thought he was as bad as his sister, but now it seemed he did have a conscience. And with his sister in jail, he had no close family.

"I should have known something was amiss," Harvey said, sounding very sorrowful indeed. "If I had only tried to stop her—"

"I know you and Louis met a fellow who told you Parkin was dead," Drew said. "Did you have a hand in it?"

"No," Harvey protested. "I thought—Louis had hired him, but I had no idea my sister—" he choked.

Patricia laid a hand on his arm. "There is nothing you could have done, Harvey. She has been willful and selfish since she was a child. I doubt you or anyone could have changed her actions."

Mr. Bentley wanted to talk to Drew further, and Harvey accompanied them to the police station after they locked up the factory. The rest of the family and Violet followed them out of the building. There were many townspeople outside, curious as to what was happening.

Violet realized as the footmen brought the horses and carriage from the nearby livery that it must have rained while they were in the factory. It was still windy and raw, but any lightning had stopped, and there was only a faint drizzle now.

It was past suppertime when they returned. Violet wasn't very hungry, but Patricia had Cook set out sandwiches and broth. They picked at the food.

All the time, she wondered what Drew was doing, and when she could be alone to talk to him. He had seemed so caring, so worried about her welfare when they were in danger—could it be his anger and disappointment were gone? And she still had to give him Charles' message.

She told Betsey and Patricia about Charles. They were amazed but thankful that he had materialized and helped her to save Drew.

By eight o'clock Harvey returned on foot, looking exhausted. They were in the parlor by then, and Patricia got out the brandy and poured glasses for them all. "We need it tonight," she stated.

"My sister has done some terrible things," he said, staring at the dark liquid in his glass. "But...I will have to get her an attorney, and Drew has offered to help, which I can not believe. She tried to kill him."

"That is Drew," Patricia said.

"She is—almost mad, I think." He swallowed his brandy in one gulp. "I do not know what is to become of her. Prison or the mad house—neither is good."

Patricia walked over to him and laid a hand on his shoulder. "Perhaps you should get some sleep, Harvey. Tomorrow I will telegraph Mary and let her know what has happened."

"And my mother, too," Betsey said. She yawned. "I declare I do not think I can stay awake much longer."

"Let us retire," Patricia urged. "Drew will be home soon, won't he?"

"He was still with Mr. Bentley when they said I could leave." Harvey stood. "I am going to bed before I collapse." He looked like he was at the end of a rope. "Perhaps one more drink." He grabbed for the decanter, poured himself more brandy, and drank slower this time.

Patricia stood too and said goodnight, then went around and hugged Betsey, Violet, and Harvey. "Don't be too hard on yourself," she told Harvey. To Betsey and Violet, she said a simple but heartfelt "thank you."

They heard her move down the hall.

"I am to bed too," Harvey said with a deep sigh, and also left the room.

Betsey looked at Violet. "Much as I would like to wait up for Drew, I must go to sleep too. Are you coming?" She stood up.

"Thank you for all you did today." Violet suddenly rushed over to hug her friend. "If you hadn't brought the police—"

"I am glad you thought to ask for help, and that I could help," Betsey said. She hugged Violet tightly. "At least the danger is over now."

Violet nodded. "Yes." All her excited energy had left, leaving her fatigued too. "I would like to wait for Drew—"

"But we don't know when he will return. And he may be too fatigued to do anything but collapse," Betsey pointed out. "You should get some rest, too."

Although she didn't want to, Violet knew that by the time Drew returned he probably *would* be too tired to talk. So she agreed and followed Betsey out of the room and up the stairs.

They parted by Betsey's door, and she returned to her room. She got ready for bed and once in her nightgown opened the door to listen. The house was silent, the sconce lights flickering only intermittently.

She sat in the bed, straining to hear if Drew was coming in.

After a while, she wondered if she would be able to sleep. She would be listening for him, she was sure, anxious to speak to him. What if he was so quiet she didn't hear him coming down the hall? Could she wait until tomorrow to talk with him?

No, she couldn't! She sprang from the bed and opened her door. All was very quiet. She tiptoed down the corridor, turning into the main hall, and walked toward his room. Her feet sank into the carpet and made not a sound. She wrapped her robe tighter about her form, feeling the chill in the hall.

She tapped on his door. No answer. She opened it slightly and poked her head in. He was not yet here.

She had only caught a glimpse of his room once. Now she entered, feeling the warmth from the small fire the servants had left burning in the fireplace.

Drew's room had large furniture, but it was classical and not too heavy looking, with wood in medium tones. The large bed dominated the room, with its stark blue coverings and blankets. A dresser and a wardrobe stood against one wall, along with a comfortable looking chair, which would be nice to read in, she thought. A small desk and desk chair were positioned in one corner. Touches of gold highlighted the room in pillows and desk accessories. On the nightstand, several books and periodicals were piled. He must like to read in bed.

She went across to the bed. It looked so nice and comfortable. She sat on it, and the thick mattress welcomed her. Feeling like Goldilocks in the fairy tale, she stretched out, hugging a pillow. She'd just wait here for Drew to return.

She closed her eyes, and relaxed. He surely would be home soon, and they could talk…

The creak of the door woke her. A glance at the clock on the nightstand showed she must have fallen asleep after entering the room some twenty minutes ago. It was nearly midnight.

She sat up.

Drew entered the room quietly and closed the door.

He walked a few feet, and stopped. "Violet?" His mouth dropped, and he sounded astonished. "What—what are you doing here?"

She pushed her hair away from her face. "I wanted

to—to speak to you, and didn't want to wait until tomorrow. I know you must be exhausted but—I hope you don't mind."

He was staring at her. "Violet," he breathed. He moved swiftly, coming toward her, and sat on the bed beside her.

Reaching out, he cupped her face in his hands. For a moment he just stared at her. "Thank God you're all right," he murmured. The he bent his head and kissed her, hard.

Ecstasy rushed through her. He cared—he still cared—despite their disagreement.

Her hands went up, and she clung to his shoulders, kissing him back without restraint. His tongue swept into her mouth, and the kiss grew hotter, wilder.

He broke away. "Violet…Violet…" he said, kissing her forehead, her cheeks, her neck and then her mouth again.

"Drew." She pulled back slightly, so she could speak. "I was so afraid for you—I didn't know what she would do—and I was so terribly afraid you'd never talk to me again—"

He shook his head. "I am so, so sorry, Violet. I guess I was just stunned by your confession. I had time to think, and I realize you didn't know if your experience with my mother's spirit were truly real, or not. But when I heard your voice and you came running up the factory stairs—I experienced pure terror. All I could think of was they were going to hurt you. I knew then that nothing would ever stand in our way again. I had to get free, had to save you, so we could be together. Always." He grabbed her hands and kissed them fervently.

"Oh, Drew." She sighed blissfully. "I was so scared—as soon as I knew you were in danger—"

"How did you know?" he asked. "You said something about—contacting Charles?"

"I asked for Charles' help. In the solarium, where I'd felt his presence before. And—I heard him! He told me you were in danger, and I knew I had to get to you, but needed help—so I ran to get Betsey and asked her to get the police." She paused for breath. "I was so scared! I knew if anything ever happened to you I'd never forgive myself—"

"Extraordinary, that you were able to communicate with Charles," he murmured.

"And what's more, he told me you should look in his nightstand, that there was a letter you needed to see," she continued.

"I will look—later," he said, and pulled her back into his arms, kissing her thoroughly.

She melted against him.

A few minutes and a dozen kisses later, he lifted his head. "Violet," he said, "I better escort you back to your room. Because if I don't, I won't be able to stop myself from—from making love to you."

She was already flushed from excitement and something else—but she felt her cheeks grow even warmer, as well as the rest of her.

"Violet," he continued, "when I knew you were in danger, I decided nothing—no one, either alive or deceased—would ever come between us again. I love you."

"Oh, Drew," she murmured against his lips, kissing him back. "I love you too, and I always will."

He pulled back to regard her, and held her hand.

"Then will you marry me, Violet? I never want to let you go."

"Oh, Drew, yes! I'll marry you!" She flung her arms around his neck and kissed him with all the love in her heart.

They tumbled down on the bed and stayed there for a long time. He kissed her, touched her...and she knew that the sensations he was eliciting in her were just the start of those she'd feel every night in his arms as his wife and lover.

"I love you," he repeated, drawing back to gaze into her eyes. "We belong together, Violet. I will always love you."

"And I you," she replied, and lost herself again in his kiss.

Epilogue

They sat around the table in the séance room, waiting.

It was November's full moon, and moonlight spilled through the windows, lighting the room with a glow. Despite the fire in the main room, this room was chilly, and Violet was glad they were holding hands. She held Drew's on her left, then Patricia's, and next to Patricia, were Betsey, Mrs. O'Grady, then Harvey and Drew.

The meteor rock sat on the table, and the trumpet lay on the sideboard.

All was quiet for a while. Violet stole a look at her finger, where the beautiful diamond and emerald engagement ring flashed. It was still exciting and hard to believe, but she and Drew would be married in two weeks. He had declared he could not wait to make her his wife, and she had agreed to have a short engagement. Their families and friends would gather here for the event. She felt a wave of happiness wash over her every time she thought about being his wife and how much they loved each other.

Henrietta remained in jail, since there was no evidence that she was mentally unstable. She kept threatening to get even someday, but it appeared she would be in prison for a very long time, so Violet chose not to worry or even think of the unfortunate, selfish woman who had arranged several deaths.

Harvey had been very subdued, depressed, and guilty. Drew had offered him a job, but he was going to return to England in the spring, since he felt that was his home; and see if he could somehow salvage the family finances there.

They had found the letter in Charles' nightstand. It was from Louis, warning Charles of imminent danger. Apparently, Louis knew Charles was going to be roughed up but not killed and had chosen to warn him but not let his associates know he was doing so. He must have felt a flash of conscience at the last minute and wanted to tell Charles to beware. So Charles had indeed been warned but chose to ignore it, Drew had declared. Any warning from Violet would have made little difference, he assured her.

Now there was a sudden heaviness in the room, and Violet sensed a presence nearby.

"Good evening, friends." It was Red Feather's voice.

"Good evening, Red Feather. Is there one who wants to come through?" Drew asked.

"One," he answered.

And then something flickered—and as Violet watched, an image slowly appeared, the shape of a body, wearing a hat, a coat—and a cigar held in his hand.

She could smell the tobacco now.

"I smell a cigar," Betsey whispered, and all around the table each person nodded.

"Charles?" Drew asked.

The figure flickered, then came back stronger, and took on the features of Charles Covington.

"I have come to say goodbye," he said. "I will be crossing over the great divide to a special place—the Great Beyond. I will probably no longer visit. I have found peace, friends. Thank you for seeing justice done and catching my killer—and Louis' killer."

"I will miss you, brother," Drew said simply.

"I know, and I wanted to say goodbye one more time. And to let you know I am glad you found the letter. I did not listen to Louis." He turned from gazing at Drew to look at Violet. "I would not have listened to you. You must feel no regrets."

"Thank you," Violet said, her heart full, as tears pricked her eyes. "Thank you for telling me that."

"Louis has already passed on," Charles reported. "Once you caught Henrietta, he was happy. And mother." He turned back to Drew. "I convinced her it was my own fault I did not take heed of the warnings, and would not have listened to an unknown woman—Violet—either. She passed to the Great Beyond too. I will join them there."

"We love you, Charles," Betsey said suddenly, her voice tearful.

"We do indeed," Drew said.

"I know. Goodbye, my friends. Drew…name your first son for me?"

"Of course." Drew met Violet's eyes, and she nodded.

"Yes," she whispered.

"Then I am content. Goodbye." The last word was whispered, as slowly, his image faded, until there was nothing but darkness and moonlight.

They sat for a while longer, but Violet knew this was the last contact with Charles.

After a few minutes, Drew said, in a voice thick with emotion," I am glad we had one more séance."

"Yes," she agreed, and the others murmured assent.

Mrs. O'Grady woke suddenly.

Drew pushed his chair back. "I believe that is the end for tonight."

Afterward, after Harvey had left with Mrs. O'Grady to walk her home, and Patricia and Betsey had returned to the house, Drew put his arms around Violet and said quietly, "We shall always remember him."

"We will keep him in our hearts," she agreed, "and someday, yes, we will have a son and name him Charles."

Drew looked at her with a gleam in his eye. "Perhaps we should start working on that now?"

Violet laughed, and moved back into his arms. "An intriguing proposition."

And as she kissed him, she knew Charles was pleased.

A word about the author...

Roni Denholtz is the award-winning writer of nine romance novels and one novella. She is also the author of nine children's books and dozens of articles and stories for national magazines.

A former president of New Jersey Romance Writers, she lives in northwest New Jersey with her family and adopted dog.